Praise for *Downfall*

"A suspenseful descent into a seldom-examined underworld . . . Well written and fast-paced."

Beverley McLachlin, former Chief Justice and
#1 bestselling author of *Full Disclosure*

"A well-crafted tale, alive with real characters and a riveting plot, making for another thoroughly compelling read."

Rick Mofina, *USA Today* bestselling author of *Search for Her*

"An unsparing exploration of the hostility between those who have it all, the members of an elite golf club, and those who've lost it all, the squatters who make the ravine near the club their home. When two of the homeless are murdered, Ari Greene, the new head of the homicide squad, wads up the banal public relations statement he's been handed and sets out to learn the truth. Rotenberg gets everything right in this stellar novel, but the scene in which 'The Three Amigas,' friends since they articled at the same law firm, have a late-night meeting in the firm's washroom is such a tender evocation of female solidarity that it brought me to tears."

Gail Bowen, author of the Joanne Kilbourn Shreve mystery series

"A riveting read that fired my conscience as well as my imagination."

Ian Hamilton, author of the bestselling Ava Lee series

"*Downfall* is so much more than a murder-mystery, opening our eyes to what lies in the ravines of our cities and our souls."

Norman Bacal, bestselling author of *Breakdown* and *Odell's Fall*

"There has never been a better time to be swept up in a new novel by Robert Rotenberg. His characters are as real as the city streets they live in: a perfect antidote to a digital world. Leave it to his imagination to spark yours."

Dalton McGuinty, former Premier of Ontario

Praise for *Heart of the City*

"The only complaint I ever have about Robert Rotenberg's novels is that he takes too long between books. . . . [Rotenberg] makes his legal-cop dramas spot-on for details, along with terrific plots and characters that evolve."

The Globe and Mail

"Pleasantly loaded with [complications], each one delivered in Rotenberg's swift and sure brand of prose."

Toronto Star

"Rotenberg has created believable and likeable characters, put them into a fast-paced story and sprinkled the mix with astute observations of contemporary urban life. What more can we ask for?"

Maureen Jennings, author of the Murdoch Mysteries series

Praise for *Stranglehold*

"His fourth and best."

The Globe and Mail

"Readers of all descriptions will get off on *Stranglehold*'s courtroom drama. . . . The action is authoritatively presented . . . and as twisty as anything from Perry Mason's worst nightmares."

Toronto Star

"Rotenberg was in the business of turning Toronto into fiction before Toronto became stranger than fiction."

Metro News

Praise for *The Guilty Plea*

"Not since *Anatomy of a Murder* has a novel so vividly captured the real life of criminal lawyers in the midst of a high-stakes trial. This is a book that every lawyer, law student, and law professor should, no *must*, read."

Edward L. Greenspan, QC

"A few lawyers are really expert in managing cases—especially criminal cases—in the courtroom. A small percentage of these are very good at making trials come alive. Robert Rotenberg is one of the few, along with Scott Turow, David Baldacci, John Lescroart. His *Guilty Plea* is a crackling good read. Plan to keep turning pages late into the night!"

F. Lee Bailey

DOWNFALL

ROBERT ROTENBERG

Simon & Schuster

NEW YORK   LONDON   TORONTO   SYDNEY   NEW DELHI

**SIMON &
SCHUSTER
CANADA**

Simon & Schuster Canada
A Division of Simon & Schuster, Inc.
166 King Street East, Suite 300
Toronto, Ontario M5A 1J3

This Simon & Schuster Canada edition February 2021

SIMON & SCHUSTER CANADA and colophon are trademarks of Simon & Schuster, Inc.

For information about special discounts for bulk purchases, please contact Simon & Schuster Special Sales at 1-800-268-3216 or CustomerService@simonandschuster.ca.

Manufactured in the United States of America

10   9   8   7   6   5   4   3   2

Library and Archives Canada Cataloguing in Publication
Title: Downfall / Robert Rotenberg.
Names: Rotenberg, Robert, 1953- author.
Description: Simon & Schuster Canada edition.
Identifiers: Canadiana (print) 20200261045 | Canadiana (ebook) 20200261096 |
    ISBN 9781476740607 (softcover) | ISBN 9781476740621 (ebook)
Classification: LCC PS8635.O7367 D69 2021 | DDC C813/.6—dc23

ISBN 978-1-4767-4060-7
ISBN 978-1-4767-4062-1 (ebook)

For my lifelong friends
Dr. Cynthia Lazar and Justice Marvin Kurz
Generous and caring beyond all measure

Outside the Church of the Holy Trinity in Toronto there is a memorial to all the homeless people who have died in the city. Frontline workers and friends have been counting for at least twenty years. The list now has one thousand names. One thousand siblings, parents, children, lovers, friends, many of whom spent the final days of their lives huddled on sidewalks as commuters stepped around them on their way to work. They died in a city awash in money with a skyline dominated by skyscrapers, where condos crowd out more of the daylight with each passing year. There are more than a million empty homes in this country, and on any given night at least thirty-five thousand Canadians are homeless. They pack into overflowing, often dangerous shelters, or they hunker down outside, hoping the elements will be kinder to them than the conditions indoors. Some of them never wake up. Most politicians treat urban homelessness as a permanent and intractable tragedy. They speculate and ring their hands while men and women freeze to death.

Michael Enright
Sunday Morning
CBC Radio
January 26, 2020

MONDAY

1

Because the subways in Toronto didn't run early enough, Jember Roshan had no choice but to ride his bicycle to work. His wife, Babita, was not pleased. "In Canada it is dark in November, and you don't even have a light," she'd said when he was getting dressed to leave. She was right, of course, but what else could he do? They needed to buy diapers for the twins, and the rent on their one-bedroom apartment was due in a week. "I promise that I will be careful," he'd told her as he was rushing out the door, but she'd refused to kiss him goodbye. In seven years of marriage, she'd never done that before.

A week earlier, the weather had turned from breezy fall temperatures to freezing cold. Yesterday, there'd even been a heavy early snowfall that had blanketed the city and closed the airport. Last winter, when he'd felt this kind of chill for the first time, Roshan had rushed out to the Variety Village at the nearby plaza and bought a used ski jacket. It wasn't warm enough, and now he wore as many layers underneath it as he could.

He didn't have gloves, and as he began his thirty-minute ride his hands stiffened on the icy bicycle handlebars. He pedalled hard. This would get his heart rate up and blood flowing to his fingers. Roshan had bought the bicycle at a yard sale for twenty dollars—the man wanted thirty—stripped it down, and rebuilt it from the ball bearings up. He liked to joke with his Somali friends that it was the only engineering work he'd done since coming to Canada.

It was quiet on the streets of the public housing complex where they lived, but once he got to the main road, the traffic picked up. This was the most treacherous part of his route, with noisy transport trucks whizzing past, leaving little space for a man on a bicycle, the acrid smell of their exhaust filling his nostrils. There were streetlights, but they were wide apart. He kept riding from light to dark and back into the light, the white steam of his breath appearing and disappearing in front of his face, like some kind of magic act at the circus.

Since his jacket was black, Babita had used her sewing machine to make him a special white T-shirt with reflecting tape sewn onto it. She insisted that he wear it on top of his jacket to make himself more visible, but in his haste this morning, and after their fight, he'd forgotten it. She would be angry with him about that when he got home.

He waved his left arm in the air as he passed through the dark patches of the road, not that it would do any good. The trucks were driving faster and coming closer, spitting up pebbles that pinged against his bicycle wheels.

At last he could see the final light stand before the turn onto the smaller, safer road, the next leg of his journey. A big transport whooshed by and barely missed him. He had become invisible. He had to get to the turn. He pedalled harder. He was heating up. Despite the cold, even his fingers were warming.

Finally he made the turn. Within seconds, the noise and the smell of the big road fell away. The only sounds were the meshing of his bike gears and the heaving of his breath. There were houses on one side of the road, and he could smell the sweet scent of smoke from a fireplace. He could relax. He felt the tension ease out of his body. He looked up and saw there was a hint of light in the dark sky. Allah had given him another day.

He always enjoyed this section of the ride. There was almost no traffic. The road curled along the edge of a riverbank, and now he could hear the rushing sound of the water coming up from the valley below.

In the late spring and early summer, when the sun was up early, he loved the scent of the trees in bloom, the singsong of the morning birds, and the warmth of the humid air. One weekend in July, he and Babita had hiked down to the river with the babies and made a lovely picnic on one of the big flat boulders that lined the shore. They'd had a fine afternoon until a group of homeless men and women showed up on the other side of the river, drinking liquor from open bottles, shouting and fighting amongst themselves.

Babita insisted they leave right away. As they climbed up the steep path carrying their two crying babies, she fell and scraped her leg. By the time they got home she was exhausted.

"Why in Canada, where there is so much money," Babita asked him as she unpacked their uneaten picnic meal, "do people live this way?"

"There are shelters, but many of these people won't go," he told her.

"Shelters? Where are their families? At home we have poverty, but not like this. Shameful."

She was right. He'd had no answer for her. These were the type of troublemakers he had to keep out of the golf club, where he worked as a security guard. Two days ago, one of them had been found dead at the edge of the property. Roshan heard that the man had had his head bashed in by a liquor bottle. Roshan's boss, Mr. Waterbridge, said it was probably a drunken brawl between two homeless people.

Roshan was interviewed by a polite young detective named Kennicott. He seemed to be the only person who really cared.

A car came up behind Roshan and whizzed past, almost hitting him. He tried to steer his bike farther off the road, but there was no curb or sidewalk, only a few inches of gravel, and then the steep riverbank.

It grew quiet again. He kept pedalling, anxious to get off his bike. In a few minutes he'd be at the club.

The silence was shattered by a loud rumbling behind him. He swivelled his head to look. A black SUV with large wheels and the driver's seat high up was bearing down on him. Speeding. It seemed to take up most of the road.

He waved his arm, but it was still too dark out. Why hadn't he worn Babita's white T-shirt? The car's front window was tinted, and he couldn't see the driver. As it got closer it passed under a street lamp, and Roshan caught a glimpse of a man driving. He wasn't looking at the road, but at a cell phone in his hand.

Roshan waved again. Frantically. He tried to hug the edge of the road and keep his bike straight without wobbling.

Bang.

He felt the impact as the vehicle smacked him from behind. The back wheel of his bike popped up and, swoosh, he was thrown off his seat toward the river, like a rock jettisoned from a catapult. In the scant light he spotted a massive tree straight ahead. He hadn't been able to afford a helmet, so he threw his hands over his face and twisted his body in mid-flight.

Now he was rolling downhill. The grade was so steep that it was impossible to stop his freefall. In desperation he grabbed a low-hanging branch and tried to hold on to it, but the force of his descent tore him away.

The sound of the rushing water below grew louder as he plunged down. It was hopeless. In seconds he'd smash onto one of those rocks by the riverside, which would surely crush his head in.

With one final lunge he kicked out at a tree stump. Crack. His kneecap smashed against it. Pain shot through him like a dagger. "Ahh!" he screamed, even though there was no one to hear him.

The move slowed his fall. He grabbed for another branch. Please, Allah, please, he prayed as he wrapped his hands around it. For my children, please let me live. He pressed his fingers together to form a grip. Perhaps it was better after all that he wasn't wearing gloves. But his arms weren't strong enough. His knee was screaming in pain. He peered down at the unbroken row of boulders below him. He was slipping.

To one side he could make out something dark and soft-looking. He couldn't tell what it was, but it didn't matter. It was his only hope.

With one last effort, he swung himself toward it as his fingers peeled away from the branch.

"Babita!" he yelled as his body flew in the air, as helpless as a parachutist whose chute had refused to open. He closed his eyes, waiting for contact.

Thud. He landed.

Not on a rock, but on the dark object. It was spongy, like a heavy pillow. He lay still. Breathing. Listening to the river. Feeling the wind on his skin. A faint smell of alcohol hung in the air.

He could hear. He could feel the pain searing through his leg. He could see the brightening sky. He could smell.

Alive. He was alive.

Clutching his knee, he rolled off the thing he had landed on and swivelled around to look at it.

"Oh no," he whispered, a scramble of thoughts and fears rushing through his mind. Although his leg was weak, he willed himself to stand and cupped his hands around his mouth.

"Help!" he yelled at the top of his lungs.

It was useless down here deep in the river valley, the sound of the rushing water drowning out all hope. His leg buckled underneath him. Still he had to try.

"Please, someone help!" he cried out as he crumbled to the ground. "There is a dead woman down here."

2

Roshan rolled onto his back, raised his knee, and massaged it with both hands. It didn't help. The pain kept getting worse. The rock he was lying on was covered with shards of broken glass that looked as if they came from a smashed liquor bottle. One piece had cut into the back of his neck.

What was he going to do? Stuck here, lying next to a dead woman. By the rags she was wearing for clothes and her long, unkempt hair, she appeared to be one of the people who camped out here in the valley. Blood had leaked out from the back of her head. Another broken liquor bottle, he thought. Was this a second homeless person killed in the same way near the golf course?

He looked around, afraid. Was the killer nearby? But there was no one, just the river, the trees, and the coming light.

His only hope was that his employer would call Babita to ask her why he was not at work. She would be frantic with fear. Perhaps someone would notice his crumpled bicycle by the side of the road and eventually—who knows how long it would take—find him.

He laid his head back on the hard rock and closed his eyes. Why had he not worn Babita's reflecting shirt? Why had he taken this job with such terrible hours? Why had he moved his family to this frigid, remote country? The only thing he wanted in life was to see his wife, hold his children.

He felt a ray of sunshine on his cheek and opened his eyes. Straight above him he saw a bird flying across the sky, the sunlight illuminating the white underside of its beating wings, flashing on and off like a rotating beacon in the night. How lucky to be a bird, he thought, free to scavenge for food and return home to his family in its nest.

A light breeze carried with it the foul smell of alcohol coming from the dead body. He tried to ignore it. Instead he listened to the sound of the rushing water behind him. It was hypnotic. Maybe he could fall asleep and this nightmare would end. He started to shiver.

Through the noise, he heard something else. What was it? Footsteps?

He pushed himself up to look. A woman was kneeling beside the dead body. Her hair was frazzled. She wore an unbuttoned coat that looked as if it had once been quite expensive, and many layers of thin shirts underneath that seemed to hang off her like the old clothes his mother used to put on the clothesline back home. Despite her unkempt appearance, the woman had a calm confidence about her. He watched her hold the dead woman's hand and feel for a pulse, then without hesitation lift her closed eyelids, as if she'd done this many times.

Where had this woman come from?

"Excuse me, ma'am," he said, his voice weak.

The woman didn't seem to hear him. She put her ear to the dead woman's mouth, and then flexed her arm. She lifted the dead woman's head and examined the back of it. Roshan could see it had been bashed in. She put her ear to the woman's nose then shook her head.

"Ma'am," he said again. Louder.

She looked back at him.

"Body is still warm. Rigor hasn't set in yet," the woman said. "Who are you?"

"My name is Roshan. I was riding my bicycle to work. A car knocked me off and I tumbled down the hill."

She listened intently. Didn't move.

"I thought I was going to die. At the last moment I saw her," he said pointing to the corpse. "I did not know it was a dead person. I landed on her. I think she saved my life."

Without taking her eyes off Roshan, the woman ran her hand over the dead woman's chest. She nodded.

Roshan didn't know what else to say.

"What happened to your leg?" the woman asked.

"I hurt my knee when I fell down here. I cannot stand."

"Don't move."

Before he could react, the woman skipped toward him, navigating the boulders with speed.

"Lie back," she said. She took off her long coat and draped it over him. There was matted fur on the collar and she tucked it under his chin. It felt nice.

"Try to straighten your leg," she said, rubbing her hands down his thigh.

"I can't." The shooting pain made him wince and grit his teeth.

"Stay still." She jumped up and rushed into the trees by the river.

He lay back, looking up at the sky, hoping to see another bird winging its way back to its nest. But none flew past. Imagine if he had died, he thought. Poor Babita, her parents killed in the civil war, left alone with the twins.

Soon the woman was back with two large branches, one in each hand. He saw perspiration forming on her forehead. She laid the branches down and then held his leg.

"I'm going to move your leg," she said, all business. "Breathe."

She eased his lower leg down until it was straight. He felt better.

"You have strong legs," she said.

"I played soccer at university. Now I play here with my friends on Saturday mornings," he said. Why was he telling her this? His mind was racing everywhere.

She didn't seem to hear him, though. She laid the branches on either side of his leg and then took off her top shirt. Working swiftly, she used it to wrap the branches firmly around his knee. She pulled a cell phone out from somewhere within the folds of her clothes.

"I'll call 911 when I get out of the valley. There's no reception down here."

"Thank you," Roshan said.

The woman bounded back up.

"Wait," he said. "Your coat."

She stared down at him. "Who is Babita?"

"My wife."

"Give the coat to her."

She walked toward the hill he'd tumbled down.

"Wait," he said again. "What is your name?"

She looked at him, shook her head, and like a mountain goat that knows its way up a steep cliff, disappeared into the trees.

3

Nancy Parish sat up in bed, pulled the sweaty T-shirt she'd slept in over her head, and tossed it on the floor.

She looked out the bay window of her second-floor bedroom. Damn it. The sky was getting light. Bad news. That meant it was morning. She'd spent most of the night staring at the ceiling, forcing herself to lie still, dozing off, jerking awake, and then doing it all over again. Now the sun was coming up, and she wasn't in any mood to meet the day. She flipped over her pillow and plunked herself face-down into it. But it was hopeless.

Every criminal lawyer had these kinds of sleepless nights. Usually it was after they'd lost a trial and had to watch their client being led away in handcuffs. For Parish, the nocturnal pattern was always the same. Her mind rolling over an endless loop of self-recriminations: What if I'd asked that question? Why didn't I think of that sooner? and How could I have been so stupid?

This night had been different. It was worse: she couldn't sleep, not because of a trial that she'd lost but because of the one she knew she was going to lose in court today. The problem was that one of her best friends, Melissa Copeland, was also her client. And, sadly, had been for years.

After she graduated from law school, Parish got a highly coveted articling job working at one of the city's most prestigious law firms. She was one of fifteen students and only three were women. The other two were Melissa and Melissa's best friend from childhood, Lydia Lansing. The two had grown up next door to each other in a wealthy neighbourhood in downtown Toronto, had gone to the same private schools and summer camps, had hung out at each other's cottages, and even belonged to the same golf club. For Parish, who came from a small town and didn't really know the city, at first this pair of super-self-confident young women was intimidating.

But being the only three women amongst all the ultra-competitive men, they supported each other through months of hellishly long hours and pedal-to-the-metal stress.

Only six articling students were hired back by the firm, and "the Three Amigas," as they were soon called, all made the cut. Each had a particular skill. Lydia was the business lawyer. Her family owned a large publicly traded pharmaceutical company, and she was a whiz at merger deals. Parish was the litigator, destined to spend her life in the courtroom. But Melissa was the star. She had an incredible head for statistics. She practically memorized the Canadian Tax Code, and she was a workhorse. After only three years she was putting in more billable hours than any other lawyer at the firm.

Tall and fit, funny and dynamic, Melissa attracted people wherever she went. She adored designer clothes and soon was doing work for major international fashion, perfume, and cosmetic companies. They loved her combination of swagger, style, and smarts.

She was also a superb athlete and the first one to get married. Her husband, Karl Hodgson, was a wealthy investment banker and top golfer she'd met at "the Club," the name they gave to the Humber River Golf Club, which was practically their second home. They'd invited Parish there a few times, and whenever she went she always felt underdressed, awkward, and out of place.

In the Amigas' fourth year at the firm, Melissa and Karl had a daughter, Britt. Much to Parish's surprise and delight, she was named her godmother.

Melissa only took one month off for her maternity leave and soon was back at it. The Three Amigas all worked killer hours, pouring themselves into the taxis that lined up outside their office at one, two, sometimes three in the morning. One night a week Parish's mother would drive into the city with a homemade lasagne or casserole. Lydia's father had an executive assistant named Rachel who'd worked for him for years. When the three women's workload got really crazy, he would send Rachel in with a "medicine chest" of pills from the company to stymie their headaches and settle their heartburn, and, for Melissa, uppers when she had to work until dawn to close a deal.

Then there was Karl. Despite his heavy schedule, at least once a week he'd bring in a catered meal and the baby. Often Melissa was too busy working to eat very much, Karl would be on his cell phone, and Parish would play with Britt. As she grew older, Britt loved to help Parish photocopy and use the binding machine, but by far her favourite thing was the paper shredder and the crunch, crunch, crunching sound it made.

Then, bit by bit, everything went sour. Melissa would be up all night poring over contracts, working all weekend preparing briefs, sleeping on the floor of her office for nights on end. Karl's catered-dinner visits tailed off and, by the time Britt was four, he stopped showing up. Melissa kept working, often, Parish thought, to avoid going home.

A year later Parish left the firm to practice criminal law, and six months after that Lydia went to work in the family business. Melissa, alone now at the firm and with no friends, practically barricaded herself in her office. Often she'd call Parish late at night and want to talk for hours about some obscure point of law she'd stumbled upon. Whenever Parish asked about Britt and Karl, Melissa would sigh and change the subject.

Very late one night, Parish got a call from the police. Melissa had been arrested for assault with a weapon. She'd gotten into a fight with Karl and cut his arm with a kitchen knife. Worse still, their now seven-year-old daughter had heard the commotion, rushed into the bedroom, and witnessed the whole thing.

Parish went to court the next morning and got Melissa bail with strict conditions: she wasn't allowed any contact with Karl and only supervised access to Britt. She couldn't go near the family home and had to get a psychiatric assessment.

Melissa went to one session with the psychiatrist and walked out. At her visits with Britt, Melissa would slip her secret notes that Britt would later give to the social worker. The notes were almost-incomprehensible rants about how she now realized that the game of golf, which she had once loved, was destructive. That golf courses were playgrounds for the rich at the taxpayers' expense. They ate up valuable land that should be used to house the homeless. And that Britt, who at seven under her father's tutelage was already a budding golf star, should immediately stop playing the evil game and dedicate herself to volunteer work for the less advantaged.

Six months later, Karl filed for divorce, applied for full custody of Britt, and won. Over the next few years, Melissa kept getting arrested for harassing her now ex-husband. Parish kept bailing her out on stricter and stricter bail conditions until even her supervised access to Britt was cut off and she wasn't allowed within four blocks of what had once been the family home.

Too smart for her own good, Melissa became obsessed with finding technical ways around every term of her bail, and miraculously, in case after case, Parish managed to keep her out of jail.

Until the bottom fell out. Karl married Lydia, who had become president of the family drug company and was making millions. For Melissa, it was the ultimate betrayal by her former *amiga*. Even worse, Karl and Lydia hired a high-priced family lawyer and went to court to completely cut Melissa's contact with Britt.

Melissa spent too much money fighting them. With her terrible track record in criminal court, her obsessive, erratic behaviour, and her steadfast refusal to attend any type of counselling or get any other kind of help, she lost.

Cut off from Britt, unable to go near her old home, and furious at

Lydia, she couldn't focus at work. Her late-night calls to Parish grew longer and more rambling. Karl became more and more obsessed with his daughter's golf career, and soon Britt was winning junior tournaments. Her results were reported online, and Melissa scoured the accounts for every detail. She'd write long letters to Karl with suggestions on ways Britt could improve her game, but he never responded.

Melissa became unglued at work and a year after Karl remarried, she was fired. Six months later she turned up at Parish's door. She'd been evicted from her condo and had no place to live. Parish took her in and even convinced her partner, Ted DiPaulo, to give her a small office at their law firm. Melissa was on her best behaviour for about a month.

Inevitably, she began to unravel. After a chaotic few weeks in which she would turn up at the office at all hours and not come home for days, one night she disappeared. She left Parish a confusing yet touching note: "I need to go work with the homeless to fight against the oppression. The assassins. The heartless corporate killers. Thank you so much Nance. You couldn't have done more."

That was two years ago. Since then Melissa had lived on the street, under bridges, in valleys, occasionally checking in to a shelter. Ted, being Ted, insisted that they keep her office open for her because "a lawyer needs an office." Melissa kept what remained of her high-fashion clothes and designer makeup there and would show up from time to time, never with advance warning. Sometimes she'd stay for a few days and do excellent research on files. Then she'd disappear again, always secretive of her whereabouts.

She kept in contact with Parish, sporadically sending her long texts: diatribes about systemic corruption of the medical profession, the establishment's war on the poor, and serial murder conspiracy plots. These were sometimes mixed with cogent analysis of Britt's latest golf triumph and heart-wrenching notes about how she longed to see her daughter.

Three months ago, Melissa had been at it again, testing the limits of her most recent restraining order. She'd been caught walking on the lawns of homes on streets at the edge of the four-block boundary circumscribed by her bail conditions. She'd done it for three days in a row, wearing different clothes each time.

Luckily the Crown Attorney, Albert Fernandez, who'd been assigned to her first case, was sympathetic to a lawyer such as Melissa who had fallen on hard times. Every time she was arrested, Fernandez took the unusual step of handling the case himself because he understood the dynamics. Melissa was lucky he did. But now even Fernandez was fed up. Last week he warned Parish that if Melissa went ahead with the trial and lost, he would ask for jail time. To make matters worse, the assigned judge, Winona Tator, was a no-nonsense fitness nut who didn't have a bone of sympathy in her ultra-sculpted body. The joke about Tator was that she had never put the word *not* in front of the word *guilty*.

Parish's problem was Melissa. Stubborn as ever, she wouldn't make any kind of deal and was insisting upon having this disastrous trial.

What was the point in trying to sleep, Parish thought as she sat back up, ran her fingers through her hair, and rolled out of bed.

Her cell phone buzzed. A text was coming in. Here we go again. This would be from Melissa. No doubt she would have been up all night and had come up with yet another brilliant idea for her defence. Parish shook her head as she looked at her phone.

"Nance, I warned you, but no one would listen," Melissa had just written. "The killings continue. There is no justice. No one is immune."

4

Despite the cold wind, Alison Greene undid the top two buttons of her overcoat. She flicked back her long, straight blond hair and held the mic up below her mouth, the way she'd been trained. She nodded an okay to Randy Krevolin, the cameraman standing in front of her, and waited for the green light on top of his camera to go on.

A moment later it lit up.

"Good morning. This is Alison Greene from *T.O. TV News* reporting live from the edge of the Humber River Valley, where for the second time in just two days the body of a homeless person has been found in what police say is a possible homicide." She turned from the camera and swept her arm to her side. "As you can see, they've set up a barrier to protect the crime scene."

She looked back at the camera. "Local residents tell me they have been complaining for years about the tent cities housing the homeless that have sprung up in this river valley. They say the situation keeps getting worse. Down the road from where I'm standing is the Humber River Golf Club, which has had well-documented fights with these homeless people. The police have told us that they will be making a formal statement soon. We will cover it as it happens. Reporting live from the scene, this is Alison Greene."

She put on her sternest-looking face and waited for the green light to turn red. The moment it did, she unhooked her mic, passed it to Krevolin, and buttoned her coat back up.

"Not bad for a rookie." He was a crusty old pro and Alison knew that from him "not bad" was a real compliment.

"Thanks for driving me out here so fast."

Half an hour earlier, she'd been finishing the Sunday-night grave-yard shift back at the TV station. Standard grunt work for a new reporter. She'd been up all night, her fifth boring night in a row, and predictably nothing had happened. As she was about to pack up, she'd scrolled through the computer one more time, and the alert popped up: "Police have received an anonymous 911 call. Person found VSA in Humber Valley near local golf course."

Wait a minute, Alison thought. The alert rang a bell. What was it? There. The Humber River Valley was the same place where a home-less man had been killed in what sounded like a drunken brawl two days ago.

She'd hustled up Krevolin and they rushed out to the station's mo-bile unit van. He was a good driver and even though by the time they arrived the police tape was up, they'd beat out the competition and parked the van in the best location, closest to the scene. The police were tight-lipped, but all the commotion had attracted a crowd of local residents, and Alison was the first reporter to talk to them.

They told her about all the trouble the homeless people in the val-ley had caused them. The noise. The litter. People being harassed on the street. Their children finding needles in the nearby park.

"We used to love going down to the river," said a middle-aged man who said he'd moved there twenty years ago. "No one dares go down there anymore."

"The murder on Saturday morning really scared us all," a young woman holding a baby in her arms said. "Now this? We keep calling the cops about the problems but no one does anything about it."

An old woman, who said she'd been born in the house across the street she still lived in, told Alison that a bike rider had been hit by a car and fallen into the valley and found the dead body.

"Where's he now?" she asked.

"The ambulance has already taken him away," she said. "My

goodness. Imagine riding along here in the dark. I saw them bring him out on a stretcher. Can you believe it? The fool wasn't even wearing a helmet."

Three other TV vans soon showed up, as well as a radio journalist and a handful of print reporters. They were swarming the scene trying to get an angle for their stories.

Even though she was inexperienced, Alison had one advantage over her competitors. Her father, Detective Ari Greene, was the new head of the homicide squad. She'd been a reporter for more than a year and had never asked him for any inside information on a case. But she'd never been the first reporter on the scene of a possible homicide.

This could be quite a story. With the second murder of a homeless person in such a short time in virtually the same location, she wondered, could there be a serial killer on the loose?

"I'll be back," she told Krevolin.

She slipped through the crowd, ducked down into the valley, and secreted herself behind the trunk of a large tree. The riverbank was steep and she heard the sound of the rushing water roll up from below and smelled the sweet scent of pine trees. Something she'd never smelled back in England where she'd grown up.

She pulled out her cell phone and pushed the pre-set speed dial number. Her father picked up on the first ring.

"Greene here."

She was taken aback. She knew that her name came up on his cell display, and he always answered, "Hi, Allie." A few months ago, she'd told him that Allie was her nickname and now he used it all the time.

The fact that he answered her call like this must mean that he wasn't alone.

"Hi," she said, not calling him Dad the way she always did. "I'm on assignment at—"

"I saw you on TV a minute ago. Good work."

"Thank you."

She waited for him to respond, but he didn't. In the year and a half since she'd moved from England to live with him in Toronto, Alison had learned that her father could be silent for long stretches of time.

"Police have everything cordoned off," she said.

"I can see that."

"None of the cops will talk to me."

"Not yet."

His speech was taciturn, even by her father's sparse standards. She tried to imagine who was standing near him. Other homicide detectives, maybe the chief of police, would be gathered at Police Headquarters to figure out how to deal with this.

"You're not alone, are you?"

"Right."

"You can't talk."

"True."

"But I can ask you questions."

"Go ahead."

Maybe she shouldn't have called. Was he angry? Was she putting him in an impossible position? She knew he'd want to help her, but could talking to his daughter the reporter this way jeopardize his investigation? She didn't want to do that, but he'd said go ahead.

"Is there a connection between this murder and the murdered homeless man found here two days ago?"

"Don't know yet."

"Do the police think there's a serial killer at work?"

"That's part of the problem."

Part of the problem? What was the other part?

"Do you know the identity of the man who was killed this morning?"

"Not exactly."

Not exactly? What was her father hinting at? They would either know or not know.

"Was he one of the homeless men living in the tent city near the golf club?" she asked.

"No, *he* wasn't."

The inflection was slight. She caught it because she knew her father well enough to hear the change of tone in his voice. No, *he* wasn't. Emphasis on *he*.

What did her father mean by that? Could it be—? "Are you saying the dead person found this morning was a woman?"

"Yes, that makes sense. Got to run." Then in a whisper. "Love you."

He hung up before she could say her usual "Love you" back. But he'd delivered the message.

What a scoop. She called her boss, Sheena Persaud, and told her that she'd learned from "a confidential source" that the dead homeless person was a woman.

"Amazing," Persaud said. "We're on commercial break for two minutes. Set up, and we'll go live." She hung up before Alison could tell her she had ducked away from the crowd and didn't know where Krevolin was.

Alison ran back to the street, her coat flapping in the wind, her hair askew. There were people everywhere. But where was Krevolin? She couldn't see him in the crush of the crowd. Maybe he'd gone back to the van. She checked it, but he wasn't there. She looked at her watch. Sixty-five seconds to go. Darn it.

She yanked open the door of the van and stood on the step to see over people.

There he was, off by the trees filming, getting cutaway shots that they could use later. Smart move, but she needed him now. She charged into the crowd. A group of teenagers were huddled together directly in her way. As she pushed through them, she smelled a wave of marijuana smoke.

"Hey lady," one of them yelled at her. "Where's the fire?"

The rest of them laughed.

Her phone rang again. It was Persaud. "We're ready in about forty-five."

"Ready," she said, trying to keep her voice level.

She got to Krevolin and tugged on his arm.

He pulled his camera from his eye and whirled around.

"Quick," she said. "We're going live in less than thirty. We have to find a spot away from the crowd where none of the other reporters can hear me."

"Behind there," he said, pointing to a nearby hedge while he clipped on his earpiece so he could also hear the producer back at the studio to get his cue.

They both ran.

"Twenty seconds," he said, handing her the mic.

She stood still, straightened her coat, undid the top two buttons, and stared at the red light on the top of his camera.

"Ten, nine, eight," he said.

She took a deep breath. Exhaled. Then another one. She lifted the mic. This was a big scoop. And it was hers.

"Three, two, and one," Krevolin said.

The light switched from red to green.

"Reporting live, this is Alison Greene with an exclusive update on this breaking story."

5

Daniel Kennicott reached across the bed for his girlfriend, Angela Breaker. They'd started living together three months earlier, and after many years of living alone, he was still getting used to waking up beside her every morning. He stretched out his fingers, but his hand landed on the mattress.

He couldn't see a thing because Angela insisted on sleeping in total darkness. She'd grown up in one of Toronto's crime-infested subsidized housing complexes, and her mother had insisted that they sleep with the blinds down and all the lights off because it was safer that way.

He couldn't hear her breathe. Nor could he feel the heat of her body. "Angela," he whispered.

No response. He turned back to his side of the bed, reached down to the floor, and groped for his cell phone, which he always left screen-side down. He flipped it over. The time was 7:05. Angela, a dedicated jogger, would have been on the road for more than an hour, starting at six sharp.

He lay back, closed his eyes, and smiled. Late last night he'd tiptoed into the bedroom thinking she was asleep. Feeling his way in the darkness, he'd slid into his side of the bed. As soon as his head had hit the pillow, he'd felt her hand on his chest.

"How bad was the autopsy?" she'd asked.

He put his hand over hers and stroked the back of her wrist.

"The man's name was Dr. Rene LeBlanc. He'd been living on the street for more than a decade. Successful pediatrician, wife an engineer, two kids, nice home in the suburbs. Then he got sued for malpractice when a baby under his care died. Couldn't take the pressure and started drinking straight vodka and doing coke. Two years later he was homeless."

"Can happen to anyone, can't it?" she said.

"For the last year he's been part of a group of homeless people who've camped out in the Humber River Valley. The pathologist said he had almost no liver left and that his platelet level was so low he could have bled to death if he cut himself shaving."

She turned her hand and intertwined their fingers.

"How was your night?" he asked her.

"Another boring board meeting." Angela was an executive in a non-profit housing advocacy group. "What happened to the former doctor's family?"

"They moved to Florida. I phoned the ex-wife to inform her."

"What'd she say?"

"She said, and I quote, 'Oh. What am I supposed to do now? Care or something? Don't call again.' Then she hung up."

Angela lay quietly beside him. With her thumb she massaged the back of his hand. He closed his eyes.

"Any leads?" she asked in a whisper.

"I've spent hours down there trying to get people to talk to me. I told them I didn't care if there was a warrant out for them, or if they were breaching their bail. I even said they didn't have to give me their names, just let me know if they saw or heard anything."

"Let me guess. No one would talk."

"Nada."

"They're suspicious of authority. That's why most of them live on the street."

"I know sometimes you run down there by the river," he said, shaking his head, "but it's another world when you get off the path. People in makeshift shelters made of plastic sheeting, scraps of plywood, or even cardboard. Some sleep right out in the open. It's third world right in the middle of the city."

She slid her hand up his arm, her fingers rubbing it.

"We found a smashed vodka bottle on the rocks beside the body," he said. "It looks as if two drunks were fighting over some booze."

He hadn't told her about the thing that had been jammed down the man's throat, which suggested something more sinister. He was holding this information back, even from her. It was one of the many mottos his mentor, Ari Greene, had drilled into him since he'd become a homicide detective: Always know more than you tell.

There was one more thing he hadn't told Angela. The true cause of death.

The pathologist, Dr. Ramos, was new. She had a lovely Spanish-sounding accent and a charming, formal way of speaking. "If you please," she'd told him, "do take a close look at the back of the victim's head."

He saw there was a hole, too wide and too deep to be caused by a glass bottle.

"Blunt force trauma?" he asked her.

"Most certainly."

"Could it have been caused by the victim falling on the rock?"

"Almost certainly not."

"Some kind of weapon. Any idea what it might have been?"

"Impossible to ascertain at the moment. One can deduce that the object was small and heavy. I shall do further investigation."

Beside him in bed, Angela had uncoupled her fingers from his hand and wrapped her arm across his chest.

"What will you do now?" she asked.

"Work the case, the same way we'd do if the guy was a millionaire."

She had pulled him gently toward her. He felt her skin, then her lips on his, her hands around his waist now, her arms, her feet, every piece of her intertwining with him.

"That's what I love about you, Daniel," she had whispered.

Being this close to death had made him crave life, need the warmth, the touch. She understood, he'd thought last night before he'd drifted off to sleep.

He heard the front door of the flat open. He put the phone back beside the bed, lighted-side down. There were soft footsteps in the hallway and then Angela was at the door, a beam of light flooding in behind her, silhouetting her fit body.

"Good run?" he asked.

"I was trying to be quiet. I thought you'd still be asleep."

"I woke up a few minutes ago. You must have been cold."

"It's fine once you get going. You must be tired."

Before he could answer her, his cell phone rang. It was the special ring tone that meant the call was from Greene, the new head of the homicide squad. Kennicott looked at Angela. She'd learned what Greene's ring tone sounded like and knew what it meant.

"Ari?" he said answering the phone. "What have we got?"

"Another homeless person murdered in the Humber Valley."

"Same MO?"

"Looks like it."

"I'll be out in five." He hung up and looked at Angela. "I've got to go."

"I know. But first, Daniel," she said, holding his face in her hands, "a kiss."

6

Only for Melissa would she come in to the office at this ungodly hour, Parish thought as she unlocked the front door of her office. Melissa always insisted that they meet early in the morning on the days of her trials, and inevitably she arrived armed with an avalanche of new ideas for her defence. Most of them were ridiculous, but as with most brilliant people, she usually had some out-of-the-box, original angle that just might work.

Parish tossed a bag of clean clothes on one of the two client chairs that faced her desk. She never knew which version of Melissa was going to show up: Would it be the ragged homeless person or the sophisticated Bay Street lawyer? She hadn't been in Melissa's office for months and had no idea if any of her clothes were still there, so as a precautionary measure she'd packed up some things for Melissa to wear in court: a navy-blue wool A-line dress, a grey tweed jacket, and suede pumps. And she'd brought a makeup kit and a hairbrush.

She was expecting the worst. For the last hour, Melissa had been sending her a stream of texts about a serial killer on the loose and an international drug conspiracy behind the deaths of the homeless, and claiming she'd come up with a new idea that was somehow going to magically win her trial.

Parish booted up her computer and checked the news. There was a breaking story about a second murder of a homeless person in the Humber Valley. This time it was a woman. Maybe Melissa wasn't crazy after all.

Parish pulled her trial binder out of her briefcase. Still, how an international drug conspiracy and a serial killer on the loose in the city could help as a defence against the charge of failure to comply with her bail conditions was something only Melissa could have dreamed up.

Don't get distracted by her bluster, Parish told herself as she read through the evidence for what had to be the twentieth time, hoping beyond hope that she'd find a ray of light in this dark forest of bad news. What was the use?

"Knock, knock," a voice in the hallway said, laughing, "knock, knock, knock."

Parish couldn't help but smile. This was the lost, happy voice of her old friend. Today she'd be the "good" Melissa.

"I'm here," she called back.

"Give me five," Melissa responded in a singsong voice, and Parish heard her open then close the door to her office.

Parish kept reading through the file. The case was a clear-cut loser. Melissa's bail conditions explicitly stated that she could not be on the four streets that surrounded her ex-husband's house. Yet she'd been seen, and photographed, by neighbours, walking on the lawns of houses on all four streets three days in a row. The neighbours were worn out by Melissa's shenanigans and would be unassailable witnesses against her.

Parish heard Melissa's door open and close, and then Melissa ask, "Are you ready for this?" from the hallway.

"Can't wait," Parish said, putting down her binder.

"Ta-dah!" Melissa jumped into the doorway, wearing a black Prada suit with gold buttons, a camel-coloured silk top self-tying at the neck, an Hermès belt, and Chanel ballet flats. Her hair was pulled back to the nape of her neck. Her skin, the one thing about her that never seemed to age, looked bright and fresh. She was carrying a Louis Vuitton leather briefcase in one hand and a large tote bag in the other. She looked wonderful.

"See," she said smiling, "once a fashion plate, always a fashion plate." She put down the briefcase and tote bag. Parish stood and embraced her. Melissa held on tight and started to shake. "Oh, Nance," she whispered, "it's horrible. You can't imagine."

"It's okay, Mel," Parish whispered back, holding her close until she stopped shivering.

Melissa loosened her grip.

Parish picked up the bag of clothes she'd brought for Melissa off the chair and tossed it in the corner. She laughed. "Look, I packed you a fresh outfit just in case."

"Nance, you're such a goody two-shoes," Melissa said, laughing too. She grabbed her tote bag and threw it on top of the other bag, where it landed with a thud. "Keep my stuff for safekeeping. You never know when it might come in handy."

They sat facing each other in the client chairs in front of Parish's desk. She pulled over her trial binder so they could look through it together. Here we go, she thought. She couldn't meet her old friend's eyes. She started flipping through the pages.

"Melissa, please listen. This time we have to make a deal or for sure you are going to end up in jail."

"Why? We have a perfectly good defence."

Wonderful. Knowing Melissa, she'd found a case in some obscure New Zealand law journal, or some such, that she'd convinced herself had a winning legal argument.

"I've scoured the case law," Parish said, "and—"

"That's your first mistake. It's never about the case. But the facts." Melissa pulled out her own binder from her briefcase and flipped to the page with the bail conditions. "Look at the word I've underlined."

Parish grabbed Melissa's binder and stared at the page. She shook her head. "Come on, this is the most technical defence I've ever seen. Even from you. No way it will fly, especially with Judge Tator."

"Nance. You remember the most important thing that we learned about litigation when we were summer students. 'Make the judge love your client and—'"

"Let the judge worry about the law," Parish said. They finished the sentence in unison. Laughing.

Melissa jumped to her feet. "Get up," she said, opening both hands and putting them in front of her.

Parish hesitated.

"Come on."

Parish knew what Melissa wanted to do.

One Friday night that first year when she'd met Melissa and Lydia and they were working late at the law firm, Parish had gone into the women's washroom and seen the two in the corner. They didn't notice her. She thought they were fighting but quickly realized they were playing a game.

They were slapping each other's hands, then the top of their own chests, then their knees while they sang a song in perfect rhythm:

> *I am a pretty little Dutch girl*
> *As pretty as pretty can be*
> *And all the boys around my block*
> *Go crazy over me!*

Parish watched entranced as they kept going, faster and faster.

> *I had a boyfriend, Patty*
> *Who comes from Cincinnati*
> *With forty-eight toes and a pickle on his nose*
> *And this is the way my story goes . . .*

They paused. Inhaled. Like a tennis player about to hit her final serve. Then faster and louder and slapping each other and themselves harder they finished.

> *One day when I was walkin'*
> *I heard my boyfriend talkin'*
> *To a pretty little girl with strawberry curls*

And this is what he said to her:
I L-O-V-E, love you
To K-I-S-S, kiss you
Yes K-I-S-S, kiss you in
The D-A-R-K dark boom boom!

They'd fallen into each other's arms laughing. Parish felt as if she'd walked in on a private party and wished she could slip away unnoticed. But she was frozen. If she moved they'd notice her. And a second later, Melissa did.

"Nancy!" she howled, still laughing. "Now you know our little secret. We've played this game since kindergarten."

"Best way ever to relieve the tension," Lydia said.

"Come on," Melissa said, "we're going to teach you."

"We have to stick together," Lydia said, "and have some girl time."

That's how her friendship with the two of them had started. They had secret code names that they'd had for each other since childhood and that they used when they were alone. Melissa was Mel, as in "melody." Lydia was Lyd as in "put a lid on it." They named her Nance as in "take a chance."

The game became their mutual touchstone. But with all that had happened, Parish couldn't remember the last time she'd played it with either Lydia or Melissa.

Melissa was looking down at her. Smiling. Hopeful.

"Okay, okay," she said, hauling herself up out of the chair and putting her hands up to her chest.

"Look at me," Melissa said. "A pretty little Dutch girl. And poor mother deprived of seeing her only child. I'm lovable, aren't I?"

Parish felt like saying, "The only thing Judge Tator loves is finding people guilty," but instead she smiled and said, "Yes, Melissa, you are. Very, very lovable."

She straightened her back, opened her hands, put them up in front of her, and pushed them toward Melissa's hands and together they began to play and sing.

7

Kennicott knelt down beside the body and let his eyes settle on the dead woman's head. Then her neck. Her shoulders, arms, and torso. Breathe, exhale, breathe, exhale, take your time, he told himself. He'd learned this from Ari Greene.

"The first time you see a body," Greene had told Kennicott in his early days on the homicide squad, "don't rush. Take it all in, every detail. This will be your only chance to see the body as the killer left it. Memorize it. A photo or video is not the same."

Kennicott's eyes drifted down to the woman's waist, her legs, her feet. Then he did it again, starting to inventory in his mind what he saw. The woman's head was small, her hair was long, scraggly, and grey, her face was round, and her skin pallid and worn. At first glance she appeared to be quite old, in her sixties or maybe more. He zeroed in on the wrinkles at the corners of her eyes, a reveal: it was the device that carnies at a circus used to guess people's ages. There were few wrinkle lines. He looked at her neck, the second reveal. The skin there was smooth. She looked older than her age. His guess was that she was in her mid- to late forties. Living on the street had taken its toll.

She was thin. And short, he'd guess about five foot three or four. Her shoulders were narrow, her arms had no muscle tone, and her fingers were callused and worn. Her fingernails were rough and bitten down to the cuticles. She wore no rings, no jewellery. Her legs were splayed out in a V-shape and her feet were unusually large for such a small frame.

Even in her supine position, without lifting her head, he could see the back of it was bashed in. A pool of blood had sprung from it and dried on the rock. There was another gash to the top of her head, and he could see bits of glass stuck in her hair. Her body reeked of death and alcohol.

Glass shards were scattered about on the rock behind her head. One of the bigger pieces had a Smirnoff vodka label attached to it.

He sat back, closed his eyes, and let the picture of the murder scene and the dead woman settle into his brain. Stay calm. With his eyes shut, the sounds of the river valley came alive. The swish of water slipping over rocks, the whistle of the wind through the trees, and the odd tweet of a bird.

Then, like changing channels on a TV, he pictured the body of Dr. LeBlanc, killed here in the valley two days earlier. Much was similar. Both had been found early in the morning, lying dead on the rocks, the back of their heads bashed in. Both reeked of alcohol, and at both scenes there were the shattered remnants of a Smirnoff vodka bottle.

At first glance the LeBlanc murder had had all the hallmarks of a fight between two homeless men. Kennicott knew the case would get minimal play in the press: it only rated two paragraphs on page ten of the *Toronto Sun*, the city's tabloid newspaper. Still he'd been careful in his press release to keep one distinct and disturbing detail secret.

"Well, well," said a booming voice that Kennicott recognized immediately, shattering the silence. "At least it's not snowing."

Kennicott opened his eyes. Harry Ho, one of the top forensic detectives on the force, and certainly the most verbose, was standing on the other side of the corpse, his large frame hovering over the tiny dead woman. Ho, an old pro, had worked with Kennicott on many murders, including Dr. LeBlanc's two days earlier.

"Here we go again, Detective K." Ho pointed to the glass shard with the label on it. "Looks as if there's a vodka killer on the loose. Smirnoff man. Me, I prefer Grey Goose."

Kennicott looked at Ho but didn't say a word.

"A lot of glass to pick up." He pulled a pint-sized vacuum out of his ever-present bag of tricks. The guy was an equipment junkie. "My latest toy. This baby will hoover up every little piece of glass."

Ho was a strange combination of self-styled stand-up comedian and ultra-nerd. Some detectives didn't like working with him because of his non-stop, attention-seeking banter. Kennicott didn't mind because he knew that Ho, despite all the quips and sarcasm, cared.

"A woman," Ho said. "This is going to cause a big stir, especially if..."

Ho, who was remarkably agile for such a tall man, squatted down until he was at eye level with Kennicott. "Did you check yet?"

"I was waiting for you."

"Might be my lucky day. Let's put gloves on."

He reached into his back pocket and pulled out two pairs of latex gloves. Passed one set to Kennicott, put his on, and then gently opened the woman's mouth.

"Yep, I see it," he said. "Here, hold her open."

Ho reached into his bag and pulled out a pair of thin forceps. Gently, he manoeuvred them deep inside.

"There, hold her still, yes, good, I've got it," he said, and pulled his hand back.

They both stared.

"Looks like the last one." He'd extracted a white golf ball with a blue, red, and gold insignia on it featuring the letters *HRGC*. He handed it to Kennicott.

Kennicott twirled it in his hand.

"Same Humber River Golf Club ball," he said, twirling it in his hand so he could read the initials below the insignia. "Same initials. K.L.H."

"Karl Leonard Hodgson," Ho said. "I worked on his trial with your boss. Ari Greene doesn't like to lose."

Three years earlier, Karl Hodgson, the former club president, was out golfing alone early one Monday morning when a drunken homeless man named Rubin Wilson accosted him as he approached the course's remote seventh-hole green. He had a knife and demanded Hodgson give him his expensive watch. Wilson had picked the wrong man to try to rob. Hodgson, known to be a vociferous opponent of the homeless people who had moved into the valley, didn't back down. Instead he took his nine iron and swung it at Wilson and bashed his head in, not once or twice but five times. Killing him.

The case caused a huge controversy in the city. Homeless advocates and their supporters organized rotating protest marches in front of each of the city's private golf clubs. They were pitted against homeowners and conservative talk show hosts who decried the increasing numbers of people sleeping on the sidewalks and begging on the streets, and the destruction of public spaces.

Greene charged Hodgson with manslaughter. It was a high-profile trial that lasted three weeks, making daily headlines. The jury deliberated for four days before coming back with their verdict: not guilty. This provoked a massive pop-up protest and demonstrators appeared without warning at rush hour on one of the city's major bridges, tying up traffic for half a day.

The acquittal only strengthened the determination of the people who supported Hodgson. Emboldened, he embarked upon a career in politics. He ran for city council as an alderman in the ward where the golf club was located. He wore golf clothes to every political event he attended, no matter how formal. In his campaign he pledged to rid the city of the homeless with the catch phrase "Work in Our City, Don't Sleep on Our Streets." He won in a landslide, and the rumour was that he was planning to run for mayor in the next election.

"You're right," Kennicott said, handing the golf ball back to Ho and watching him put it into a fresh evidence bag and seal it. "Ari doesn't like to lose."

8

Alison realized that this was going to be tricky. Here she was reporting on a protest on College Street in front of the place where her father worked—Police Headquarters. She had a job to do, and it was important that she not let her personal life interfere with her professional life. Still, it felt weird. And she didn't know how her dad was going to feel about it. She had to be careful.

The scene was crowded. The centre lanes of College Street were taken up by streetcars, which left two narrow lanes each way for vehicles. It was the morning rush hour, and police were keeping the protesters confined to the meagre sidewalk in front of the building. Add to that the reporters and their TV vans parked on the sidewalk up the street, as well as the usual pedestrian traffic, and this whole thing had the potential to spin out of control.

The protesters were a small but rowdy bunch. They carried what looked like hastily made signs, with slogans such as "Cops Don't Care," and "Police + Politicians + Homeless = No Action," and "Stop Killing Our Most Vulnerable." Alison watched them. She spotted their leader, a young, athletic-looking man with straight blond hair and trendy-looking wire-rimmed glasses. He started to chant, "The homeless have rights, the homeless have rights," and his followers joined in.

Alison looked back at Krevolin and pointed to the man.

"Follow me. I want to try to get in and interview him."

She manoeuvred her way through the crowd, venturing onto the street when there was a gap in the heavy traffic, to get near to him. Krevolin stuck with her. When the chanting stopped, they approached the man.

He saw them, turned to his followers with his arms outstretched like a southern preacher whipping up his congregation, and said, "Look, people, we have a TV reporter here. I predict she'll seem really sympathetic when she interviews me, but on the news today not a word I'm saying will make it to air."

He turned back to face Alison. His face was smooth. He was handsome and he knew it.

"Hello, Madam Reporter," he said, in an obsequious voice.

She held out her hand. "Alison Greene, *T.O. TV News*."

"Dr. Arnold Burns, People on the Street Health Care Clinic." He shook her hand. His skin was soft and warm and he gave her a wide grin.

"Like most reporters," he said, "I doubt you know the real statistics of poverty in Toronto, the fastest-growing city in North America. And one of the richest in the world."

Alison let go of his hand. She wasn't going to let this guy intimidate her. "Why don't you wait until I get my cameraman set up?" she asked. "We'll go live, and you can tell me and everyone else your comments."

His back stiffened. Gone was his smile, replaced with a serious look. "They're not comments, they're facts."

She put up a finger to quiet him while she listened on her earpiece to her producer back at the station.

"We're live in one minute, Doctor."

She motioned Krevolin forward.

"Really?" He was trying not to sound impressed that she was putting him on the air live, but she could tell he was.

"You'll have about ninety seconds."

He waved to his supporters to gather around him, positioning the ones with the placards in the front. This guy was no fool, she realized. He knew how to play the media and make his little demonstration look much bigger on TV than it really was.

"Going in twenty," she told him.

"Do you want me to repeat my name and the name of my clinic for you?" he asked, grinning again.

He had sparkling white teeth, a surprising dimple when he smiled, and deep brown eyes that he focused on her. The guy was damn charming.

She could see how this charismatic young doctor had attracted these followers on such short notice. He probably had a lot of young woman followers too.

"Not necessary," she said.

She turned her back to him and faced the camera. The green light went on. "This is Alison Greene reporting live on College Street in front of Toronto Police Headquarters. Earlier today the second homeless person in two days was found murdered in the Humber Valley. The victim this time, as reported first here on *T.O. TV News*, was a woman. Behind me, as you can see, protesters have gathered to voice their concerns about the unseen poverty in Toronto, Canada's wealthiest city. With me now is Dr. Arnold Burns, a physician at the People on the Street Health Care Clinic."

She turned and stared straight in his eyes.

"Doctor Burns. You work on the front lines. How pervasive is homelessness and poverty in Toronto?"

She put her mic below his chin.

Instead of looking at the camera, as the amateurs did, he looked right back at her.

"Alison, I'm glad you asked me that question." He was calm and relaxed, talking to her as if they were best friends having an important conversation. "Sadly, too few people really care about what is actually happening in our city. They see beggars on the street, homeless people sleeping on sidewalks and in parks, and walk right past them while holding their five-dollar lattes or drive by in their imported luxury vehicles. They don't recognize the pervasiveness of the poverty, the true extent of the hunger, the real desperation in Toronto. It's a crisis but people want to pretend it doesn't exist."

He was good at painting a compelling picture.

"What do the statistics tell us?" she asked him.

"Did you know that one hundred fourteen homeless people died in Toronto last year? That's one hundred and fourteen of our fellow citizens. This should be headline news. And more than a third of them were women."

"That's startling."

"More than sixteen thousand people use the shelter system, and countless others simply live on the street or in the ravines and river valleys in third-world conditions. And how about this? One in every four children in this city lives in poverty. Tell me the truth, Alison, how does that make you feel?"

It made her feel ill. She had no idea the numbers were this bad. But she couldn't show emotion. Her job was to be an objective reporter.

Burns was smooth. In seconds he'd turned the interview around and was questioning her. She was the one who was supposed to be doing that. She had to regain control.

"Is that why your group is protesting today?" she asked him.

"No." He faced the camera. This guy knew how to sell it. "The inaction of the police." He waved at his little gang of supporters, cupped his hands as if he was talking to an enormous crowd, and shouted, "Two homeless people have been murdered this week, and what are the police doing?"

"Nothing!" they shouted back.

"Do the police care?" he bellowed.

"No," they yelled back.

"What do we want?"

"Action!"

They were so loud that it took a few seconds for Alison to hear her producer shouting in her ear: "Wrap it up, wrap it up." Oh no, she realized. She'd been so entranced by the doctor that she'd been watching him in action and not reporting. She'd lost track of the time. And she'd

allowed him to tarnish the Toronto Police Force, and by proxy, her father, without challenging him at all. Too late to fix it. Damn.

She swung back to the camera, positioning herself at an angle that
put the sign holders right behind her. "Reporting live for *T.O. TV News*,
this is Alison Greene on the street in front of Toronto Police Headquarters."

She watched the green light above the camera, willing it to go to
red. It stayed on for a few more painful seconds, as Krevolin panned
behind her to take in the scene.

Finally the red light went on. Behind her, the protest instantly went
quiet, like an electric radio when the plug was pulled from the wall.

"Not bad," Krevolin said, pulling the camera off his shoulder.

She shook her head. "Nice of you to say, but we both know it was a
disaster."

She felt a tap on her shoulder. It was Burns. Smiling again, looking
less condescending. Warmer.

"Thank you," he said.

"Just doing my job."

"I think you were doing more than that. You seemed genuinely surprised by the grim statistics."

"I'm still quite new here. Toronto seems wealthy compared to
London, where I grew up, which has its grotty parts. Here the poverty
seems to be hidden."

"Hidden. That's the problem."

"Do you think you are being fair to the police?"

He wasn't smiling anymore. "The police, the politicians, the corporations, what's the difference? They're all on the same team."

She was tempted to argue with him. But what would she say? *You're
wrong. My father is the head of the homicide squad and I know he cares.* It
would sound ridiculous, and besides she didn't want him to know.

He pointed to her cameraman. "Why don't you come to our clinic
and do a story about the real Toronto?"

He whipped a business card out, like an expert poker player flipping over his winning card, and slid it into her hand. Their fingers brushed across each other as she took it.

"I can't bring my cameraman, we've been up all night and I'd need to get approval," she said. "But I'd like to see it for myself."

He pulled out a pen from nowhere, flipped the card over, and wrote out the name of a café. "Meet me here at noon, the best coffee in the city."

He put the card back in her hand.

She read what he'd written: "Fahrenheit Café, Lombard and Jarvis." He'd elongated the bottom of the final *s* into a large bubble and drawn a smiley face inside it.

She looked back at him but he'd already turned back to his gang of followers.

"What are the police doing?" he shouted again.

"Nothing!" they shouted back.

"Do the police care?"

"No."

"What do we want?"

"Action!"

She slipped the card into her pocket and looked up at Police Head-quarters, where, she knew, her father was probably looking down from his fifth-floor office.

9

By any measure, the provincial courthouse called 1000 Finch West was a disgrace. Built as a "temporary" facility back in the 1980s, it was located in a rundown strip mall miles from any decent public transportation routes. Outside its front door, across the cracked-concrete parking lot, sat a massive used-car shop plastered with cheesy advertising signs—"Need immediate dough? And have nowhere to go?" "Need a Car Loan? Captain Car Loan Approves Everyone!" And signs for paralegals—"Need to get a criminal pardon? See if you qualify?"

If a Hollywood producer were searching for a location to film a scene in a decaying courthouse in the middle of nowhere, this would be perfect.

The inside of the courthouse was no better than its exterior. It was a windowless cavern. The washrooms were dirty, the downstairs prison cells decrepit. There wasn't a comfortable place for people to sit, only a few hard wooden benches under cold fluorescent lights. Nor was there anywhere to get food or even a vending machine for drinks or coffee. Young children, dragged to court by their poor parents, had nowhere to play.

The only saving grace was the second-floor Crown Attorney's office that, unlike every other Crown's office in the province, was not barricaded with bulletproof glass. Many years ago, the popular head Crown who ran the office had insisted on an open-door policy, welcoming defence lawyers and making every effort to work with them to resolve all but the most contentious cases. Although he had passed away decades earlier, his legacy remained and after all this time nothing had changed.

That was why, despite the horrid facilities, the boondoggle traffic jams to get here, and the wasteland of strip malls and fast-food joints surrounding the courthouse, the best and the brightest Crowns all wanted to work here.

This was good news for Parish, who walked in to meet with Crown Albert Fernandez. It was nine thirty, the witching hour for prosecutors, when the pressure of the ten o'clock court start time was kicking in.

Fernandez was alone in an office he shared with two other prosecutors. Three desks were crammed into the small room, all facing blank walls. The tops of two of them were filled with messy combinations of law books, court files, pads of paper, black binders, and scattered pens, pencils, and coloured markers. Fernandez's desk was spotless except for one binder with a label that said R. v. COPELAND, MELISSA.

He saw Parish and smiled as she plopped a cup of coffee down in front of him.

"Albert, a real latte from a real downtown coffee shop," she said.

Fernandez, who was born in Chile, and who Parish knew was a coffee connoisseur, grinned.

"I double-cupped it for you to try to keep it warm," she said.

He took a long sip. Closed his eyes, savouring it like a wine connoisseur. "Mmm. Downtown. Civilization."

"Don't think I'm trying to buy you off."

"Ah, but we both know you are." He picked up his binder and opened it. "Unfortunately, Ms. Parish, if your client goes through with the trial this time, I will have no choice but to ask for her to be incarcerated. We've got Judge Tator. You know she loves to convict, and she loves to sentence even more."

"Look. We'd both like to settle this. But I'm stuck. Melissa wants a trial."

It was a stratagem that her senior partner Ted DiPaulo had taught her when she first joined his firm. Never, ever, refer to your client as "the defendant," "the accused," or "my client," or even by their last name, but use only their first name when you talk to the Crown, the judge, even the jail guards.

Fernandez pulled a typewritten page from the inside sleeve of his binder. The heading read: "AGREED STATEMENT OF FACTS."

"It's her choice. She's going to piss off the judge. I have four civilian witnesses subpoenaed to be here today," he said, handing the pages to her. "One's a teacher who has a special needs class waiting for her, one's a lawyer who is supposed to be in the Court of Appeal this morning, one's a surgeon who will have to cancel her surgery if you make her stay and testify, and one's a stay-at-home dad who is missing his spin class for this. If we can agree on these facts, then I can send them all on their way."

Parish took her time reading through the agreed statement of facts. It was well written, concise, and reasonable. She handed it back to him.

"Sorry. No can do. You need to call them."

"All four? Even the surgeon?"

She shrugged. "Call her first and she can get out of here."

Parish had done trials with Fernandez for years. He rarely got angry or flustered. But now he looked upset.

He flipped through his well-organized binder and stopped at a tab labelled "DR. ENNIS," clicked open the binder, pulled out a three-hole-punched set of pages stapled cleanly in the top left-hand corner and showed it to her, keeping it in his hand. He'd used a yellow marker to highlight the key points of the doctor's testimony. The guy was a good lawyer.

"Look, right here on page two." He flipped to the page and read out loud: "'I've lived on Park Road for fifteen years and I knew Ms. Melissa Copeland when she lived four blocks away on Bedrock Drive. We used to carpool our daughters to Gymboree classes. The police have informed me that her current bail conditions prevent Melissa from walking on my street. During the week of August fifteenth, I saw Melissa walk across my lawn directly in front of the kitchen window three days in a row while I was preparing dinner for my family. Although each time she was wearing different clothing, I clearly recognized that it was her.'"

Fernandez threaded the pages back into his binder and closed it with a loud snap. He threw his hands up in frustration. "Come on. What else do you want?"

"What I want," she said, "is for you to call the doctor and the other three civilian witnesses. Those are my instructions from my client. Don't worry, I'll be nice to them."

"Really?"

"Really. I'll see you in court at ten."

She stood up to go.

"Wait," Fernandez said. "Shut the door."

She shut it and looked back at him. "What's up?"

He pulled out a chair for her, and she sat.

"Lydia came to talk to me yesterday."

Fernandez knew this file so well that he was on a first-name basis with all of the players. He knew the whole story of Melissa and Lydia and Karl and Britt.

Parish looked at him but didn't say anything.

"She started crying. She doesn't want Melissa to go to jail."

Stay silent. Let him talk, Parish told herself.

"She wants this nonsense to stop."

"But she keeps charging Melissa."

"Because Melissa won't stay away."

"Because her former husband and her former best friend won't let her see her only child."

He shook his head. "This is the fourth time she's breached her conditions."

"And you've been incredibly tolerant and sympathetic. I totally appreciate it."

He sighed. "Nancy, you're in the middle of this. These women are your two best friends."

He just called me Nancy, she thought. Fernandez wasn't usually this informal. He must know the first-name stratagem too.

"Lydia told me that they're having a party tonight at their golf club for their daughter," he said.

"She's Melissa's daughter and her name is Britt. She won the trophy as the top-ranked female golfer in Ontario under age thirteen. I'm her godmother, and I'm going to be there too."

"Lydia said they're terrified Melissa will show up and cause a scene. She said if Melissa will agree to not come to the party tonight, she'll allow her supervised access with Britt again. I'll find some excuse to adjourn this trial and get you away from Judge Tator. And if things settle down, we won't even have to proceed."

Parish stood. "I'll ask her. But Albert, be prepared. I know Melissa better than anyone. She won't go for it."

Fernandez stood, cutting her off from the door. This was totally out of character for him.

"Tator will convict Melissa and toss her in jail without a second's hesitation, even if I don't ask for jail time. This morning I tried to trade courts with other Crowns, but we're stuck."

"Albert, if only every Crown Attorney and judge were as fair-minded as you are. Sometimes we're just stuck in our roles. If Melissa wants it, we have to have a trial."

He moved aside. "I tried," he said, frowning.

She stepped past him. "See you in court," she said. It was curious. He seemed to be even more upset about this than she was.

10

Ari Greene took off his jacket, draped it over the back of his chair, and sauntered over to the window of his corner office on the fifth floor of the Toronto Police Headquarters and looked down at the small but rowdy crowd of protesters on the street below. Four TV news trucks were up on the sidewalk, their antennae reaching high into the sky. Cameramen were busy setting up their tripods, and well-dressed reporters were straightening their clothes and fixing their hair, waiting to go on air. He spotted his daughter. Unlike the other reporters standing on the periphery of the demonstration, she'd wormed her way right into the middle of it, pulling a cameraman in along with her.

That's my Allie, he thought, right in there ahead of the competition.

The protesters carried handmade signs turned up toward the building: "Stop Killing the Homeless" one read. "Cops Don't Care" read another.

He looked back at the large computer screen on his desk. In the last ten minutes, forty-three new emails had come in from reporters and news outlets asking Greene to comment on the latest murder in the Humber Valley.

There was a loud knock on his open door and the chief of police, Nora Bering, strode into his office. They'd joined the police force at the same time decades earlier and had quickly become fast friends. As their careers progressed, they'd worked together off and on for years. The upshot was that they spoke in the kind of shorthand that only so many years of mutual respect and experience could foster.

"You'll hate this," she said, putting a sheet of paper on his desk.

Greene came back from the window and looked at it. "Press

Release" was typed in bold letters below the Toronto Police Service logo. He gave Bering a wary look before he picked it up and began to read aloud.

"'Toronto Police Service have responded immediately to the latest apparent homicide in the city. Every effort will be made to . . .'" He stopped reading, scanned the rest of the page and put it back down. Shook his head.

"They pay someone a lot of money to write these," he said.

"Good work if you can get it," Bering said. She motioned out the window to the demonstration on the street below. "Welcome to being the Big Cheese."

"The protesters don't waste any time, do they?"

"The modern age. Everyone knows everything right away."

"And everyone has an opinion," Greene said.

"You going to go down there?"

"Absolutely. It never pays to hide."

"What are you going to say?"

He shook his head. "I can tell you what I'm *not* going to say." He picked up the paper again and read aloud: "'Toronto remains one the safest cities in Canada, with by far the lowest homicide rate per capita of any large city in North America.'" He crumpled the page into a ball and tossed it to Bering.

She caught it. "This murder? Same MO? Same golf ball in the victim's mouth? Same initials on the ball?"

He nodded then motioned toward the window. "The media will have a field day when they find that out."

"Who knows about it?"

"You, me, Kennicott, and Ho, the forensic officer. Tight circle."

"Then there will be the pathologist who does the autopsy and the staff at the morgue. And the ambulance attendants. And the funeral home, with the press circling like sharks," she said. "I give you three or four days until this leaks out. Max."

"That's encouraging," he said. There was someone else who knew, but as much as he trusted Bering, he wasn't going to tell her who it was. Old instincts die hard. He always protected his sources.

Greene watched Bering walk over to the window and look down. "All the usual suspects down there," she said.

She turned back to him. "A female victim ramps up this whole thing. Even before they find out about the golf balls stuffed in the victims' mouths, how long until the press starts speculating there's a serial killer on the loose."

"Probably a matter of minutes not hours," he said.

She tossed the paper ball up in the air, caught it, tossed it up, and caught it again. "We can't win. If we say there's a serial killer out there and we don't make a fast arrest, then we're incompetent and uncaring. If we don't tell the public there's a serial killer and someone else gets murdered—"

"Then we're incompetent and uncaring," Greene said.

She threw the ball up, caught it for a third time, and then squeezed it tight. "The mayor's already called me."

"Tell her not to worry. Kennicott's on the case. You know Daniel better than anyone."

When Kennicott joined the force, it had been a big news story because he was the first lawyer in Toronto to become a cop. The press loved the drama of his personal story. Kennicott's older brother, Michael, was a successful businessman who was murdered in broad daylight on an outdoor patio in Yorkville, one of the city's trendiest neighbourhoods.

Greene was assigned to the case and, after a year of his getting nowhere, in frustration Kennicott quit his job as an up-and-coming Bay Street lawyer at one of the city's largest firms and joined the force. Bering was a veteran cop then and was his first partner. Under her tutelage he made homicide in record time and began to work with Greene. They were very successful. But when Greene's lover was strangled to death in a cheap motel where she was supposed to rendezvous with Greene, it was Kennicott who arrested Greene for murder. Now Greene was his boss, and Kennicott's brother's murder still remained unsolved.

"Two murders, looks as if by the same killer," Bering said, glancing out the window. "This little demonstration is nothing. We've already heard that coalitions of protest groups are planning a massive pop-up demonstration in a few days to tie up traffic. It could be anywhere in the city. The mayor wants another detective to work with Daniel on this."

She tossed the paper ball to Greene.

He caught it.

Her message was clear.

He looked down at his computer screen. Another twelve emails had come in.

"Tell the mayor I'll be the lead detective."

"That's what she wanted to hear." Bering pointed to the window. "What are you going to say to the rabble out there?"

He rolled the ball between his two hands to tighten it even more, turned, and threw it at the window. It made a tiny *poof* sound when it hit the glass and fell silently to the floor. He reached behind him for his jacket and pulled it off the back of his chair.

"To tell you the truth," he said, putting his arms through the sleeves and shrugging the jacket over his shoulders, "I haven't got a clue."

11

One of the joys for Kennicott of being a homicide detective was that he could recruit younger officers who had made a good impression on him. Last year, he'd met Constable Sadie Sheppard and sensed a determined confidence in her. It was impossible to quantify but one of those things that you knew when you saw it.

He'd had to speed to the scene of the murder of a well-known condominium developer. It was rush hour. Sheppard was in the nearest patrol car and got the call. She'd picked him up and the first words she said to him were, "I love to drive, buckle up." He'd barely got his seat belt on when she took off like a rocket, flew through traffic, executed a perfect U-turn, and delivered him in record time. He kept her for the whole investigation, and she performed like a pro.

This morning she was driving him to the housing complex where Jember Roshan, the golf club security guard who'd been knocked off his bike and tossed down into the Humber Valley, lived. He'd been checked out of the hospital and sent home.

"Don't speed around here," Kennicott said to Sheppard.

"Never. Kids at play," she said. "I appreciate you letting me work on this case with you. Is there anything you want me to do when we interview Mr. Roshan?"

Sheppard was a self-starter. She'd already read everything about both murders in the case notes.

"Just watch and take your own set of notes," Kennicott told her. "He's probably still in shock. You have to handle a witness such as this gently and make this family feel comfortable with us being there. His recollection will most likely improve in time."

They parked in the big lot in the centre of the complex and took the three flights of stairs up to the Roshans' apartment. Kennicott had asked Sheppard to call ahead to tell them they were coming, and he had her knock on the door. A woman with a baby in her arms answered.

"Hello," Sheppard said, smiling. "You must be Babita. I'm Officer Sheppard. This is Detective Kennicott. Your baby is beautiful, which one of the twins is she?"

Babita had a shy, warm smile. She held out her hand to Sheppard. "This is Obax. Her sister, Sagal, is sleeping. Please come in."

She opened the door to a modest apartment with minimal furniture. Kennicott noticed a sewing machine on a table in the corner.

"Detective Kennicott," she said turning to him. "Thank you for coming. My husband is in the bedroom resting."

"Thank you for allowing us into your home."

She led them down a narrow hallway to a small room dominated by a bed in the middle. Roshan was sitting, propped up by a few pillows. He flashed a gracious smile when Kennicott and Sheppard walked in. Kennicott said hello to him and introduced Sheppard.

"Welcome," he said in a gentle voice.

There was room for a chair in the corner beside the bed and Babita sat in it cradling the baby.

"We wanted to see how you are doing and ask you a few questions," Kennicott said.

"Thanks to Allah, I am alive. The doctor said my leg is bruised and nothing is broken."

"He insists on going to work tonight," Babita said, frowning.

"There is a party at the club and they will pay overtime. Mr. Waterbridge, my employer, says he will send an Uber to pick me up. I will not walk the perimeter but drive the security cart."

"You see," Babita said.

"We're glad you weren't badly injured," Kennicott said.

"My children and my wife, they are what kept me alive."

Kennicott took out his notebook and saw Sheppard do the same. "We've read the statement you gave to the police earlier today. You were riding your bike to work when a dark car hit your back wheel and you landed in the valley. Can you describe the vehicle?"

"It was an SUV. Black."

"Anything more?"

Roshan shook his head. "It was still dark and the windshield was tinted. I only saw it for a second. I don't think the driver even saw me."

"Can you tell us anything about the driver?"

He shook his head. "I wish I could tell you more."

"Could you see if it was a man or a woman?" Kennicott asked.

"Yes, it was a man."

"And could you see his face?"

Roshan shook his head again.

"How about his hands. Could you see where they were?"

Roshan closed his eyes, and then opened them. "The man had a cell phone in his hand. That is why I could not see his face." He paused. "I am supposed to wear a reflecting T-shirt that Babita made specially for me when I ride my bicycle to work but unfortunately I did not wear it this morning."

Kennicott saw Roshan sneak a peek at his wife, who shook her head. She did not approve of his forgetfulness.

"Babita is an excellent seamstress," he said. "It was negligent of me to forget to wear it."

Kennicott started writing in his notebook. He heard a baby crying in the next room. Babita stood.

"Here," Sheppard said, stuffing her notebook in her pocket and holding out her arms. "I'll hold Obax while you go get Sagal."

"Thank you so very much," Babita said, comfortably handing the baby over to Sheppard.

"Try to remember everything that happened after," Kennicott asked after Babita left the room. "Please tell me all you can about the person you met down there."

Roshan nodded. Shook his head. Kennicott could see this was hard for him.

"I rolled off the woman I had fallen on, and I realized she was dead. I tried to yell for help but it was of no use. I lay on the rocks, and I saw a bird in the sky. It was a sign from Allah that I was going to live. Then I heard footsteps, and a woman appeared."

"Can you describe her for me?"

"She was a white woman. She was tall. She wore many layers of clothing."

"You're a security guard at the golf club and deal with the people who live there," Kennicott said. "Ever seen this woman before?"

"Never."

Roshan described for Kennicott how the woman examined the dead body, then looked at his leg and bound it with some tree branches before she climbed out of the valley.

"She had a cell phone," he said. "She told me that she was going to get me help."

Kennicott nodded. A homeless person with a cell phone, who seemed to know the basics of first aid, if not more. Who was she?

"Can you tell me anything else about this woman?" he asked.

Babita walked back in the room, holding the second baby, and took her seat again. Sheppard was still holding Obax, who seemed very comfortable in her arms.

"She wore an overcoat that she put over me to keep me warm," Roshan said. "When I tried to give it back to her, she said, 'Keep it for your wife.'" He looked at his wife. "Babita, please show Detective Kennicott."

Babita stood and Kennicott noticed that a long overcoat was draped over the back of her chair. She handed it to Kennicott. It was dirty, but he could see it was beautifully designed. He looked at the label. It was a Max Mara cashmere coat. Kennicott's former girlfriend was a fashion model, and she'd done a number of photo shoots for the company. He knew how expensive this coat would have been.

"Detective," Babita asked him, "why would someone with such a costly overcoat and a cell phone be living this way?"

"I don't know," he said.

The coat had many pockets. He slid his hand into the outside ones. Nothing. Then the inside ones. Nothing. But wait, there was a hidden little pocket down near the hem. He reached in and pulled out a business card with the letterhead of a well-known law firm on it and the name Melissa Copeland, Barrister & Solicitor written in bold letters.

Kennicott turned it over. A phone number was written on the back in black ink.

He handed the coat back to Babita.

"Enjoy it," he said.

"Thank you."

Without Roshan or Babita seeing, he slipped the business card in his pocket. He knew the number well. It belonged to Ari Greene.

12

"**O**yez, oyez, oyez," the court clerk said, her voice ringing out in the near-empty courtroom. "All rise, the Honourable Justice Tator presiding."

The clerk sat as Tator strode from a door behind the bench and raced up to her seat on the raised dais. She was a thin, fit woman, with strong arms that she spread out as if she were stretching in a gym class, before she opened her court book, picked up a pen, wrote something in it, looked up, and scanned the courtroom.

It was a wide, windowless room lit by dull fluorescent light. There was nothing on the pallid beige walls except for printed-out sheets with the next four calendar months that were messily taped to the wall to the left of the witness box.

The seats in the body of the court were hard, functional wooden benches. The only people in attendance were the court staff, an elderly attendant dressed in uniform stationed by the door, Parish, Melissa, and Fernandez standing behind the counsel tables, and a pair of young people in the back row with clipboards taking notes. They looked like college students doing an assignment.

Tator scowled. "Good morning, Ms. Parish, Mr. Fernandez."

"Good morning, Your Honour," Parish said.

"Your Honour," Fernandez said.

Tator grabbed the court docket from her desk, glanced at it, tossed it down, and stared down at Parish, her eyebrows arched.

"Ms. Parish, your matter is the only one on my docket. Are we having a trial today or is this being resolved in some other way?"

Parish knew the question was judge-speak meaning: What the hell is going on? Are you really going to have a trial about this? A mere breach of bail conditions? She was a busy judge with serious trial matters to deal with.

But Tator was wily. She knew that even though her voice was full of sarcasm, none of this would come through on the court transcript, which would read as her being an even-handed and reasonable jurist.

Parish stiffened her back. It was important to look strong in Tator's court or she'd run right over you.

"Thank you very much, Your Honour. Yes, we are here for trial."

Tator gave a slow nod. She looked over at Melissa, who was still standing at Parish's side. "Tell your client to be seated," she said. Then to Fernandez, "Mr. Fernandez, call your first witness."

"The Crown calls Doctor Rebecca Ennis."

Doctor, Parish thought.

Fernandez could have simply referred to Ennis by her full name: "The Crown calls Rebecca Ennis." Instead he'd made sure that *Doctor* was the first word that Tator heard about his first witness. It was a signal to her about how credible *Doctor* Ennis would be. And what a waste of time it was to have her appear in person in court.

Tator looked at Parish and frowned.

Damn.

Fernandez turned to the court attendant by the door and nodded. The attendant nodded back, and opened the door.

Ennis walked in, looking tentative. For most people, their only image of what a courtroom looked like came from TV and movies, where the courtrooms were big and luxurious and packed with spectators. It was disorienting for them to enter this ugly, utilitarian room.

"Doctor," Tator said, breaking out into her first smile of the morning. "Step right up beside me to the witness box here, to my left, your right."

Doctor, Parish thought. Great.

Ennis looked to be in her mid- to late forties. She wore a crisp white shirt under a modest sport jacket. She stood in the witness box and scanned the courtroom. Parish watched her carefully. As she suspected, Ennis looked everywhere but at Melissa.

The woman is embarrassed to be here, Parish thought. Uncomfortable.

"Good morning, Doctor Ennis," Fernandez said, after rising to his feet and making eye contact with her.

"Good morning," Ennis said, looking relieved to have someone to talk to.

Doctor, doctor, doctor, Parish thought.

Fernandez was an efficient advocate. He quickly established Ennis's qualifications and her address.

"Now, Doctor, do you know a woman named Ms. Melissa Copeland?"

Ennis bit her lip. "Yes, I do."

"And Doctor, do you see that person in the court today?"

She stole a glance at Melissa. "Yes, I do," she said again.

"Could you point her out, please?"

She flicked her finger at Melissa.

"Indicating the accused, for the record," Fernandez said.

The rest of his examination was standard examination-in-chief by an experienced prosecutor who knew how to get a witness's story out efficiently: How did the doctor know Melissa? They'd been neighbours for about ten years, until Melissa left the neighbourhood. How did Ennis know about Melissa's bail conditions? The police had informed her and her neighbours, who all lived four blocks away from the Hodgson home. How often had she seen Melissa walk on her front lawn? Three days in a row until finally she felt compelled to call the police.

"Are you certain the person you saw was the accused?"

She nodded, with a sad look on her face. "It was Melissa. Even though she wore different clothes every time. We used to take our

daughters to Gymboree classes together. Sometimes we'd go for coffee while the girls played. One winter my husband and I built a skating
rink in our backyard, and Melissa would bring Britt over on the weekends if she wasn't working."

This was why it was usually better for the defence to work out
an agreed statement of facts with the prosecutor before a trial if the
evidence was uncontested, to avoid having a witness such as Ennis take
the stand. Not only did it anger a judge that you were wasting court
time and dragging a law-abiding citizen into court unnecessarily, but
when people testified in court, they were more compelling than dry
words on the page. Inevitably, just as Doctor Ennis was doing now, the
witness remembered more detail than when interviewed by a police
officer.

"Thank you," Fernandez said. "Those are my questions." He turned
from the witness stand, caught Parish's eye, and gave her a little tilt of
the head, his way of saying, "Well, you asked for it."

Ennis looked at the judge, confused. "Am I done?"

"I'm afraid not, Doctor Ennis." Tator turned her head to ensure the
doctor couldn't see the sour look on her face as she faced Parish. "The
defence lawyer may have some questions for you."

Parish stood. She avoided the judge's eyes, instead looking directly
at Ennis, who seemed to steady herself, as if she was expecting some
kind of assault. The other thing people saw all the time on TV and in
the movies was defence lawyers who berated witnesses, harshly cross-
examining them about the minutest details.

Parish knew that would have been the worst possible approach with
such a credible witness. The key was to acknowledge, and indeed celebrate, her honesty, not to question it.

She smiled. "Doctor, I understand you are anxious to get back to
work."

"I am."

"You have patients at your clinic who are waiting for you."

"Yes, I've rebooked people, and I'll work tonight."

"Thank you for coming to court. This won't take long. I've only got a few questions."

"Okay," Ennis said. Relaxing.

"Melissa and you were neighbours for years." Parish put her hands on Melissa's shoulder. She intentionally referred to Melissa by her first name. Make the witness feel they were having a conversation about a mutual friend.

"That's right."

"You yourself never had any problems or conflict with her, did you?"

"Me? With Melissa? No." Ennis looked relieved to be able to say something positive about her former neighbour. "Well, sometimes Melissa got stuck at work," Ennis added, still sounding nervous. "Then I'd pick up Britt and take her if Karl, her husband, wasn't available."

"Normal parenting stuff, correct?"

"Yes, normal."

"And you're still friends with her ex-husband, correct?"

"I wouldn't say friends, but we know each other. It's a tight-knit neighbourhood." She was starting to sound wary.

"Can we agree you were normal friendly neighbours?"

"That's right."

"In other words, you are totally neutral about this matter. You're not taking sides."

"Absolutely not," she said, shaking her head.

"You are here for one reason, and only one reason. To tell us exactly what you observed the three times you say you saw Melissa walk across your lawn."

"Yes, and it was Melissa." She was starting to sound defiant. Exactly what Parish wanted.

"You saw her clearly all three times."

"Yes, I did. She was right in front of the window."

Parish glanced up at the judge. Tator looked surprised that Parish seemed to be conceding what she assumed was the key point of the defence—the identity of the woman walking across her neighbours' lawns.

Parish was still standing behind her desk. She pulled out three sheets of paper, walked over to Fernandez's desk and dropped one in front of him, and then went up and gave another copy to the court clerk, who gave it to the judge. She approached the witness box with the third and last copy in her hand.

"Doctor," she said in a soft voice, "I went on Google Maps this morning and printed out a photo of what I believe is the front of your house. Can you look at this, please."

"Sure." She took the photo.

Out of the corner of her eye, Parish could see Tator looking closely at the photograph she'd been handed.

"This is our house," Ennis said.

Parish put her arm on the edge of the witness box as if she were leaning on the fence of a friendly neighbour, about to have a casual conversation. "You'll agree with me that at the bottom of the photo we can see your street, above that the sidewalk, and above that your front lawn and then your house and front window you were looking out of."

Ennis nodded.

"Excuse me, Doctor," Parish said. It was her turn to play the *doctor* card. "You will need to say the words *yes* or *no* for the court record."

"Oh, I'm sorry. Yes. Yes, it's our house."

"Can you do me a favour then?" Parish asked, pulling out a red marker and uncapping it. "Please mark with an X where you saw Melissa walking in front of your house and the path she took."

"Sure," Ennis said, happy to do such an easy task. She took the marker and put an X mark in the middle of the lawn and drew dotted lines going across it parallel to the sidewalk.

Parish took the photo and examined it. "And did Melissa walk on the same part of your lawn each time?"

"She did. The same way all three times."

Parish took the marker and marked-up photograph back and walked over to show it to Fernandez. She could tell by the look on his face that he'd figured out what she was doing. He glanced at it, frowned, and said, "Thanks." She took it back to the clerk, who passed it up to Tator.

Parish watched her study the photo for a minute with a quizzical look on her face. Parish could tell that, unlike Fernandez, Tator didn't get it.

"Proceed, Counsel," Tator barked. "This witness has sick people waiting for her."

Parish smiled at the judge and turned to the witness stand.

"Doctor, you'll agree with me, your front lawn is quite large."

"Yes. Our house is set back twenty-five yards from the street."

"You saw Melissa walk across the middle of your lawn, as you've indicated here on this photo. Three times." Parish was using her kindest voice.

"Yes."

"You never saw Melissa set foot on the street itself, did you?"

"Absolutely not." The doctor let herself smile and stole a glance at Melissa.

"You never saw her set foot on the sidewalk, did you?"

"No. I never saw Melissa walk anywhere but across our lawn. I'm one hundred per cent sure of that."

Parish turned from the witness and now it was her turn to catch Fernandez's eye. He put his head in his hand and nodded ever so slightly.

"Thank you, *Doctor*," she said, adding her own emphasis to the word, "those are my questions."

Parish took her seat before she looked up at Tator. But the judge already had her head down reading through the court documents. Her focus would be on the key line in the charge, that Melissa had breached her bail by being "on the street . . ."

Tator glared up at Parish. But Parish could see she was also thinking, *I get it. Clever.*

Never gloat in court, Parish told herself. Words of wisdom Ted Di-Paulo had drilled into her when she first joined his practice. "Modesty is a weapon," he'd told her. "And it's your natural personality. Use it."

Tator turned back to the doctor. "Thank you for coming today, Doctor," she said.

"May I go?" Ennis asked.

Tator held up her hand. "One moment. Mr. Fernandez, any questions in re-examination?" There was a hopeful tone in her voice.

Fernandez stood. "No, Your Honour. I have no further questions."

He looked at Parish. Gave her a hint of a smile.

"Your Honour," he said. "I'm going to ask that we take the morning break earlier than usual this morning. There are some matters I'd like to discuss with counsel before I call my next witness."

Tator shook her head at Fernandez. Then she turned on Parish.

Uh-oh, Parish thought. She'd just poked the bear.

13

Although Kennicott and Greene had been through many ups and downs, they were still a highly effective team when they worked together. And Kennicott found he learned something new from Greene every time.

He pulled his car in behind Greene's vehicle. It was parked on a side street in a working-class neighbourhood in the west end of the city. The street was lined with modest bungalow homes and meagre front lawns. The second victim was from here. Kennicott grabbed a file he'd put together on her background and walked up to Greene's car.

This was one of the toughest parts of the job, informing the family of the deceased that their loved one was dead. Murdered. It was impossible to know how people would react to the shocking news.

As Kennicott opened the passenger door, Greene looked over and nodded. Kennicott knew how quiet his former partner could be. He could see that Greene was preparing in his mind what he was going to say to the dead woman's husband. This was no time for small talk.

Kennicott sat down in the car, closed the door, pulled out the file, and began to read aloud: "'Name, Deborah Lemon, forty-one years old, grew up a few blocks from here, studied nursing at University of Toronto and worked at the Humberside General Hospital.'"

"A real west-ender," Greene said.

"'When she was twenty-five, she married an orderly, Marvin Lemon. They have two boys, Mark and Mitchell, now fourteen and fifteen. Five years ago she had a bad fall in the hospital stairwell while escorting a psychiatric patient to an appointment and broke her leg in three places. She needed four operations and ended up addicted to opioids. Two years later, she was fired when she was caught stealing oxytocin from the hospital pharmacy. The report says she was up to twenty-four a day.'"

"Twenty-four? Phew. Was she arrested?"

"Yes. She went to Florida for a three-month rehab stint, wrote a letter of apology, did one hundred hours of community service, and the Crown dropped the charges."

"The right thing to do."

"Two months later the family filed a missing person's report. Days later they found her in line at the Law Society Feed the Hungry Program and brought her home. That's the last thing we have on her."

Greene looked over at Kennicott. Shook his head.

"The house is near the end of the block," Greene said.

They got out of the car and walked down the street. Kennicott had called ahead to tell Lemon that they were Toronto police officers—Greene had taught him to never identify himself as a homicide detective on an initial call, to wait until he saw the victim's family in person—and were coming over to talk to him and his sons. He didn't give any details.

Lemon was waiting for them on the small front porch that fronted his two-storey home. He was a short man wearing a Toronto Maple Leafs baseball cap. His face looked grim. Kennicott and Greene went together up the cracked concrete walkway. Lemon came down from the porch to greet them. They shook hands.

"Mr. Lemon. I'm Detective Ari Greene. This is Detective Daniel Kennicott."

"Homicide detectives, right?" he said.

Greene nodded.

"It's Deb, isn't it?"

"Yes."

Lemon flinched. "I saw it on the news. They didn't say her name, just that it was a homeless woman who was murdered. When you guys called, I put two and two together. I called the medical clinic and talked to Sylvia, the woman who runs the place. She said it was Deb. Still . . ." His voice trailed off.

"Where are your sons?" Kennicott asked.

"Inside. I told them they had to stay home from school. I prepared them for this."

"Do you want us to talk to them?"

He shook his head. "Deb's been dead to them for a long time."

Dead to them, Kennicott thought, but not to him.

Kennicott could see the shock and sadness turn to anger on Lemon's face. "That bloody hospital. She worked there her whole damn life. Did you know she was born there?"

"No, I didn't," Greene said.

"So was I. A week later. We used to laugh about that." He gave out a bitter chuckle. "Her fall was all their fault. One hundred thousand per cent. The cleaners didn't dry the floor, and the patient was known to be violent. She should never have been escorting him by herself."

Kennicott glanced at Greene. He hadn't taken his eyes off Lemon since the moment they'd met. Every bit of his attention and compassion was with the man.

"What did the hospital do?" Lemon said, his voice rising. "Pump her up with those drugs and kick her out the door."

Greene nodded.

"I hate what they did to her," Lemon said.

"The drugs," Greene said.

Lemon looked down and tied his hands in knots. "The drugs, the hospital, and the drug rehab places that sucked up all our money. And the Nursing Association, oh, they were a big help. Star Chamber is what I call them."

He was spitting out the words.

"Any time Deb started to recover, they'd drag her in for an interview. Their overpriced lawyers in their fancy suits all making tons of money off our backs. Assholes. They'd cross-examine her as if she was a criminal. Urine tests, blood tests. They poked her like she was a pincushion. Then we'd get those long cover-your-ass letters on their embossed letterhead."

He made a fist with one hand and hit it into the other. He stared at Greene. "I'm sorry."

"No need to apologize," Greene said.

Lemon pounded his fist into his hand again. His voice softened. "She'd come home from one of those hearings, and I knew in a few days she'd be gone. Did you know I had to re-mortgage this house to pay for that clinic in Florida?"

"No, I didn't," Greene said in an equally soft voice.

"She wasn't home a month, and she started stealing from us. Living back on the street. One afternoon she took the boys' hockey equipment and sold all of it at the Hockey Exchange for a hundred and twenty dollars. Right before the playoffs. I told the owner what happened, and he gave me the stuff back. Her own sons. A hundred and twenty bucks."

Big pain and little pain, Kennicott thought. When people were faced with overwhelming tragedy, it was often the small things that hurt them the most.

Lemon looked back up at Kennicott, then Greene.

Greene put his hand on the man's shoulder. "I have to ask you. When was the last time you saw Deb or heard from her?"

Deb, Kennicott thought. Greene picked up on the nickname Lemon called his wife. Greene spoke about her as a real person, instead of using impersonal words such as "your wife" or "the deceased" or even "Deborah." It was good to be working with Greene again.

"Seven weeks ago. On a Tuesday night after I'd come home from baseball. Our last game of the season. It was midnight, and she started pounding on the front door. I came right out here on the porch and locked the door behind me. I wouldn't let her in. We had a horrible fight."

Midnight. After his baseball game. Last one of the season. When a witness was this detailed about something, it was seared in their memory. Kennicott could see that Lemon knew exactly how long he'd endured the agony and uncertainty of wondering if he'd done the right thing: Seven weeks ago last Tuesday night.

"It was the first time I'd locked her out," he said. "I had to."

"The boys," Greene said.

He nodded. "They couldn't take it anymore. For years everyone— my sister, the kids' therapist, even my friends at work—they all told me I had to draw the line. So there. I drew the line. And see. This is what happened."

Kennicott looked at Greene. He still had his hand on Lemon's shoulder and was still entirely focussed on the grieving man.

"Thanks, Detective," Lemon said. "I've got to go inside."

"Go be with your boys."

He nodded. Saddened and defeated. "Cremate the body when you're done with it. Sylvia is going to arrange for a memorial service this afternoon. I want this over with."

He shook hands with both of them, turned, and walked up the steps.

Back in the car, Greene said to Kennicott, before starting the engine, "Come back tomorrow and ask Mr. Lemon what his wife said to him when they had the fight on the porch."

Mr. Lemon. Kennicott realized Greene was showing the man respect even when he wasn't there. Another lesson learned.

14

"It's called a cortado," Burns said to Alison, referring to the two coffees he brought over along with a pair of little white napkins. She was perched on a high stool looking out the south-facing window at Fahrenheit Café, the trendy spot where he'd asked her to meet him. The coffees came in small clear glasses, the image of a swan neatly drawn in white foam on top.

"I know all about cortados," Alison said. "I was a barista when I lived in London." She was going to add she worked at a café when she was a university student two years ago but didn't. It would have made her sound too young.

He gave her a sly look. "You've never tasted one as good as this. They're real coffee snobs here."

"Good. I need the caffeine after a sleepless night. You a regular?"

"I come here every morning."

Alison felt someone come up behind her. She turned and saw a man with short-cropped hair and an impish grin on his handsome face. He slapped Burns on the shoulder and spoke to her.

"Arnold took my five-hour barista course. Star student. I keep trying to convince him to quit this medicine stuff he does and get a real job pulling shots."

Burns grinned. "Alison, meet Sameer, world-champion barista and teacher extraordinaire."

"Do you like my coffee?" Sameer asked her.

"I've yet to try it."

"Two sips. The first one only sets your palette," Sameer said.

"See," Burns said.

She took a sip. The coffee was not too hot but deliciously warm, the way a cortado was supposed to be. The flavour was bold. Naturally sweet. She took a second sip. He was right. Now she could really taste the richness of the coffee.

"Pretty good," she said.

"That's British for 'very good,'" Burns said.

"Pretty damn good," she said, in as North American an accent as she could muster.

Both men laughed. Sameer slapped Burns on the back again and went back behind the counter.

She lifted her glass and clinked. "To fighting the good fight."

"To the fight," he said, a serious look replacing his smile.

She tossed back the rest of her cortado in one gulp and used one of the napkins to dab her lips. Carefully. She'd put on some lipstick before walking into the café and didn't want to rub it off.

He sipped his cortado without talking. This was the other side of his loud public persona, she thought. The quiet, committed side. She felt at ease to be with someone who wasn't afraid of silence, like her father.

"How long have you been in Canada?" he asked her after he'd finished his drink.

"About a year and a half. It's a long story."

She'd grown up in England with her mum, who'd told her that her father had left when she was a baby, moved to New Zealand, and started a new family. That wasn't true. Alison was twenty years old when her mother was stricken with a brain tumour. Unbeknownst to Alison, her mum reached out to Ari, whom she'd lived with two decades earlier when she was finishing her graduate degree in Toronto.

A week after her mum died, Alison went to a solicitor's office and was introduced to this stranger: Toronto homicide detective Ari Greene. Her father. He stayed in London for months, and eventually she decided to try living in Toronto with him. It turned out she had an unknown grandfather as well.

"Do you like the city?" Burns asked.

She looked back into the café. It was filled with well-dressed, energetic young people brimming with confidence and enthusiasm.

"It certainly is modern with the high-rises going up, the building cranes everywhere, and all the glass. People always on the go. It seems there are a lot of rich people here."

"Seems," he said with a note of bitterness. "That's the point. If you want to see the real heart of the city, come with me."

Outside, he had a smart fixed-speed bicycle that he'd locked up with a thick chain and a heavy-duty square-shaped lock.

"A socially conscious doctor with a super trendy bike," she said, chiding him as he bent down to unlock it. "You're such a hipster."

He laughed a self-deprecating laugh. She liked that.

"I love my fixie. I put on special tires in the fall and ride every day of the year."

"Rain, snow, sleet, or hail?"

"Three sixty-five. Saving the environment," he said, stringing the chain around his neck as if it were some kind of warrior's necklace.

"Cliché millennial," she quipped.

They walked up Jarvis, a north-south street filled with sleek new condos and office buildings. But after only a few blocks everything changed to empty parking lots, car rental places, and graffiti-filled walls. Instead of well-dressed young people, the sidewalks and alleyways were now filled with hunched-over men and women wearing dirty clothes, huddled together, smoking cigarettes, drinking cheap coffee outside shelters and free-injection sites.

The People on the Street Health Care Clinic was in an old storefront, with chipped-paint-covered bricks and a thick metal door. Inside, the reception room was filled with ragged-looking women sprawled out on low-slung couches, each with a crinkled shopping bag at her feet. To one side an older woman sat behind a linoleum-topped desk that looked to be twenty years old, shuffling through a mound of paperwork.

"Sylvia, meet Alison Greene," Burns said to the woman. "The TV reporter who covered the protest and actually gave me ninety seconds of air time."

"Looked more like a minute to me," Sylvia said. Her voice was gruff and monotone. She rolled her eyes over to Alison. "Welcome to Women's Day in Paradise."

"Women come Mondays and Wednesdays," Burns explained. "Men Tuesdays and Thursdays."

"Fridays we do Pilates, take vegan cooking classes, and tend our organic garden," Sylvia said, her deep voice flatter than a pancake.

"Translation," Burns said. "Paperwork for the government so we can get paid. It's massive."

"And emergency appointments," Sylvia said.

"Well, I'm jolly pleased to be here," Alison said.

Sylvia raised an eyebrow and rolled her eyes back to Burns.

"Forgive Sylvia's skepticism," he said. "We've had a boatload of reporters come through here all enthusiastic about doing a story on our clinic and nothing ever happens."

"Perhaps I'll be different."

"Why don't you start by covering the memorial service," Sylvia said.

"Memorial service?" Alison asked.

"For Nurse Deb," one of the women on the couches behind Alison said.

"Nurse Deb?" Alison asked.

"The woman who was killed in the valley today," Burns added. "Word travels fast in our little world. That's how we got the demonstration together so quickly this morning. Deb was a registered nurse until her life fell apart."

"Oh," Alison murmured, feeling foolish.

"Don't look so shocked, Miss Reporter," Sylvia said. "Just because these women are down on their luck doesn't mean that they're not smarter than half those assholes in the office towers a few blocks from here. Everybody loved Deb. She got lots of people off of the needle."

Sylvia picked up a clipboard and handed it to Burns. "Fatima's in Room A. The CAS grabbed her kids again, and she overdosed on the weekend."

Sylvia returned to her paperwork without another glance at Alison.

Burns took the clipboard and motioned to Alison. "The women here live in constant fear that a social worker from Children's Aid Society will show up at any time and they'll lose their children. For years kids were taken away because of false drug tests."

"That's horrible."

"That's reality. Let's go see Fatima."

Alison started to follow him, then turned back. She cleared her throat. "Excuse me, Sylvia."

The woman looked up from her desk. Annoyed.

Alison crept back toward the reception desk. "Can I ask you about the memorial service?" she asked.

Sylvia stared at her.

Alison stepped closer. "The details perhaps?" She was trying not to sound as if she was pleading. "Ah, when? Where the memorial is being held?"

Sylvia frowned. She rummaged through the piles of papers, moved a pack of cigarettes out of the way, and somehow found a pad of Post-it notes and a pen. She wrote something on a note and stuck it on the end of her desk.

"Marvin told the cops to do what they want with her body."

"Marvin?"

Sylvia frowned again. "Deb's husband."

"She was married?"

"Yes, lady reporter, Deb was married. For twenty-four years. Marvin wants this over and done so we're doing it this afternoon. Better for his boys' sake."

"Oh, she had a son?" Alison said, feeling like a total idiot.

"Two. Mark and Mitchell. Good kids. Both are in high school, and they do their volunteer hours here."

"That's good," Alison said. Her words sounded so hollow.

"Good? Good would be if the pharmaceutical companies hadn't made a small fortune turning their mother into a drug addict. Then maybe she'd be alive today."

"Yes, yes." Alison reached over to the desk and picked up the Post-it note.

"Thanks for this," she said.

But Sylvia was already back at her paperwork and didn't reply.

15

"You want to take the morning recess now?" Tator said to Fernandez. Shaking her head. She looked at the clock on the courtroom wall. "You realize it's not even ten thirty."

"I do, Your Honour," Fernandez said, still standing.

Parish sat at her desk watching, not moving a muscle. What was playing out in court was a battle of wills. Court started at ten. The morning session went until one o'clock with the usual coffee break at 11:30. Tator could refuse to allow the morning recess this early and force Fernandez to call his next witness. But Fernandez could choose to not call any more witnesses and the case would collapse.

"We've set aside the whole day for this trial," Tator said, practically growling. "You know, Mr. Fernandez, that if we don't finish today, then the next trial date will be months from now."

"I'm well aware of that, Your Honour."

Parish smiled to herself. The two of them were playing a chess match and everything they were saying was in code.

Tator wasn't persuaded by this technical defence about the lawn's not being the road. Parish could already imagine her ruling. She'd roll her eyes and say, "Really, Counsel, clearly your client understood the intent of her bail conditions and even tried to hide her identity by wearing different clothes three days in a row. This was a clear violation."

Classic Judge Tator. She couldn't wait to get the trial over, convict Melissa, and throw her in jail.

But Fernandez thought the judge was wrong about the law. He knew that if Melissa was found guilty, Parish would appeal and possibly win. Or at least keep Melissa out on bail and drag this out even further. He wanted to have a recess and use the threat of Tator's convicting Melissa to try again to make a deal with Parish.

"I'm well aware of how crowded this courthouse is," Fernandez said in his most deferential tone.

This was code for: I know, Your Honour, that you need to make it clear on the record that you are concerned about wasting court time, but I need to get out of here.

"Now are you proposing we waste more time, Mr. Fernandez?"

This was code for: I *am* making it damn sure on the record that I'm concerned about the efficient use of court time.

"My hope, Your Honour, is that if I have an opportunity to speak to defence counsel, I could, in fact, save time."

Code for: No. If you force me to continue, I'm going to close my case. I think you are wrong on the law and besides I don't want you to throw Melissa in jail.

Tator shook her head. "I don't understand why this wasn't canvassed with defence counsel before trial."

Translation: Why didn't you see this coming?

"It's an issue that only arose out of my friend's cross-examination. Unfortunately, the defence has made no concessions in this matter, leaving many issues that the Crown must be sure to cover. I still have three more civilian witnesses to call and the defence is insisting that I call the officer-in-charge, and then there's Ms. Lansing, the complainant in this matter."

In other words: Give me a break, Parish is being a pain in the ass because of her impossible client, and I can't think of everything.

Tator stared down at Fernandez. She tapped her fingers on her desk, fast and hard, making a typewriter-like clicking sound that echoed around the near-vacant courtroom. She looked at the clock again as if to confirm her anger.

"You *hope*, Mr. Fernandez, that this recess will save time. But if you are unsuccessful in your efforts, then you'll agree you would *waste* more time. To say nothing of the time we are using up right now arguing about this."

Meaning: For the record, you're going to take the blame for this, not me.

"I'm well aware of how precious our court time is, Your Honour. As you know, our Crown office is one of the busiest in the country."

Right back at you: I'm not going to be bullied.

Tator pursed her lips. Frustrated with Fernandez, she turned to Parish. "Counsel," she barked.

"Yes, Your Honour," Parish said, springing to her feet.

"What do you say?"

Parish had to be careful. Fernandez was trying to do her a favour, and she wasn't going to throw him under the bus. But she didn't want to get Tator any angrier.

"Your Honour, my client has been on bail for months and is anxious to have this matter dealt with today—"

"Good. You agree with me. There's no need to recess now and we should get on with the trial."

Parish waited until Tator finished. A judge could interrupt a lawyer at any time, but it was never a good idea for a lawyer to interrupt a judge.

What Tator had meant was: Come on, Parish, don't play cute. You're dying for this early recess to make a deal for your loser client. All you're doing is pretending you're concerned about court time for the record if there's an appeal.

"But on the other hand," Parish said, once it was clearly her turn to speak, "Mr. Fernandez is an experienced counsel and if he thinks that recessing at this point would be productive and save the court time, I believe it's in the best interest of *all parties* to see if we can enter into a fruitful discussion."

Parish's code: Best interest of *all parties*, including you, Judge. How will it look on appeal if you deny this request? Parish knew that if there was one thing that judges hated even more than lawyers who wasted their time, it was being overturned on appeal. No one saw what happened in ninety-nine per cent of the trials they presided over, but appeals were reported for all of the judge's colleagues to see.

Tator gave a long, loud exhale. She remained seated.

Both lawyers were still standing, looking down at their feet like a pair of troublemaking teenagers hauled up before an angry school principal.

"Mr. Fernandez, just how long do you need for this extremely early recess?"

Code: You win, but I'm going to limit the damage.

"I think half an hour will suffice."

The usual morning break was fifteen minutes. Fernandez was saying he needed some time to hammer out a deal.

"Half an hour?" Judge said in mock horror. "Ms. Parish?"

"I agree with my friend. I think it might be best to have a longer-than-usual recess if there's a hope of resolving everything. That would save the rest of the day, allowing Your Honour to assist other courts with their matters."

Her code for: Thanks, Fernandez. I have your back.

Tator slammed her hands on her desk and stood up abruptly. "Fifteen minutes. That's it. I'll be back here and counsel had better be ready to go." She grabbed her court book, looked straight at Parish, smiled, and flew off the bench, out the door, her court clerk trailing behind her like a nervous courtier following her queen.

What did Tator's smile mean? Parish wondered. Maybe she'd read this all wrong. Maybe the judge was trying to force Fernandez on with his case because she was going to acquit. Maybe she was trying to tell Parish: Don't make a deal.

Or was there more to it than that? Tator had read all the court documents. Maybe she was saying to Parish, Hurry up and make a deal. I'm trying to scare your client for her own sake. If I find her not guilty now, she'll just get herself into more trouble.

That was one thing about being a trial lawyer. Unless you got to the end of a case, you never knew what a judge was thinking. Ever.

16

After having to notify the loved ones of a murder victim that their family member had been killed, attending the autopsy was the second-toughest thing for a homicide detective to do.

Kennicott always felt as if he were an intruder. Seeing the dead person, their naked body laid out on a stainless-steel operating table. Silent, motionless, all their past secrets an open book, the way their bodies were sliced apart, their insides pulled out, weighed, bottled, and sent off to a nameless lab.

Over the years he'd grown accustomed to the gruesome medical parts of the procedure: the slick swishing sound of the sharp knife slicing through skin, the high-pitched whir of the circular saw cutting off the top of the head, and the horrid stench of an opened body, which was inescapable in the sterile room. But the thing he never got used to was going through the personal effects of the deceased.

He'd examine the usual things: money, credit cards, cell phones, makeup kits, sunscreen, lip balm, pens, Post-it notes, Tylenol bottles, mints, gum. Then there would be the clues to a normal day in a normal life cut short: a pair of tickets for a show, a receipt for an item they'd bought and intended to return, a shopping list, a letter not yet put in the mail. The hardest part was the clothing, rummaging through their pockets, their shoes, their socks, even their underwear.

No one gets up in the morning expecting to be murdered. They left behind all the minutiae of their day-to-day existence. It all seemed innocent, typical of another day in the life. Not death. As if their lives were a clock, ticking along, and in an instant, smashed, never to start again. Kennicott's job as a homicide detective was to try to trace their life from that moment backwards, live the life the dead person had lived before it was snatched from them.

That's what made this autopsy and the one he'd attended last night unusual. Both were homeless people who had lived in the Humber Valley, and neither of them had any of the accoutrements most people took for granted. No wallets, no driver's licences, no cell phones, no identification, no money. They literally had nothing but the shirts on their backs. Shirts plural, not just one shirt, because they wore layers and layers of clothes. Their only real possessions.

"Back so soon," Dr. Ramos, the pathologist, said greeting Kennicott. She was a stylish, agile woman with long thin fingers. She had the look of someone who, in another life, could have been a concert pianist.

"Thank you for coming in on such short notice," he said.

"I appreciate that this is urgent. Another homeless person from the same location is what I understand," she said in her lovely accent.

"A woman this time," Kennicott said.

"We've had Adam, now we have Eve."

"Both from the Humber Valley. Hardly the Garden of Eden."

"Let's have a look, shall we," she said, as casually as a dentist about to examine a sore tooth.

Kennicott watched as she opened up the body efficiently, cut away and scooped out the key organs, all the while narrating her actions into a small mic clipped to the top of her white coat. An assistant followed her every move, anticipating the tools she would need and preparing the appropriate jar or steel plate with which to take and store the various body parts.

In less than an hour she was done, pulling off her surgical gloves, using her elbows to turn on the long-stemmed taps over the deep sink in the corner of the room and washing her hands. "Cause of death is easy," she said to Kennicott as she scrubbed away. "Smack on the top of the head with a glass bottle—lots of fragments in her hair and scalp— and the head bashed hard in the back."

"Which killed her?"

"The bash to the back of the head. The glass bottle would have stunned her but wouldn't have been fatal."

"Can you tell which came first?"

"Wouldn't want to speculate. The back of the head was bashed in with one blow from a blunt-force object."

"Any idea what it could have been?"

She kept cleaning her hands. "Can't say. I think that's your job, Detective."

"Similar to the male victim we had last night."

"Appears to be."

She used her elbows again to turn off taps and then pulled down a roll of fresh paper towels to dry off her pristine hands. She scanned the operating room. Her assistant was at the other end, labelling the samples.

"This woman had cervical cancer. I suspect it was totally untreated. It had spread throughout her body."

"Life on the street for her must have been rough."

"Horrible." She lowered her voice. "There's one thing about both of these cases that I find unusual."

This could be useful, Kennicott thought. But he didn't say anything.

She took off her white coat and hospital scrubs and neatly folded them up as if she were packing for a trip, before putting them squarely in the laundry bin.

Be patient, Kennicott told himself. The way Greene would be.

"If one does this job long enough, one does get a feel for things." She headed for the door. Kennicott walked beside her.

"You mentioned that both times a vodka bottle seems to have been used on the back of their heads."

"Yes."

She opened the door and politely stood aside, insisting that Kennicott go first.

Kennicott understood what was going on. She wanted to tell him something completely off the record and was being careful. Pathologists were meant to be scrupulously objective and to never speculate about the crime itself.

He walked through the doorway and Ramos followed behind him. She waited patiently for it to close before she spoke.

"One also develops this extraordinary sense of smell," she said quietly. "You see, Detective, when I opened up both of these people's stomachs, I didn't smell any alcohol. Anywhere."

"No?" Kennicott said, surprised. "Meaning?"

"Meaning, it will take a few days to get the laboratory results of the blood tests to confirm this," she said. "Perhaps this was not a fight between two drunkards or a battle concerning a bottle of alcohol, as it first appeared to be. Perhaps someone wished to create that impression. No?"

17

Greene drove slowly through the stone gates of the Humber River Golf Club. He'd been here many times a few years earlier during his investigation of Hodgson's murder case, and he remembered how everything about the place had the feel of old money. The sculpted gardens, the granite steps leading to large clubhouse double doors, the high-ceilinged foyer with its elaborate moulding, wainscotted walls, and dark oak floors.

Established in the 1920s when the area was a wealthy Toronto enclave, the club had expanded over the years and now owned a swath of beautiful property that backed onto the Humber River. As with all the golf, tennis, and social clubs in the city back in the early twentieth century, originally membership was restricted to keep out Jews, Asians, Blacks, Italians, Greeks, and Irish Catholics. That had changed slowly over the years, but these days the club faced another type of foreign invasion from the homeless people who'd taken up residence across the river.

Repelling them wasn't an easy task. The club built a fence around the property, only to find it cut through, climbed over, or dug under. Members reported finding liquor bottles and needles on the putting greens, and tents made from plastic sheets in the nearby woods. In the parking lot, members' luxury cars regularly had their windows smashed in and their contents stolen. As the tent city across the river grew, things got worse. Despite the club's hiring security guards to patrol the grounds 24/7, there was a string of robberies out on the course's more remote holes: members forced to surrender their watches, jewellery, and cell phones at knifepoint. It all culminated with Hodgson's killing the man who tried to rob him.

Greene pulled into the parking lot. Since it was mid-November, there weren't many cars, but a bunch of colourful trucks were lined up by the far fence: Disco Dan's Dancing Show; Peter's Party Photo Booth; Barbara's Big Balloons; Greg's Golf Games.

These would be the suppliers for the party that Hodgson was throwing tonight for his daughter, Britt, the young golf protégé. Like everything Hodgson did, it was going to be a big event.

Greene took his time going over to the main clubhouse. It was a point of pride amongst homicide detectives that they walked and didn't run—unless, of course, the situation was urgent. There was also a good reason for this: they always wanted to project calm. Confidence.

Gerald Waterbridge, the club's general manager, was waiting for him at the bottom of the stairs. Greene had met Waterbridge when he worked on Hodgson's case, and Waterbridge had been unfailingly cordial and cooperative. His prime concern back then was the reputation of his club. He must be doubly concerned now.

"Detective Greene, welcome back to Humber River," Waterbridge said, holding out his hand.

Dressed as always in blue blazer, white oxford-cloth shirt, old school tie, grey flannel pants, shining black loafers, and conservative eyeglasses, Waterbridge projected what Greene thought was the perfect buttoned-down image for the perfect citizens at their perfect golf club.

"Nice to see you again too," Greene said.

"I can't honestly say it is good to see you again *here*," Waterbridge said with a nervous laugh. He looked worried, but ever the gentleman, gave Greene a warm handshake.

"Perils of the job," Greene said. "No one likes to see a homicide detective show up at their door. Especially for a second time."

"You are right about that," Waterbridge said, trying not to sound nervous but not succeeding.

A large van pulled up beside them. The signage on this one read

Barry's Big Blow Ups and featured poster-sized photos of people in various poses. The driver and a workman jumped out and opened the van's sliding side door.

"Excuse us, gents," the driver said. "Major delivery."

The workman popped inside the van and handed a life-sized poster out to the driver. It was a glossy photo of a young girl in mid golf swing.

"That must be Britt," Greene said to Waterbridge.

"Her father's pride and joy," Waterbridge said.

"Can one of you gents get the door?" the driver asked. "We've got a bunch of these babies."

Waterbridge rushed up the stairs and opened one of the big oak doors. Greene joined him and opened the other as he watched the men carefully unload four huge photos of Britt in various stages of her young golfing career.

"It's going to be quite a party," Greene said, when the deliveries were done.

"And I'm going to make a point of *not* being here," Waterbridge said.

They went inside and climbed the main staircase. It was lined with portraits of the club presidents, all men with classic old Toronto names: Laidlaw, Osler, Burnamthorpe, Islington, Witherspoon, Johnson. Hodgson's was the second-to-last one on the wall. It was like walking through a time machine starting back in the 1920s, when the men had long bushy sideburns and large, thick eyeglasses, and wore dark business suits with wide lapels and even wider ties. Over the decades the facial hair disappeared, the eyeglasses shrunk in size, the suits grew lighter, the lapels and ties thinner.

At the top of the stairs Greene stopped to look at a photograph of a conservatively dressed woman in a plain business suit, a string of pearls around her neck. The label identified her as Alice Burnamthorpe and gave the years of her birth and death. She'd died twenty years ago at the age of thirty-seven.

"Beautiful, wasn't she?" Waterbridge said, standing by Greene's side.

Greene turned to him.

"Alice was my wife," Waterbridge said. "First and only woman club president. Scratch golfer. Wonderful mother. You know, Detective, when you're young and in love and get married and have kids, no one tells you that on your fifteenth anniversary your beautiful wife is going to become ill and die three months later. Do they?"

"I'm sorry," Greene said.

"It was hard on the boys. They were young." Waterbridge pointed back to a portrait midway down the stairs. "Horace Burnamthorpe, club president nineteen forty-two to forty-seven, was Alice's grand-father."

"Her family were lifers at the club."

"And extremely proud of it. I'm doing everything I can to carry on the tradition."

Waterbridge led Greene into the enormous dining room. Three massive chandeliers hung from its wood-panelled ceiling. There was a stage at the far end, and to one side floor-to-ceiling windows looked out onto the manicured back lawn. The big room was buzzing with activity as workers set up various booths and stations for the night's activities. A small army of waiters were scurrying about setting the tables with white tablecloths and sterling silver cutlery.

"As you can see," Waterbridge said, "Mr. Hodgson is having an intimate little party for about two hundred of his closest friends."

"He never does anything small, does he?"

"I'm afraid not."

In his time here, Greene had learned much about the intricate dynamics of this private golf club. It was situated on prime green space, in a city sorely lacking in parkland, and the last thing the members wanted was any kind of publicity. Especially since the taxes the club paid were a pittance of what the city could earn if the land were divided up into much-needed residential homes.

Every once in a while the idea of expropriating the land bubbled up in the press, spurred on by a crusading journalist or activist. A few years ago the club quietly made a deal with the city to quadruple the taxes they'd pay for the next fifty years. To finance this, and because many of the old-money families their members came from were dying off, they opened up club membership. The new members with their new money were brash and flashy. None more so than Hodgson. He'd been a pariah here even before he was charged, and now he was a cross they were forced to bear.

"I've saved us a seat in the corner," Waterbridge said, leading Greene to a table near the stage. Greene sat and looked out the windows at the manicured back lawn. A golf cart with the word *Security* displayed on its side, driven by a man in uniform, zipped along the paved path that bisected the lawn before it scooted off toward the river below.

An athletic-looking young man with a set of golf clubs slung over his shoulder walked along the stone path by the window. Seeing Greene and Waterbridge, he stopped and waved before continuing on.

Waterbridge's face lit up and he waved back.

"That's Jack, my youngest son," he said to Greene.

"How many children do you have?" Greene asked. It was good to make small talk before asking the harder questions.

"Two boys. Losing their mom when they were young was tough on them and, let me tell you, they're a study in opposites. The older one is the academic. He hates golf, won't even set foot in this place anymore. Jack, he was never a great student. He's doing a slow victory lap at community college right now. He loves golf and works here part-time. I'm grooming him for my job, that is if the club can survive this mess we're in."

"Two murders in the valley in two days."

"Terrible. What can we do? Last year the members put together a Help the Homeless Fund. We raised more than twenty thousand dollars and bought all sorts of sleeping bags, ski jackets, gloves, socks, and toques. It's a drop in the bucket and, between you and me, I'm not sure it didn't make matters worse. Just made it easier for people to camp out over there."

"The members must be frustrated."

Waterbridge threw up his hands. "Nothing we do seems to work and, frankly, all this bad news is hurting our new membership drive. Besides, these young people all want to do yoga and cycling and circuit training. Some of our newer members want to build a gym and hire personal trainers. Imagine what the founders would think of that."

"It's hard to envision one of those old men with the sideburns and the heavy suits going to a spin class," Greene said.

"Right you are," Waterbridge said, smiling.

He looked at Greene. They both knew the preliminaries were over.

"How can I be of assistance, Detective?"

"One of your employees found the second dead body down in the valley this morning."

"Mr. Roshan. Works in our security detail. Excellent employee. Thank goodness he wasn't too badly hurt. We've sent a gift basket to his home. So dedicated, he's insisted on working tonight."

Greene looked back out the window. Before coming here he'd checked the police reports for the last twelve months. There had been twenty-five reported incidents at the club, everything from golf pins broken in half, to human feces left in holes on the greens, to members' cars being broken into and scratched, and their tires slashed and deflated. Hodgson's vehicle in particular had been the target of much of the vandalism.

"I have to ask you about Karl Hodgson," Greene said.

Waterbridge nodded. "I thought so."

"A week before the first murder, the tires of his car were slashed."

"I was here when the police arrived."

Greene looked back at Waterbridge. Nothing happened at the club without his knowledge. Waterbridge bit his lip. What Waterbridge didn't know, and Greene was not going to tell him, was that Greene had checked Hodgson's car registration. He drove a large black SUV, which was consistent with the description of the vehicle that Roshan said had knocked him off his bike.

"Does Mr. Hodgson still play his solo rounds early on Monday mornings?"

"Rain or shine."

Waterbridge looked off to his side. A server was approaching with two menus in her hand, and he caught her eye and waved her off. When Greene was here three years earlier, Waterbridge kept offering Greene free food, and Greene kept refusing.

"It's late in the season. Did he still play this morning?"

Waterbridge tried to keep his face neutral, but Greene could see he was not happy with the answer he was about to give. He took off his glasses, pulled a handkerchief from his coat pocket, and cleaned them. Greene knew it was a stall.

"He did, by himself as usual," Waterbridge said, after he'd finished with his glasses.

Greene nodded. They both knew what this meant. Hodgson might have had the opportunity to kill the homeless woman. And for Waterbridge, this meant more bad publicity for his precious golf club.

"Did you see him after he finished the round?"

"No. But I never do."

"Why not?"

"To tell you the truth, Detective," Waterbridge said. He poured himself a glass of water and took a sip. He was stalling again.

"I'm afraid that Mr. Hodgson doesn't use the locker facilities anymore. He keeps his clubs and his gear in his vehicle. The course is still open, he played his regular Monday morning nine holes before anyone else was on the course."

"Would someone have seen him come or go?"

"Seen him? No. I checked this morning and he registered online as usual, but you see, Mr. Hodgson is not, how can I say it, not one of the club's most popular members, even though he was acquitted at his trial and he has won the seat on city council . . ."

His voice trailed off.

"I understand," Greene said.

The old guard, the old money, had given Hodgson the cold shoulder for the sin of bringing bad publicity to their private enclave.

Greene had to be careful with his next questions. It was dangerous to reveal too much. But he had to find out about the specially made golf balls with members' initials stamped on them.

"One more question. Do many members get their golf balls embossed with their initials?"

Waterbridge jerked his head to look at Greene. "Many do. Mostly the newest members, to be frank."

"Who does that for them?"

"We send them out to a printing company down by the lakeshore."

"How does it work?"

"Simple. A member puts in a request at the pro shop. We scan and send them over the order and once a week they deliver the golf balls."

"Can you give me the name of the company and your contact there?"

Waterbridge appeared confused. "I can." He pulled out his cell phone and began looking through it. "I assume, Detective, that if I ask you why you want this information, you'd suggest that I don't ask."

Greene smiled but didn't respond.

Waterbridge found the contact and flipped his phone around. Greene wrote the information down.

"Thank you," Greene said, standing to leave.

Just then a loud booming sound came at them from the stage. "Sound check, sound check," someone said.

Waterbridge cringed.

"I'm sure you'll enjoy your night," Greene said. "Away from all the hoopla at the club."

18

Melissa was agitated.

"Nance, what's going on?" she asked after everyone except the court clerk had left the court.

"The judge is sending you a message. She thinks our defence is nonsense. Fernandez sees she's going to convict you, and he's giving you one last chance to make a deal or you're going to jail."

If you've got the cards, play them, Parish thought. Even with your own client.

"That's not fair," Melissa said. Her face tensed up.

Parish had seen this too many times. Melissa's composure would start to crack, and in the blink of an eye she'd become unpredictable.

Parish tried to get Melissa to look at her but she wouldn't meet her eyes.

Melissa was wringing her hands together.

"Melissa, please." Parish was practically begging. "This time you need to listen."

"Ms. Parish." The court clerk behind them cleared her throat. "Sorry, but I have to lock up. You and your client need to clear the courtroom."

Melissa nodded. Parish took her by the arm and led her down the centre aisle. She was afraid Melissa was going to collapse.

She opened the courtroom door and Lydia was standing right in front of them. Her arms firmly folded across her fitted Chanel jacket, looking perfectly put together in her corporate uniform.

"Good morning, Mel," Lydia said, sounding as if she were talking to a client, not her oldest and once-best friend.

Melissa stared at her, unable to speak. Parish could feel her tense up. For a moment she thought Melissa was going to hit Lydia. She held Melissa's arm tight.

"I am fully cognizant of the fact that you wish to attend at the party tonight for Britt at the golf club," Lydia said. This was the way she spoke at work. Slow and deliberate and technical. Melissa and Parish had once dubbed it her "Legal-speak Lydia Voice." "You are aware that such action is prohibited by the terms of your current bail conditions."

Melissa stiffened. It seemed to take every bit of her resolve to speak. Her voice pitched high. "Britt . . . is . . . my . . . daughter . . . not . . . yours."

Lydia took a deep breath. Uncrossed her arms. "Mel," she said, her tone of voice softening. "I want you to see her, I really do. I've instructed my lawyer that if you agree not to come to the party tonight, I'll agree to give you more supervised access to Britt again." Lydia was speaking fast, as if she had to get it all in. "You can see her, but please not tonight. It will be too much for her."

Melissa kept glaring at Lydia.

"I'll talk to the Crown Attorney, Mr. Fernandez, right now," Lydia said. "I'll tell him that if you agree, I want him to drop the charges. He will. Even now. No one wants to see you go to jail."

"No," Melissa said, her voice louder.

Parish peered over Lydia's shoulder at the police officer on guard by the security entrance. He was a broad-shouldered, fit-looking guy with a close-shaved haircut. She watched him swivel in his chair and look at them. People in the hallway were starting to stare.

"Mel." Lydia looked desperate. "Please." She held her hands up in front of her chest, opened her palms, and tried to smile. "It's still me. Your oldest friend. The Little Dutch Girl?"

She slowly moved her hand toward Melissa, hoping Melissa would respond.

"Lydia," Parish said, alarmed. "I don't think you should—"

Melissa ripped her arm out of Parish's grip. "No," she said, her voice even louder.

"I know you hate me," Lydia said, putting her hands down in defeat. "This is not about you and me. It's only for Britt's sake. All her friends will be there and—"

"And you don't want her freak mother to ruin it," Melissa shouted.

Parish looked back down the hall. The policeman was on his feet, walking toward them.

"No, that's not true." Lydia turned to Parish. Tears were streaming down her face, streaking her carefully applied makeup. She looked at Parish in desperation. "Nance, we all used to be best friends. I'm trying."

"Mel," Parish said in a hushed tone, "you can't raise your voice here. They'll remove you from the courthouse."

Melissa kept glaring at Lydia. She didn't seem to be hearing anything Parish was saying.

Lydia wiped away her tears with the back of her hand. She reached out and touched Melissa's arm.

"Lydia, no," Parish said, trying to stop her.

Melissa jumped back, a wave of fear crossing over her face. "You hit me!" she screamed.

The policeman broke into a run. His heavy boots made a stomping sound on the hard floor.

Melissa raised her fists. "You stole my husband." Her voice was at full volume. "You stole my daughter."

Everyone in the hallway had frozen.

"Ma'am, stop right there," the policeman called out in a loud, authoritative voice. He was steps away.

Melissa jerked her head up, aware of the policeman for the first time. She stared back at Parish, horror filling her eyes.

She swung her head toward Lydia. "I . . . hate . . . you . . ." she blurted out.

Before anyone could move, she bolted, tearing right past the policeman.

"Nance, I warned you," she screamed just before she crashed out through the courthouse door. "They want to kill everyone!"

The door slammed behind her. There was a stunned silence. The police officer looked at Lydia and Parish quizzically.

"Did she hurt you, ma'am?" he asked Lydia.

Lydia's head hung down, her shoulders were folded in. "No. No, she didn't," she said, not even looking at the officer. "Please, let it be."

"She's my client," Parish said. "She needs some time to cool down. There were no threats, no assault."

The policeman took out his notebook and a pen from the bulletproof vest he was wearing. His name tag identified him as Atanasov. He turned back to Lydia. "Can I get your name please, ma'am?"

Lydia looked up at him. Bit her lip.

The policeman clicked his pen.

"I don't want to file a complaint."

"I understand, ma'am, but—"

"We're old friends. It's just a personal matter."

Atanasov's pen hovered above his notepad.

Lydia straightened her shoulders. Looked him straight in the eyes. "I'm a lawyer, and I know my rights. I have informed you that no criminal activity took place, therefore you have no reason to embark on an investigation, therefore I have no legal obligation to identify myself to you at this time."

Legal-speak Lydia is back, Parish thought.

"Okay," Atanasov said, unclicking his pen and putting it away. "But if she comes back in and this happens again—"

"It won't," Parish said.

He shook his head before he walked slowly back to his seat.

Lydia looked at Parish.

"She's not coming back, is she?"

"No."

"I want her to stop trying to sneak up on us. I don't know what to do."

"In a few minutes when court resumes, the judge will issue a bench warrant for her arrest," Parish said.

"That can't happen. If the police find her, they'll put her in jail."

Parish put her hands up in frustration. "What else can we do? I'll bail her out again."

"I don't want Melissa to ever be in jail."

"What did you think would happen when the police were called?"

Lydia's eyes widened. "I didn't call the police. It was the neighbours. We met in kindergarten. *Kindergarten.* She's my oldest friend. I don't want any of this. People blame Karl, but they have no idea what he put up with all those years. The time she cut him with the knife and he finally called the police—"

"I know."

"No, you don't. It wasn't the first time. You should see all the cut marks he has on his chest, his arms, and his legs from her attacks. He had to report her that time, to protect Britt."

Parish looked at Lydia. She could see she was telling the truth. Parish wasn't surprised. Part of being a good defence lawyer was trying to limit the damage for your client. Keep the issues as narrow as possible.

They stood looking at each other. The other people in the hallway had moved on, the hum of their many conversations criss-crossing and floating through the air.

"It's not my fault I fell in love with Karl," Lydia said.

"No one's blaming you."

"Ha," she said. "Tell that to Melissa. She will never believe me, but I want her to see Britt, I want her to be there as her mother. I want her to be healthy again."

"We all do."

"Before court starts, please come with me up to the Crown office," Lydia said. "I'm going to tell Fernandez to drop the case."

"Sure."

Lydia put her head on Parish's shoulder. It landed like a dead weight. She reached out, and they held hands.

"What happened to the Mel we knew? The Mel we loved?" she whispered. "Nance, what happened to her?"

19

Alison was beyond exhausted. Not only from the lack of sleep, but from the emotional turmoil of the last twelve hours. She was walking up the steep hill to her dad's house, perched high at the end of a cul-de-sac.

The house was elevated from the street, and there was a long staircase up to the front. Last year her Grandpa Y had turned the bottom floor into a separate apartment for Alison, with her own side-door entrance off the driveway on the south side.

Alison was thrilled. She'd adored her grandfather from the moment they met at the airport the day she arrived in Canada with her father. They'd just got through passport control and customs and walked out into the hall packed with anxious friends and relatives waiting for passengers from all over the world when, without warning, a short, surprisingly muscular man with a magical glint in his green-blue eyes rushed up and wrapped his arms around her.

"Welcome, welcome, welcome," he said in his warm, laughing voice. The way he held her somehow made Alison feel for the first time since her mother died that she was at home. She soon nicknamed him Grandpa Y.

His wife had died a few years earlier, and Ari was their only child. Ari's surprise discovery of Alison, his unknown daughter in England, meant that for the first time in his life Grandpa Y had a grandchild.

She couldn't even begin to imagine the horrors he'd been through in his long life. He'd grown up in a small town in central Poland. Half of the four thousand people who lived there were Catholic, the other half were Jewish. The two groups got along without incident for centuries, until the night in September 1942 when the Nazis arrived. Grandpa Y's first wife and two children were murdered, along with all the other two thousand Jews. He and one other man were the only ones who survived. In 1945, when the American 82nd Airborne liberated the concentration camp he was in, he weighed eighty-five pounds. After three years in a displaced persons camp in Austria, where he met Ari's mother, they arrived in Canada virtually penniless. Despite all this, Grandpa Y was the most positive and wisest person she'd ever met.

Alison climbed the three flights of stairs to the front door. She'd called ahead to tell Grandpa Y that she was on her way home, and he was sitting at the kitchen table. He'd made her lunch: a tuna-fish sandwich, which he'd cut in half on a diagonal, a pickle, and fresh pot of tea.

She hadn't realized how hungry she was, but just the smell of the food made her stomach churn. She was starving. She picked up half of the sandwich.

"Eat, eat," he said. "I saw you on TV. Congratulations. You were the first reporter on the scene."

"I was lucky," she said, polishing off the first half of the sandwich in a few bites and reaching for the second half.

He shook his head. "I don't believe in luck." This from a man who'd survived three years in the camps. "Drink some tea," he said. "I made it the British way."

That was a running joke between them. He liked instant coffee because it was the first thing the paratroopers who freed him had given him to drink. Alison's mother was a tea fanatic. When she lived for a year in Toronto with Ari, she'd taught him the "correct method" to make a pot of tea. Alison had shown Grandpa Y how to do it the same way.

He poured the tea, and she watched the steam rise. When he was done, she cradled the cup with both hands, the warmth comforting.

"I saw you reporting from the protest," he said.

"They were angry at the police."

"I could see that on the TV."

"Do you think Dad will be upset at me for covering this?"

"Why? It's your job. That young doctor you interviewed is quite dynamic, isn't he?"

Yes, *dynamic*. That's the word. That's what had attracted her to him. She'd spent two hours with Burns at his clinic and watched how he treated his sad and broken patients with remarkable kindness. How could Grandpa Y be so smart to see she liked him?

"He took me to his medical clinic for the homeless today. He's very committed," she said, polishing off the second half of the sandwich. "You won't say anything to Dad if I see him again?"

"Never," he said.

"That's why I love you," she said, after crunching into the pickle. "I never knew there was this much poverty in Toronto. It all seems so very hidden."

"It all seems so very hidden?" he said, echoing her British accent. He was a great mimic. Said he learned it in the war. "The poverty is not hidden from your father. A police officer sees all sides."

She sipped her tea and put the cup down. She had to screw up her courage to ask him a question she'd been afraid to ask since they'd met.

"The tea is lovely," she said.

"You're a good teacher."

Maybe she wasn't ready yet to ask him about something that meant so much to her.

Before she could say a word, he reached across the table and took her hand. "Your mother was a good teacher too."

She exhaled. Tears clouded her eyes.

"You knew her? I was afraid to ask."

"I was waiting until you did. Did I know your mother? Of course!"

"But—"

"Ari didn't know she was pregnant."

"I know but—"

"My wife had early onset of Alzheimer's. Some days Ari would come to visit us and she'd scream at him, thinking he was a Nazi guard."

"He couldn't leave you alone with her."

Grandpa Y shrugged, a shrug that said: *This is life, what are you going to do about it? You have to get on with things.*

"Dad never told me any of this."

"Why would he burden you with it?"

She had one more question. The toughest one. Grandpa Y was still holding her hand.

"The answer is yes," he said, before she could speak. "Your father loved your mother. I know she loved him. You never have to worry about that."

She hadn't cried since her mother died. Now she couldn't stop. Grandpa Y waited patiently.

"Grandpa Y?" she asked him at last. "Did you like my mum?"

"Me?" he said, laughing. That warm laugh of his that she had come to treasure so very much. "Like her? Did I like her? I loved her. I told Ari to go with her to England, but he wouldn't leave. It was the biggest mistake in his life."

Her parents loved each other. She was conceived in love. She wasn't sure why it meant so much to her, but it did.

She got up and bent over to kiss his cheek.

He pulled her close for another one of his hugs. This one was tighter than ever. "The Nazis took them all away from me," he whispered, his lips close to her ear, "then God gave me you."

20

Greene had known Julian Keswick, the supervisor of the parking lot below City Hall, for decades. Keswick was in charge of the secured section where judges who sat at the nearby Old City Hall courthouse parked, as well as a second secured lot reserved for city politicians.

Greene tapped on the perpetually dirty glass door of Keswick's little office, located deep in the bowels of the parking lot, and walked in. The place hadn't changed from the day Greene had first come here decades ago. Same steel desk. Same classic old Farrah Fawcett poster behind Keswick on the otherwise bare wall. Same seemingly endless stacks of paperwork on the desk. Same plaque on the desk: "Honk If You Need Service . . . Then Wait Until I'm Damn Good And Ready."

Keswick looked up from behind a fat old computer monitor that must have been there for at least fifteen years.

"Ari." He leaned back in his old wooden chair, then, like a boy on a swing, he used the momentum of his chair to propel his enormous body back toward the desk so he could stand up. He gave Greene an exaggerated mock bow.

"Hail to the Chief," he said. "I heard about your new gig. Couldn't keep away, could you? Once a copper always a copper."

"It's a job," Greene said, reaching out to grasp Keswick's extended, meaty paw.

Keswick shook his hand. "A job? Excuse me, you're the *head of homicide*. And to think, I remember when you were a little *pisher* division detective doing purse snatchings and house break-ins. To what do I owe the honour, sir?"

He sat back down, relieved to be off his feet.

Greene took a seat across from him in the old stack chair that also had been there forever. He pointed to the poster. "I see Farrah's still keeping you company."

"It's an ideal marriage. We've been together for forty-five years, and to me she's as beautiful as the day we met."

Greene laughed, even though he'd heard the joke many times over the years. "I need to take a look at a vehicle," he said.

Keswick turned his head back toward the restricted judges' parking lot. "One where our 'vulnerable' judges park?"

Greene shook his head.

Keswick turned his head in the other direction.

"Oh. You want to look where our 'hard-working' politicians leave their cars."

Greene nodded.

"And I assume, Chief, that we don't want anyone to know about this, do we?"

Greene shrugged.

Keswick leaned back again. His chair groaned. "Ari, I haven't laid eyes on you since you beat that murder rap. I hated seeing you charged."

"I wasn't too fond of it, either."

"I knew you were innocent all along. When I heard you went to England after, I didn't think you'd ever come back."

"Neither did I."

"Maybe you should have stayed away. Look at what's happening to this town. All these murders. Kids. One of them looks at another the wrong way and out come the guns. It's ridiculous."

"Standards have slipped," Greene said.

"Now what? We have a serial killer murdering homeless people?"

This was the way Keswick worked. First, he wanted some conversation, some gossip, before he'd agree to let Greene do whatever he wanted to do.

"We're working it," Greene said. Which he knew Keswick would understand to mean, I can't tell you anything more right now.

"It's not right. This isn't the Toronto the Good that it used to be."

"Big-city progress, big-city problems."

Keswick chuckled. "When I started this job, what were my lunch-time options? Burgers and fries. Fish and chips. Fried chicken. Now? Within two blocks of here there's Japanese, Thai, Korean, Indian, Jamaican, Italian, Greek, Middle Eastern. Back then who'd ever even heard of pad thai or sushi or jerk chicken? Now I can eat delicious food from anywhere in the world, so long as I don't get hit by a stray bullet."

The two men had a long history. Keswick and his wife, Beulah, had a daughter named Daphne who was a bad crack addict. When she had a daughter, Francine, Children's Aid swept in and scooped up the baby. The upshot was that Keswick and his wife had raised their grand-daughter since a month after she was born.

"How old is Francine now? Three?" Greene asked.

"You never forget, do you?"

"How's she doing?"

"She's a handful for old folks like us. Never stops moving. She calls me Papa. You know, Ari, we're blessed."

Keswick pulled out the top drawer of his steel desk, extracted a fob key on a thin metal ring, and pointed it toward the politicians' parking lot.

"The vehicle you're looking for is the black Ford SUV. Spot four-teen, on the left wall."

Keswick had already figured out that Greene wanted to check out Hodgson's vehicle on the QT. He slipped the key ring onto one of his fat fingers and twirled it around.

"Bastard killed that homeless guy with a golf club," Keswick said. "Now he struts around here as if he owns the city."

Greene had an idea. "When's the last time you heard from Daphne?" he asked.

Keswick twirled the fob faster. "You won't tell Beulah?"

"Of course not."

"She thinks I go out for a beer with my pals after my Monday Night Bowling League, but I see my daughter at the Coffee Time at Sherbourne and Jarvis. The twenty-four-hour one."

"How's Daphne doing?"

He shook his head. "She won't go to a shelter and I won't give her money. Instead I buy her coffee cards."

"Still won't go back into treatment?"

"You mean follow-up treatment after Beulah and me drained our savings to get her into rehab? You know, Ari, she had one relapse."

He stuck his forefinger in the air.

"One damn relapse. Oh no, no, no. The government can't afford to pay for follow-up treatment for an addict who relapses. Ask the fucking bureaucrats. And the politicians, why should they care? The homeless don't vote. All they want to do is balance their budget. That's a joke. Did you know they spent three quarters of a million dollars retrofitting this garage to make our precious judges 'feel safe' when they park their Lexuses and Teslas here? No one gives a damn about the poor anymore."

Greene sat still and waited for Keswick to catch his breath.

"Where's Daphne living?" he asked.

"She won't tell me. I'm worried sick she's in the Humber Valley where all the homeless are getting killed. Sometimes she stays under the Danforth Bridge. She's told me there's all sorts of hidden encampments down there that nobody even knows about."

He puckered his lips, stopped twirling the fob, and pulled it off his finger.

"Last winter almost killed her. And now it's getting cold again. Thank goodness for the lost and found here. I got her scarves and gloves and toques. Someone even left a Canada Goose coat. Worth about a thousand bucks. Amazing what some of these rich people buy and don't even care about."

He looked Greene square in the eye and handed the fob over to him.

"Is there really a serial killer on the loose murdering the homeless?"

Greene met his eyes. "It's Monday. You seeing Daphne tonight?"

"Ten o'clock."

"I'll meet you there."

"Really, Ari, you don't have to—"

Greene put up his hand to stop him from talking.

"Thanks," Keswick said. "Daphne was such a beautiful child. Now she looks older than her mom."

21

Parish opened her car door, threw her briefcase onto the passenger seat, plopped into the driver seat, and slammed the door shut.

"Damn it!" she yelled. She lifted her hands and smashed them down on the steering wheel hard enough that it hurt. Then she did it again. She was tired. She was hungry. She was frustrated as hell, even though she had somehow "won" another case for Melissa.

After Melissa ran out of the courthouse, Parish and Lydia went up to the Crown's office to see Fernandez. Lydia told him she didn't want him to go ahead with the charges. He then walked with the two of them back into court, precisely at the end of the fifteen-minute recess.

Judge Tator marched in, took one look around the courtroom, and demanded of Parish: "Counsel, where is your client?"

Fernandez explained that he'd spoken with the complainant, Ms. Lydia Lansing, who was standing beside him in court. And that he had decided at Ms. Lansing's urging to withdraw the charge.

Parish eyed Tator carefully. Was she angry or pleased to hear this? Tator gave no indication. She spoke to Lydia in a matter-of-fact voice, like a customs officer going through a checklist on a form, making it clear for the court record that she was doing her due diligence.

"Ma'am, I understand from the materials I've read about this matter that you are a lawyer."

"That's correct," Lydia said.

"You understand the nature of these proceedings."

"I do, Your Honour." Lydia was staring straight up at the judge. Parish could see she looked determined to maintain her composure.

"No one has tried to influence you to make this decision."

"No, Your Honour."

"No threats or promises."

"None."

That should do it. Parish expected Tator would end it now, but she didn't. Instead she dug back into the court documents in front of her. Reading.

It is rare to have total silence at any time a group of people are gathered together. But it is particularly awkward, and intimidating, when a courtroom falls silent. The judge had the floor and no one else could speak in a place designed for talk.

Tator kept reading, slowly shaking her head.

Parish looked over at Lydia, who seemed to be teetering on her designer shoes.

Tator finally raised her eyes and zeroed in on Lydia. The judge had been an excellent lawyer in her day, and Parish could see why. She knew how to command a courtroom, capture the moment.

"Ms. Lansing, I don't want to tread too much on the personal issues behind all this, but to be clear for the record, you and the accused were colleagues at the same law firm?"

"Yes, Your Honour."

"I believe you articled together?"

"We did."

"I see," Tator said. She hesitated. "How should I say this? There are some complicated family dynamics at work between the two of you, are there not?"

Lydia closed her eyes, and started to nod, as if she were in a trance. She swayed on her feet.

For an instant Parish thought she might even lose her balance. She had seen this many times before in the courtroom, people thrown back into their past recollections. Forgetting where they were, or even that other people were there.

Lydia kept nodding.

"Ms. Lansing," Tator said, her voice warming. "I do need you to answer yes or no for the record."

Lydia snapped her eyes open. Flustered.

"Oh, excuse me," she said. "Yes, it's true. Things with Melissa and me are complicated. They certainly are. I wish they weren't."

"I understand. To be absolutely clear, despite what I'll call, if you don't mind, your mutual history, you are confirming on the record that you are content with Mr. Fernandez's decision."

This happened with some judges. Especially the ones who had been good courtroom lawyers. Like a retired hockey player who was now a coach behind the bench but couldn't control their urge to get back on the ice, they couldn't control their urge to cross-examine a witness.

Lydia started nodding again. Then realized that she had to speak. "Yes, yes, I am."

Now Tator was nodding too. "You two have known each other for a very long time," she said, sounding more like a friend than a judge.

Lydia's lips began to quiver. Then she broke, crying. She covered her face with her hands. "We went to kindergarten together, camp, school, university," she said, struggling to get the words out. "She was my very best friend. I want her to get help, to get better."

The courtroom fell silent again.

Lydia looked alone, naked and exposed.

Parish took a step forward to take the spotlight off her.

"Your Honour," she said. "I think this witness has made herself clear."

Tator realized that she'd gone too far.

"Yes, thank you, Counsel," she said quickly. "The Crown has complete control of his case, and if he chooses to withdraw a charge, there is nothing this court can do. I have no further jurisdiction."

Tator turned to Fernandez. "Mr. Fernandez, tell your colleagues that my court is now free. I can assist with any overflow cases."

And with that, it was all over. The spectre of Melissa going to jail, the nightmare scenario that had kept Parish up all night, vanished into thin air not with the stroke of a pen but with a few words from a judge. After all these years of practice as a criminal lawyer, it still amazed her how a handful of words one way or the other could change forever a person's life.

Lydia came over to her, and they walked out of the courtroom together, past security, through the heavy metal front door, and into the treeless parking lot. With nothing to stop it, the wind was strong and cold.

Lydia looked across the pavement at the used-car lot. "Nance, such an exotic place you get to come to for your work."

"A hundred miles from the corporate boardrooms you spend your life in."

"Imagine if all three of us had stayed at the firm. Mel went so far downhill when you and I left."

"Who knows." Parish shrugged.

"I'm not evil. Anything I do, Mel is going to turn against me."

"I know."

"I want her to see Britt. I really do."

"It's freezing," Parish said. "Go home and I'll call you later."

"They say it's going to warm up tonight. See you at the party."

They hugged and Parish watched Lydia walk away before she went over to her car. She turned on the engine and blasted the heater, plugged her cell phone into the charger, and tapped out a text. "Mel. Lyd was good as her word. The charges against you are withdrawn. She wants to work out a way for you to see Britt after the party tonight. Please call me. Please. Nance."

Parish knew that trying to reach Melissa now was almost certainly futile. It was like sending a message in a bottle, because when Melissa blew up like this, it could be weeks, even months, before Parish would hear from her again. Still, she had to try. Maybe it was the lawyer in her, or the loyal friend, or whatever. She pushed send.

Her cell rang while it was still in her hand. Was Melissa miraculously calling her back? Instead, the call display read "Detective Kennicott, Toronto Homicide." She had his name in her contacts because he'd been one of the detectives on a murder trial she'd done a few years earlier.

"Hello, Detective," she said.

"Good morning, Ms. Parish. I've just spoken with Albert Fernandez. I understand you are Melissa Copeland's lawyer."

"I am," she said slowly. Why was Kennicott, a homicide detective, calling about Melissa? She couldn't be a suspect, could she?

"I want to talk to you about her."

"I can't do that right now." Parish knew that Kennicott had been a lawyer before he became a cop. "You understand solicitor-client privilege. I'd need her permission."

"I understand, but you don't need Ms. Copeland's permission to listen to what I have to say. It's important and urgent, but I'd rather not talk on the phone."

She sighed. "I've had a long morning, Detective, and I'm stuck up here in the North York Courthouse."

"I know where you are."

"You do?"

She heard a tap on her window and turned. Kennicott was standing there, a grim look on his face.

She rolled down her window.

"Detective Kennicott? What's going on? Is she all right?"

"I don't know. I drove up here and just missed her," Kennicott said. "We think she's in danger."

22

"**D**etective Greene," Hodgson said. "What a most *unpleasant* surprise."

"Not many people are happy to be visited by a homicide detective."

"Especially for a second time." Hodgson was a broad-shouldered man who wore his initialled shirts undone at the collar, as if his neck were too big to enclose in a shirt. He had a full head of thick hair and a nervous tic of tilting his head to the side and running his hand through it.

"I figured you'd show up on my doorstep this morning when I heard about the second murder in the valley. I've already called my lawyer," Hodgson said. "Your pal Phil Cutter."

Cutter had been Hodgson's lawyer at his murder trial. Years earlier, he'd started his career as a Crown Attorney and soon developed a reputation as a rabid advocate, determined to prosecute every case to the max. Greene had worked a number of murder trials with Cutter and never felt comfortable with him. Eventually Cutter's zeal led him to cross the line, and Greene was the one who caught him and got him turfed out of the Crown's office.

He'd become a defence lawyer—"I've gone over to the dark side," he liked to brag—and had been up against Greene on a number of murder trials. As a defence lawyer, his ultra-combative style, drilling down on even the most minute detail, was at times brilliant. But often his obsessiveness wound up being detrimental to his clients' best interests. Greene didn't trust him, and Cutter knew it.

Greene looked around Hodgson's office. It wasn't so much an office as a shrine to his daughter's golf achievements. Photos of Britt playing adorned the walls, along with tournament champion banners, and an array of brass trophies on a special shelf. A collection of putters was mounted behind his desk, each one longer than the next, tracking his daughter's growth.

Greene sat across the desk from Hodgson. He didn't attempt to shake hands, and he didn't acknowledge any of the golf-shrine décor.

"I'll take a wild guess," Greene said. "Cutter told you not to talk to me."

"You are correct."

"Then why did you agree to see me at all?"

"Because I wanted to tell you something important, Detective Greene." Hodgson leaned forward. "I didn't kill that bum who was killed in the valley a few days ago, and I didn't kill the one who died today that's all over the news this morning."

"Bums?"

"Yeah, bums. I never use the word *homeless*. That glorifies it. Makes it sound as if these leeches had no life choices. They have plenty of choice. There are available shelter beds in the city every night. Nobody has to live in the valley or sleep on the street."

"Sounds like a political speech."

"It is. And yes, the rumours are true. I'm running for mayor in the next election, and I plan to win." He sat back and smiled. Ran his fingers through his hair.

They both knew what that meant. If Hodgson became mayor, he'd be Greene's boss.

Greene stood. "I'm apolitical."

Hodgson stood too. "That's it?"

"You told me you didn't kill them," Greene said.

"You don't believe me?"

"It's not my job to believe or disbelieve. I'm interested in facts. Do you want to tell me where you were earlier this morning?"

For the first time since Greene had walked into his office, Hodgson wasn't looking cocky. He crossed his arms. Defiant. Silent.

"Perhaps you would like to explain this to me," Greene said, fishing his cell phone out of his pocket. "I'm curious. How did the right front fender of your SUV get scratched?"

"Right front fender?" Hodgson said, unable to contain himself. Answering a police officer's question with a question was a classic stall. He was playing for time.

"Long and narrow," Greene said. "Have to see what forensics says, but it looks to me as if it's the shape of a bicycle fender. Back wheel."

Hodgson looked flustered. Even though his lawyer had advised him to keep his mouth shut, it wasn't easy for an extrovert like him. He loved to talk, and the best way to break his cone of silence was to be quiet. Surprise him.

Greene slowly raised his cell phone, punched in some letters, and pulled up a set of photos. He fiddled with the phone, rotating it, upwards and sideways. He didn't look at Hodgson, but he could feel his agitation and impatience growing.

"There it is," Greene said.

"What?" Hodgson said, his anxiety getting the best of his vow of silence.

"I took some pictures of your SUV in the parking garage. Want to see?"

Hodgson shrugged.

"Is that a yes or a no?" Greene asked. Without waiting for an answer, he reached across the desk and put the phone right up to Hodgson's face.

Hodgson couldn't resist looking at the photo. He shook his head. "Ever since the trial and my acquittal, my car gets vandalized all the time."

"This scratch looks fresh."

Hodgson stared at him and didn't respond. Back to trying to not speak.

"I'll ask you again. Where were you this morning, say at about five thirty to six a.m.?"

"I don't have to answer any more questions."

Suspects often said this. But even saying they didn't have to talk meant they were still talking. And that was the key. Keep them talking.

Greene reached back into his pocket and pulled out a piece of cloth. He bent over Hodgson's desk and began to unfold it.

"You recognize this?" he said, taking his time pulling off the last bit of material to reveal a golf ball with Hodgson's initials on it.

Hodgson stared at it.

"K.L.H. Your initials, and here's the club crest," Greene said. "Leonard's your middle name."

"Where did you get this?" Hodgson asked. Once again, unable to maintain his silence.

Greene folded the cloth back up around the ball. It was his turn to go silent. He turned to leave.

"I order two dozen balls every April," Hodgson said, animated now. "It's a point of pride for me that I never lose all of them during the season."

This made sense. Hodgson had testified at his trial that he was a scratch golfer. And his order of twenty-four balls in the spring was true. Greene had checked with the labelling company. But that wasn't the whole story.

"But then you ordered a half dozen two weeks ago," Greene said.

"One morning a few weeks ago when I was out on the course playing a round, someone broke into my car and stole my last six balls."

"Did you report the theft?"

"There's no point. Waterbridge and the old farts who run the club, do you think they give a damn? They're probably happy about it. They'd love nothing better than to see me gone."

Greene pocketed the wrapped-up ball.

Was Hodgson being set up? Or had he let his rage get the better of him when he killed the two homeless people? Had he cleverly concocted a plausible explanation? Impossible to tell.

"Pleasure to see you again, Councillor," Greene said. "And don't take your vehicle to the car wash." He opened the door and left without looking back.

23

Alison had Krevolin park the TV van a block away and around the corner from the church where the memorial service for Deborah Lemon was being held. It was impossible to be unobtrusive if you were a TV reporter, but at least this way they wouldn't be on the street where the mourners were gathering.

The service was set to start in about half an hour. Alison was scheduled to broadcast live when the church doors opened fifteen minutes before it began. She and Krevolin got out of the van and walked around the corner. The little church was at the far end of the block, and she could see a crowd had already gathered outside. This was a close-knit, working-class neighbourhood. They passed homes on the street where families, despite the blustery cold weather, had come out into their small front yards to watch.

At times like this, Alison wished she were a newspaper reporter and could sit quietly in the back of the church to watch the service and listen to the eulogies without being noticed. Talk to people privately. Write up her story on her own time. Cover the event and not become part of it.

But being a TV reporter meant showing up with a cameraman and everyone knowing you were there. She couldn't film inside the church and was limited to interviewing people as they came in and out of it. To bulk up the story she had to get tape of what they had to say.

She was under a lot of pressure to deliver a good report. Her boss was skeptical about her doing this story, and Alison had fought hard for it.

"We cover funerals of rich and famous people all the time," she'd argued, "why don't we ever cover the funeral of a homeless person?"

"Hundreds of people die in this city every week," Persaud had said. "That doesn't make it news."

"Deborah Lemon was the second murder victim in the valley this week."

"True."

"We never do real stories about the poor or the homeless."

"We cover the homeless issue."

"That's my point. We talk about the issue. Interview experts. But when do we do stories about the people who actually live on the street? And the people they leave behind?"

Persaud had agreed. Even though Krevolin had been up with her since they'd rushed out to the Humber Valley early this morning, the cameraman had volunteered for the assignment.

As they approached the church, Alison could see people were huddled together in two different groups. The first group was well dressed. Some wore Humber River Hospital togs with name tags clipped on them and badges dangling around their necks. The people in the second, smaller group were poorly dressed and most of them were smoking. Alison recognized some of the faces from the protest that Dr. Burns had led outside Police Headquarters. There was no sign of the dead woman's family.

Sylvia, the receptionist from the clinic, was there. She spotted Alison and gave her a condescending glare. Alison looked for Burns and was surprised that he wasn't there. She had a fleeting thought: Was she *only* looking for him for professional reasons? Did she have personal motives for setting this whole thing up?

She had called him this morning when she got the go-ahead for the assignment.

"I'm impressed," he said.

"I think it's an important story."

"Especially if there's a serial killer out there."

"That's what sold it," she admitted.

As Alison walked closer to the church, Krevolin put his hand out to stop her. "I need an establishing shot," he said, hoisting up his camera. She stood beside him as he filmed the scene. She looked around. More people were becoming aware that they were there. Some were pointing.

"Done," Krevolin said. "Let's go."

They started by interviewing the health-care workers. Lemon's former colleagues from the hospital spoke eloquently about what a dedicated and professional nurse Deb had been before her fall. Many were crying.

Alison checked her watch. Fifteen minutes to go. There was still no sign of the family or Burns.

She approached the homeless crowd and smiled at Sylvia.

"Good afternoon," Alison said.

"Arnold told me you were coming," Sylvia said, as unimpressed as ever. "You interviewed all those hospital workers first. You going to bother to talk to some of Nurse Deb's real friends?"

"That's why I'm here." She motioned Krevolin to follow her. She took out her mic, he rolled the camera, and she started to talk to people. Some were articulate, others rambled, and others were almost unintelligible. The one thing they all said was that "Nurse Deb" assisted people in the valley and was always trying to help them get off drugs.

All at once the crowd grew quiet as a black limo drifted along the street and parked in front of the church. A middle-aged man and two teenage boys got out. They looked awkward in their badly fitting suits. A few of the hospital workers went up to hug the boys and their father.

Alison looked around for Krevolin. He'd quietly slipped back from the crowd and was filming from a respectful distance.

The family climbed the steps to the church. The moment they were inside, Alison heard a loud noise behind her. She turned, and there coming around the corner was Burns out in front of a group of protesters, carrying a new set of signs: "Remember Nurse Deb" and "Nurse Deb Helped the Homeless," and "Cops—Help Us Now!"

Burns led them as they chanted: "Toronto police, save the homeless," over and over again.

Alison walked over to Krevolin. They both knew what had happened. Nothing like a TV camera to create a story.

He looked at his watch. "You're going live in thirty seconds," he said, hoisting his camera on his shoulder and stepping behind her so the protesters who were gathering on the sidewalk were squarely in the background of his shot.

Alison looked at Burns and caught his eye. He grinned at her. She didn't smile back.

He'd set her up and they both knew it.

He shrugged his shoulders as if to say, "Come on, we all know this is how the game is played."

Should she be angry with him? Or impressed with the depth of his commitment to get this story out? After all, rich people and big corporations and popular entertainers had publicists and handlers who knew how to play the media game and get maximum coverage. Why not a homeless advocate?

"Toronto police, save the homeless!" his little crowd was shouting louder and louder. "Toronto police, save the homeless!"

She rolled her eyes at him. With a hint of a smile.

"Five, four . . . ," Krevolin said.

She turned her back on Burns and the protesters and put on a serious face.

"Three, two, one."

The green light went on.

"This is Alison Greene," she said. "Reporting live for *T.O. TV News*."

She finished her report and again, the protesters stopped their chanting.

"That's enough," she said to Krevolin. They walked back around the block and had just finished packing up the TV van when she heard the sound of a bicycle riding up.

She whirled around. Burns was standing there, his hands on the handlebars of his bike, his chain and lock dangling around his neck, that charming smile of his dancing across his face.

"I should be quite cross with you," she said, arching an eyebrow at him. "Shouldn't I?"

"Why?" he said. "For helping people exercise their right to protest?"

"Perhaps for talking me into doing a story so you could get more publicity."

The grin disappeared from his face. "Drug companies spend millions on their high-priced publicists to get stories about their so-called new miracle drugs or breakthrough cures for cancer, and nobody says *boo*, do they?"

When he turned off the charm, he was much more convincing.

"You're right," she said. "I used the same argument to convince my producer to let me do this story." She turned to Krevolin. "This is Randy, my cameraman. He's working on his own time even though we've been up all night."

Burns reached out and shook hands with Krevolin.

"Appreciate it," Burns said.

"No worries," Krevolin said, and walked around the van and got in the driver's door.

Burns smiled at Alison.

"You free tonight?"

"What do you have in mind?"

"How about helping feed some hungry people?"

"That sounds like a hot date. Where?"

"There's a church across town on the Danforth that runs a program on Monday nights. They're always looking for volunteers."

24

Among the many subtle lessons Greene had taught Kennicott over the years, there was one that would never be found in any training manual: Wherever you are in the city, find a decent spot to eat or at least to get a good cup of coffee.

It was not easy to do when he got stuck up here on a case at the North York Courthouse, stranded in the sprawling suburban wasteland that surrounded the wealthier, leafier downtown. They called it the donut effect: The rich live inside the donut in their protected neighbourhoods, while the poor were stranded in a world of crumbling high-rise buildings, too-wide-to-do-anything-but-drive-on streets, and scant public transportation, dooming those with cars to continual driving and those without to near impossibly long bus commutes to get to practically anywhere.

The upshot was that the choice of eateries in this barren landscape was limited to characterless chain restaurants, submarine sandwich shops, pizza parlours, fried chicken and hamburger joints. But Greene, ever resourceful, had shown Kennicott the Nino D'Aversa Bakery, a lively, sprawling Italian restaurant and café that he'd somehow found hidden away in the middle of an industrial park.

Kennicott had convinced Parish to let him take her out for a cup of coffee, and she'd followed him through a maze of side streets until they pulled in to the restaurant's crowded parking lot. She got out of her car and gave him a curious look.

"Here?" she asked.

"You'll see," he said.

They walked in together. The bakery was huge, with floor-to-ceiling windows, hard tile floors, tables on one side, a buffet-style restaurant and café and gelato bar in the middle, and rows of baked goods and pasta for sale on the other side. It wasn't even noon and the place was bustling with customers, all seemingly happily engaged in loud and animated discussions. The air was filled with the scent of fresh ground coffee.

"How in the world did you ever find this place?" she asked him, looking around in amazement.

"Cops. We have informants all over the city."

She laughed. He directed her to a table in the corner by the window. The only people nearby were a pair of young women chattering away, clearly oblivious to everyone around them. Kennicott made sure Parish took the seat looking into the restaurant with the window at her back. He sat facing her.

There were two used coffee cups and two plates still on the table. The waitress, a busy older woman with her hair up in a bun, arrived and efficiently cleared everything off. They both ordered cappuccinos.

"Smells so good," Parish said. "I want to relive the last ten years of my professional life so I could come here every time I'm stuck up here in Nowheresville."

"Wait until you try the coffee," he said.

The waitress soon arrived with their order. The cappuccinos came with a hard biscotti and a glass of water. Parish sampled the coffee and gave him a thumbs-up. She bit into her biscotti. It made a hard, snap sound.

"About Melissa," he said.

She swallowed, sipped her coffee. "I'm listening."

"I know she's one of your best friends."

Parish snapped off another bite of her biscotti. She was trying to act nonchalant, but he could see he had her attention.

He looked around, to make sure no one could overhear them. He put one elbow on the table, cupped his face in his hand, and moved closer to her.

"It's a good thing you're sitting down. There's something you need to know about Melissa."

Parish looked over his shoulder. He could see she was confirming that no one was near. She looked back. Concerned. She was about to take another bite out of her biscotti.

"I'll keep it simple," he said. "Melissa's a police informant."

Parish bit down on the biscotti instinctively, almost like a child biting down on her thumb. He could see the surprise register in her eyes.

She swallowed then said, "Melissa?"

He nodded.

"For how long?"

"Soon after her first arrest."

"You're kidding. That was years ago."

He didn't respond, giving her time to process this.

"Seven years, and Melissa never let on." She blew out her cheeks. "Who's running her?"

"This might surprise you too," he said. "It's Ari Greene."

"Greene? Really?"

She'd first met Greene when he'd been the detective on a murder trial that she'd done a few years earlier. He was a close friend of her partner, Ted DiPaulo. Greene was an intriguing, sometimes slightly intimidating guy.

Her face broke out into a huge grin. She began to chuckle, and then burst into a loud laugh.

"What's so funny?" he asked her. He was pretty sure he knew what she was going to say.

"You burst my bubble. All these years, all of Melissa's cases, here I thought I was a brilliant lawyer keeping her out of jail."

"I didn't say you're not a brilliant lawyer," he said.

"That's a good lawyer's double negative," she said. They both laughed.

"This means that Albert knew all along," she said, still processing all this. "That's why he kept Melissa's files to himself."

"Fernandez never let on?"

"Not for a second. I should nominate him for an Oscar."

Parish dipped what was left of her biscotti in her cappuccino and swirled it around.

"I know it's gauche to do this, but it tastes good." She waved the biscotti in the air like a conductor's wand before she ate it. "Mmm," she said after she swallowed.

He dunked his still-untouched biscotti too. "It's November. You can indulge."

"And getting cold. I'm worried."

"We need to find her," he said after taking a bite. "Is there anything you can tell me? Solicitor-client only goes so far."

She picked up a small metal spoon and used it to scoop up the last dregs of her cappuccino. She shook her head.

"Did you notice the two people with notebooks in the back of the court?"

"The students?"

"They weren't students. They were armed undercovers."

"Had me fooled."

"Your friend Melissa knows how to disappear. Apparently she bolted so fast they couldn't find her."

"That's Mel for you."

"And those two women talking away at the table behind me," Kennicott said, pointing his thumb over his shoulder.

She looked at them, then back at him. "Who are *they*?"

"Two more undercovers. They got here before us and made sure we got this table so we'd have a private place to talk. The dirty dishes were left here intentionally. Greene knows the owner."

Parish put her hand to her forehead and rubbed it. "You guys are taking this seriously."

"Very. Two homeless people killed in two days. I'm asking you straight out. Did Melissa tell you anything that might help us?"

Parish picked up her spoon and licked it clean.

"Understand, with Melissa everything is high drama. She sees conspiracies everywhere."

"She's paranoid but that doesn't mean she might not be right sometimes," he said. Pressing her. "If she was a witness to these murders she might be in danger."

Parish reached into her briefcase and pulled out her cell phone.

"Melissa sends me hundreds of text messages. This morning I got a whole bunch."

Kennicott watched her tap her phone and scroll through her messages, biting her lip. She shook her head. "I don't know."

"I can't force you to show them to me."

She put her phone face-down on the table, reached into her briefcase again, and pulled out a pen and paper.

"Here," she said. "I'll show you one text Melissa sent me early this morning that had nothing to do with her case. Write this down but as soon as you don't need it you'll destroy this piece of paper. No texting or emailing about it. And no one knows where you got it from."

"Agreed."

She turned her phone so he could see it.

"I can tell by her jumbled spelling that Melissa was worked up when she wrote this," Parish said.

Kennicott started to write, reading the words out loud softly as he went. "*Nance I warnd you, but no one wd listn. The kilingz contnue. No one is imune. There is no justice.*"

"I got it this morning," she said. "I assumed it was another one of her rants. I had no idea she had reported a murder."

"Melissa calls you Nance?"

She frowned. "It's an inside joke. Melissa and Lydia were childhood friends and they had nicknames for each other. Mel and Lyd. When I became friends with them, they thought I was too small-town cautious, so I became Nance Take a Chance."

"The three of you really cared about each other, didn't you?"

"Sisters in arms."

He folded the paper carefully and put it in his pocket. "We have to find her. Do you have any ideas where she would go?"

"No idea."

"Fernandez told me about the party for her daughter tonight at the golf club. Will you be there?"

"It's not my kind of thing, but yes, I'm going."

"Do you think she'll show up?"

"I hope not. It would cause a scene and be painful for Britt. But . . ."

"She's obsessive and this could be her chance to see her daughter," Kennicott said, picking up on Parish's thought.

"This is between you and me. I'm going to work there tonight, undercover. Just in case, here's my cell number."

He passed her his business card.

She photographed the card with her phone and passed it back to him.

"If you see me," he said, "don't wave."

25

Greene had to find Fraser Dent. Once a top bond trader who spoke fluent Japanese, Mandarin, French, and Spanish, in his early forties Dent became a fall-down drunk and had lived on the street for more than a decade. "Just following the family tradition," he liked to say, referring to his father and grandfather, drunkards who'd both ended up dying of liver failure.

Over the years Greene had kept him going, "lending" him fifty dollars each time they met, getting him into rehab when Dent was willing. In return, Dent funnelled Greene information from the street. When Greene was charged with murder, Dent helped him out, big-time, behind the scenes.

It had been months since they'd talked, and it could often take Greene a few days to find Dent, who didn't have a cell phone. Greene didn't have time to waste. He went downtown and started hunting for his old friend.

His first stop was Seaton House, the biggest men's shelter in Canada, which housed more than eight hundred men. It was located in an area of the city that for years had had both the largest concentration of street people and new condo developments at the same time, and local politicians had often talked about renovating the shelter and moving most of the residents out to smaller suburban locations. But Greene had his doubts that the downtown clientele, some of whom had lived in the area for decades, would leave the neighbourhood, even though a flood of new money was moving in and gentrifying everything in sight.

He checked the logbook at the front desk. In spite of the chaos of these men's lives, the one thing that they were rigorous about at Seaton House was record-keeping. No one got in without proper ID. The last time Dent had checked in was twelve days ago, and no one had seen him since.

Greene's next stop was the Law Society of Ontario Feed the Homeless lineup. Every day at about four thirty a line of homeless men and women formed in the City Hall square. When the doors opened, they'd walk into one of the city's most beautiful buildings that dated back to the early eighteen hundreds. There, they'd be served dinner by some of the city's best and most high-priced lawyers.

Greene walked up and down the line, nodding to familiar faces. Chatting with some. No one had seen Dent for days. Once the hall opened, Greene walked in with the crowd and checked the sign-in sheets. Dent had last been there a week earlier.

His third stop was the Canterbury Clinic, a drug and alcohol rehab clinic that worked with street people. For years, it had scraped by on donations and bake sales, until, as the drug problem in the city escalated, the government came through with just enough funding to keep the doors open. Dent had been a client there and, when he was straight, volunteered as a counsellor.

As Greene walked out of the elevator and into the barebones waiting room, Trish, the clinic's veteran receptionist, greeted him.

"Detective Greene, where've you been?"

"Keeping Toronto the Good safe, one day at a time. Is Michael here?" he asked, referring to the clinic's dynamic, sometimes mercurial director, who had somehow kept the place afloat for years. Like his clients, he had his own paranoid peculiarities, one of which was that he never spoke on the phone. If Greene wanted to talk to him, he had to come over. Greene suspected it really wasn't a paranoia but a ploy to make Greene show up from time to time. He didn't mind.

Michael had spent years working with Dent, and the two had a strong, if troubled bond. Probably because they were both bright and because Michael, like many good counsellors, was himself a recovered addict.

As Dent once told Greene, "The trouble with Mike is that I just can't bullshit him."

"Too bad," Greene said.

"Rough," Dent agreed.

Trish smiled at Greene. "You know how Mike is. An hour ago one of his clients came in high as a kite. He was furious. He'd made a deal with her dealers that they weren't going to sell her anymore stuff so the CAS wouldn't grab her two-year-old. Mikey stormed out to go hunt them down. Who knows when he'll come back. Can I help?"

"I'm looking for Dent."

"It's your lucky day. He dropped by a week ago looking clean as a whistle and Mike put him to work. Right now, he's interviewing a Vietnamese kid hooked on heroin. Has about ten more minutes to go. You in a rush, want me to buzz him?"

"No," Greene said, sitting down on a dusty old sofa and picking up a three-year-old *Time* magazine. "I'm more than happy to wait."

Dent emerged ten minutes later. He wore a pair of green khaki pants and a clean dress shirt with the sleeves rolled down and the collar buttoned up at the neck. Greene knew the shirt was to hide his considerable tattoos. He looked clean and clear-eyed. A skinny Asian man with pink and green streaks in his black hair slunk out behind him.

Dent, who had not expected to see Greene, didn't flinch. He winked at him as he put his arm around his patient.

"Tran, you're doing well." He pulled out a tiny old cell phone. "You had a bad weekend, that's all. Something comes up, you call me twenty-four/seven."

"Yeah, thanks," Tran mumbled, and walked out without another word.

Dent smiled at Greene.

"You look good," Greene said.

"Saving the world one soul at a time for fifteen dollars an hour."

"Since when do you have a cell phone?"

"This crappy old thing?" he said, twisting it in his hand. "When I worked on Bay Street I had two full-time secretaries, my office phone, and two cell phones. Now I have this old piece of junk the clinic gave me since I'm working here more than twenty hours a week."

"That's great."

"Not great, but it's good. With all these murders, I was waiting for you to find me. Come on in to our luxurious boardroom."

The boardroom was a square windowless room with a beat-up round table and a mishmash of chairs pulled in around it. Towers of paper towels, toilet paper, and tissue boxes were stacked high against the walls.

Dent pulled out a chair and motioned Greene to take another. He pointed at the wall. "What do you think? A modern art piece, or a donation from one of our clients—no names mentioned—who works in the grocery business?"

"People appreciate what you do for them," Greene said.

"Once in a while. What do you need, Detective?"

"To find out what's going on in Humber Valley. None of the homeless people will talk to us."

"That surprise you?"

"Not one bit," Greene said, "That's why I smoked you out."

26

Alison had worked as a food server one summer at a posh restaurant in Sloan Square. Now she was working in the basement of the Eastminster United Church. She'd been instructed by the people who ran the feed-the-hungry program that all the homeless people were to be seated at a properly set table, complete with cutlery, napkins, and glasses, and that they be served fully plated meals—no one was forced to stand in a humiliating food line—and that once they'd finished eating, their dishes should be cleared promptly, as in a real restaurant.

Alison was taken aback by how many people were there—more than a hundred—and by how many of them were women. She counted forty-two. One old woman caught her attention. She was thin and frail, but she had an erect, dignified posture and excellent table manners. Alison watched her eat. She grasped her soup spoon between her thumb and forefinger and scooped outward before bringing it to her mouth. She held her fork facing down, then piled small portions of food on the outside of it with her knife—which she held with her forefinger on top of the blade. When the woman finished her meal, she put her knife, then her fork on the plate in a line at the exact five o'clock to eleven o'clock angle, the way Alison's mum had insisted.

Serving was surprisingly hard work. As she rushed in and out of the kitchen, Alison saw Burns. He was on dishwashing duty, his hands in long yellow plastic gloves, intent upon scrubbing down a pile of large pots in a deep industrial sink. Out of the limelight, when he'd turned off the charm, she could see that he took what he did seriously.

On one of her passes through the kitchen, he noticed her and smiled.

"I'll have to add 'fine dishwasher' to your list of accomplishments," she teased.

"I'm a doctor. I'm used to scrubbing in." His face turned serious again. "It's important. The last thing any of these people need is to pick up an infection."

When the meal ended, she joined Burns and the staff in the kitchen and ate mushroom soup with rice and chicken stew. The volunteers were tired and no one was talkative. It had been sobering, seeing so many people in such desperate straits.

By the time she and Burns went outside, it was dark. He had his bicycle with him and he walked with it as they strolled along the Danforth, a wide thoroughfare filled with restaurants and shops. A limp blue-and-white sign hung across the street announcing, "Welcome to Greek Town." She'd been out here a few times in the summer and it was always packed with people, but on a cold November night it felt deserted.

"What did you think?" Burns asked her.

"I was most impressed with the dignified manner with which the people were treated, with real plates, napkins, and cutlery."

"It all matters."

"One older woman I noticed had perfect British table manners."

"You must mean Pipa. Comes every Monday. She showed up about two years ago after her husband died. He was a plumber, never had much in the way of savings. They didn't have children. Then the landlord renovicted her."

"Renovicted?"

They'd reached the start of Danforth Bridge, the long span over the Don River Valley below. He stopped and looked at her. Shook his head. "You do have a lot to learn. Rents are skyrocketing in the city and landlords want to cash in. A renoviction is when they kick out a tenant to do some minor renovations so they can jack up the rent for the next tenant. Renoviction applications in the city were up three hundred per cent last year. Tons of people are homeless now just because they can't pay the rent. It's only going to get worse."

"And Pipa?"

"She used to live in a spacious two-storey flat with a sunny balcony she filled with flowers in pots every spring. We were lucky to find her a basement apartment, and it costs twenty-five per cent more."

They started walking again. Traffic was light. There was no one else around. At the halfway point across the bridge there was a circular alcove that extended over the river and highway below. They stepped out to take in the view. The lights of the office towers, each one topped with the logo of a bank or a big corporation, high-rise condominium buildings, and illuminated construction cranes sparkled across the horizon. It was stunning.

There was an old-fashioned circular telescope on a stand facing south. Alison had seen the same things last winter when her father took her and Grandpa Y on a day trip to Niagara Falls.

"Let's try it," she said, fishing out some coins.

"I hope it works."

She put a quarter in and looked through the viewfinder. It was dark.

"It doesn't," she said.

"Let me see," he said, leaning close to her. Their heads touching briefly.

"You're right," he said.

She stared at the downtown towers and thought of how the people who lived and worked there were a million miles away from Pipa and the others they'd fed in the church basement. Before she came to Canada, Alison had barely heard of Toronto. She had no idea it was this large or this affluent. She'd since learned that it was the fourth-largest city in North America and by far the fastest-growing one. Despite all the glitter, now she was seeing its dark underbelly of extreme poverty and hunger.

The view from the bridge was partly obstructed by a steel barrier that rose high above the stone railing. As Alison straightened up, Burns put his hand on one of the metal bars. Coloured lights rolled back and forth across it in what looked to be a random pattern.

"Do you know what this is?" he asked her, trying to shake the bar and showing her it was firmly fixed in place.

"Some strange type of modern sculpture, perhaps?"

He gave out a bitter laugh and jumped up on the ledge. "It's a suicide barrier," he said, spreading his arm out wide. "This used to be a favourite place for people to jump. All these lights are supposed to turn it into an art piece. They were added later to try to pretty it up."

"London is full of bridges, and I can't imagine them covering one up like this. Did it work?"

"Yes and no. Nine or ten people a year used to jump from here. Now there are lots of other bridges in the city that they use."

The night air was cold, and whether it was because of the wind coming up from the valley below or the thought of Pipa, alone in her life with her excellent table manners, Alison started to shake. Burns jumped down and put his arm around her.

"I didn't expect to see so many women there tonight," Alison said.

"Thirty-six per cent of the homeless are women. Do you have any idea how many homeless people there are out in the cold in this city every night?"

She shook her head. Even though he had his arm around her, she was still shivering.

"Take a guess."

She held her hands up. "A few thousand?"

"Estimates go from seventy-five hundred to ten thousand. The average lifespan for people in this city is eighty-two years. Want to guess what it is for homeless people?"

"Not really."

"Half. Think of ten thousand people dying on average at age forty-one." He turned and looked at the shimmering view before them. "All those cranes throwing up condos for the rich, and so many people without any home at all."

"It hurts you, doesn't it?" she said.

"What?"

"Seeing people suffer. Dying so young."

Alison wasn't quite sure how what happened between them next happened.

She let her head drop onto his shoulder, and her lips lightly touched his neck. He held her closer. What little noise there was from the traffic seemed to disappear. And then they kissed.

27

Parish was checking her hair in the rear-view mirror of her ten-year-old Toyota as she sat in the long line of pricey cars and over-sized SUVs, waiting on the street to enter the Humber River Golf Club.

She hated getting dressed up. On the rare nights when she wasn't at work in the office meeting with clients or preparing for court the next day, she liked to stay home and loll around in sweatpants. But tonight she was wearing the only cocktail dress she owned, pearl earrings, a matching necklace, and an almost-new pair of Manolos. She'd bought the shoes last winter, the last time she had a serious date.

A month ago, Lydia sent her the invitation for tonight's event. It called for "golf-club formal dress."

Parish phoned her. "What the hell is golf-club formal?"

"Get out your best cocktail dress."

"As if I have more than one. Tell me you're kidding."

"I know. The party's kind of over the top for an eleven-year-old winning a golf trophy."

"You think?"

"It's Karl. When it comes to Britt and golf, the sky's the limit."

Ever since Karl divorced Melissa and married Lydia, Parish had been caught in the middle between her two close friends and former colleagues. She was determined to remain neutral, but it wasn't easy. Especially because Karl's whole life was wrapped up in his daughter, and his obsession with keeping Britt away from her mother, while at the same time Melissa's behaviour became more and more erratic. Which was the cause, and which was the effect? It was impossible to tell.

"Nance," Lydia said, filling in the silence on the phone line. "You still there?"

"I'm here."

"You're going to come to the party. Please."

"I'll be there," Parish said, knowing she had to go.

Parish hadn't heard anything from Melissa since she'd stormed out of the courthouse this morning. There was a chance she might show up tonight, and Parish was afraid there'd be a major confrontation. Maybe by attending the party, Parish could mediate if anything happened.

A woman in a black jacket with the label "Concierge for Hire" was stationed at the entrance, inspecting invitations. Parish rolled down her window and felt the night air. Typical see-saw November weather in Toronto: it had warmed right up and a light rain was starting to fall.

"Welcome to Britt's party," the woman said to Parish. "Your name, please."

Parish gave her name and the woman checked it off on her clipboard. Something about her looked familiar. Then Parish placed her. She was one of the "students" sitting in the back of the courtroom. An undercover officer.

"Here's your Britt scarf," she said handing Parish a scarf with Britt's name in bold letters above the club's colours and insignia.

"Thank you," Parish said, then added the word, "*Officer.*"

The woman was composed. She smiled back at Parish. "Have fun, Counsellor," she said, then waved Parish through.

Parish drove along the winding golf-club driveway to the front entrance, where three young men wearing the same concierge jackets were perched on the carpeted front steps that led to the clubhouse. One of them rushed out to the car in front of her and opened the driver's door, unfurling an umbrella as he went. A second young man opened the passenger door to let out a woman wearing an elegant sheath, covering her with another umbrella. The driver, a man in a tux, passed his keys to the young man along with a dollar bill—of what denomination Parish couldn't see—and took a ticket from him. The young man hopped in the car and sped away into the darkness.

Incredible, Parish thought. Valet parking when the lot was a two-minute walk away. And damn, she was going to be underdressed.

She pulled her car up. The third young man scooted down, easily taking the steps two at a time, swooped over, and opened her car door all in one smooth motion.

"Good evening. I'm Jack," he said, covering her with an umbrella. "Welcome to Britt's party."

He had a beaming smile on his handsome face. Parish guessed he was in his early twenties. Very fit. Perfect teeth too.

Her foul-mouthed friend Zelda, who worried about Parish's lack of a sex life since her divorce four years earlier, loved to tease Parish about how younger men were attracted to her. "It's your great hair," Zelda said. "To say nothing of your great ass and your goddam perfectly aquiline nose."

Although Parish liked to deny it, perhaps Zelda was right. There'd been Bert, the young waiter, whom she met one night when she was out with Zelda at a vodka bar. He'd slipped her his phone number on the back of the check. Then Harry, a young guide, when they went on a canoe trip up north last summer. Both times, the flings only lasted a few weeks.

"There's nothing to talk about with them," she complained to Zelda the last time they were out at a Law Society trivia night and Jeff, a first-year lawyer, tried to pick her up.

"Talk? What the fuck do you need to talk about, girl?"

She swung her legs out of the car. Jack reached over and took her arm. She shook her head back and forth so that her hair flopped over her face and swung back away. What the hell, she was having a good hair day.

Up close, she put Jack at maybe his mid-twenties. Still boyish, and she could see he was in great shape.

He handed her a card with a picture on it of Britt holding a trophy in one hand, her golf club in another, a rather shy look on her face. Underneath the words *Britt Is Number One, Your Car Number Is* were typed out, and someone had handwritten in her number, 77.

"Thanks," she said, taking the card and examining it. "Lucky sevens. This could be my night."

"Hey, you never know," Jack said, all smiles.

She noticed him looking sideways at her old Toyota and caught a smirk on his face.

"Maybe you should park my old jalopy at the dark end of the lot," she said.

"Sorry." He chuckled. "It's just most people here drive ridiculously expensive cars."

"You could finance a third-world nation with them," she said.

He laughed. "That's a good line. I'll have to tell my business professor that one."

"Where do you go to school?"

"Community college. Special course in golf-club management. I'm kind of doing my victory lap. Two more credits to go."

"Happens." Parish was in no hurry. It was easier to make small talk and flirt with this good-looking young guy than face the high-powered crowd inside. "This looks like a good job."

"It's just part-time. Dad's the general manager. He named me Jack after Jack Nicklaus. I've been golfing here my whole life."

"You must be good."

"Seven handicap," he said, rubbing his hands together.

Parish realized he wasn't only making small talk with her but was expecting her to give him a tip.

"Wait a minute." She fished around in the little change purse inside her shoulder bag. The smallest bill she had was a ten, and she wasn't about to ask him for change.

"Here, thanks," she said, handing it over to him.

He glanced down. She expected him to be surprised to get such a big tip, but he momentarily frowned. The other members in their fancy cars must give these kids at least twenty bucks.

What the hell was she doing at a place like this? She was so out of her league.

She swiftly calculated. If she was seventy-seven, and there was still a line of cars behind her, say there were a hundred. If most of them gave only ten, that was a thousand dollars divided among four kids. Cash. Say the average tip was fifteen dollars. Or twenty. The rich, she thought, just get richer.

"Ah, thank you," Jack said, seeming to remember his manners.

The car behind her beeped its horn. Jack looked at it and waved. "Got to go. Have a good time in there, lucky sevens," he said, before he sped away.

Inside the ornate clubhouse, she was accosted by a photographer. He insisted on getting her to pose beside a life-size cardboard cutout of Britt swinging a golf club. Then a woman with a video camera directed her to a booth where she was asked to recall her greatest memory of Britt growing up.

"Hi, Britt. It's me. I'll always treasure the nights when your dad brought you to the law office where I worked with your mom." She waved at the camera. "Remember the paper shredder? *Cccrunch Cccrunch.*" It was Parish's private way of messaging Britt about Melissa. Karl and Lydia wouldn't want to hear about Karl's ex, but too bad.

Parish had taken her godmother duties with Britt seriously. They met three times a year. Once at Karl and Lydia's annual pre-Christmas open house. Parish would bring her a present, and they had a tradition of sneaking out and going to Starbucks for hot chocolate. At March break, before the golf season, and in the fall after the season ended, Britt would come and stay with Parish for a weekend. It was a big thrill for her to be downtown, and they'd spend most of their time shopping. Her dad wanted her to be in golf clothes and sweatpants all the time, but Britt had some of her mother's flair for fashion.

The club's vast ballroom was festooned with banners and balloons with *BRITT* stencilled on them. The walls were covered with more life-sized photos of Britt golfing from the age of three on up. Parish noticed that Melissa wasn't in any of the pictures. Her very existence in her daughter's life had been erased.

The dance floor was already packed with kids Britt's age. A hip-looking guy was leading them in moves to the music of a DJ on the stage at the end of the room. A photographer was taking pictures and a videographer was taping the whole thing. Tuxedo-wearing servers circulated with precious-looking hors d'oeuvres and glasses of champagne. Parish grabbed a glass and downed it in two gulps.

She found the place with cards on it for table assignments. Hers was named the "Twelfth Hole." She got another glass of champagne and walked over there. People were already seated at a round table busily talking to each other, old friends who all knew each other. She didn't know any of them. The only seat left was by the window. She sat and took in the room.

There were some prominent politicians and local celebrities, whom she recognized, but she didn't know anyone here. She wasn't surprised. Ever since Lydia had left the law firm and married Karl, she'd hung out with this new, wealthy crowd.

Parish gazed out the window. A lone golf cart with the word *Security* painted on its side drove along the path that cut across the back lawn and disappeared into the darkness.

Keeping the barbarians at the gate, she thought, trying to imagine what it was like for the homeless people across the river sleeping out in the cold. And wondering about Melissa: where oh where could she be?

"Hi, I'll be your server tonight, ma'am," a familiar male voice behind her said.

She swivelled around to look at a server, who was holding up two bottles of wine.

"Will you be drinking red or white?" he asked.

"I'm thinking red. Fill it right to the top please."

He bent over to pour the wine and whispered, "Good choice, Ms. Parish."

"You need to keep me well lubricated tonight to get through this," she whispered back. "But don't worry, Detective Kennicott, I'll take a cab home."

28

Kennicott had decided to work the party as a waiter—Greene knew the caterer and made the last-minute arrangements—so he could keep an eye on Hodgson. It was important that he not realize the police were watching him. There was a small chance he might recognize Kennicott because he'd appeared on TV during some of his homicide cases, but that was in another context. People tended to look at the uniform and not the person.

Kennicott wore a black suit, white shirt, and black tie, like all the other servers. He'd put on a pair of thick glasses, with non-prescription lenses, as a final touch. He had one other undercover working with him, Constable Sheppard. She was at the entrance checking people in. Then she was going to help the young men who were parking cars and keep her eyes on the entrance.

The party was buzzing. Before dinner was served, the kids danced away on the dance floor while clusters of adults socialized at the bar. Ever energetic, Hodgson jumped right in and circulated among the crowd. Various "golf stations" had been set up around the edges of the room: a mini–putting green; a chipping station; a driving range. Kennicott watched Hodgson take Britt with him and go from station to station, glad-handing, both he and Britt then taking clubs and using them. Hodgson was good, but it was obvious that, even at her young age, Britt was better. The videographer followed them, capturing it all for golf-posterity.

Britt seemed camera shy, embarrassed by all the attention her extroverted father was lavishing on her. Kennicott saw her look longingly at the dance floor, where the other kids her age were jumping up and down, having fun.

Kennicott also saw Hodgson's wife Lydia come out from the kitchen and walk up to an older woman with a clipboard, who Kennicott assumed was the party planner.

Lydia checked her phone, bit her lip, said something to the party planner, then walked purposely over to her husband and tapped him on the shoulder. She pointed toward the head table. Hodgson gave the golf club he'd been using to one of the guests, took Britt by the arm, and paraded her through the crowd up to the microphone in front of his seat at the head table.

"Thank you, thank you, everyone," he said in his booming voice. He took off his Britt scarf and waved it over his head.

The rumbling sound of conversation in the room died down. A number of people in the audience took their scarves and waved them too.

"Good evening. Lydia and I are overjoyed you could all be here to celebrate with us Britt's tremendous victory. She's the number one golfer for her age group in all of Ontario!"

Everyone clapped. Even the servers.

"This is Britt's night. No long speeches. Dinner is being served, so please take your seats. Then there'll be a special video presentation I'm sure you'll all enjoy. In the meantime, dig into the club's delicious food, and then take your turn at our golf stations."

For a while Kennicott was busy serving tables and keeping an eye on Hodgson. The man was back in constant motion. He didn't bother to eat but flitted about from table to table, shaking hands, taking selfies with people. After about half an hour Kennicott slipped into a hallway and texted Sheppard.

"See anything unusual out there?"

"No. Just a few million dollars' worth of cars and bored rich kids."

Kennicott went back into the hall. He looked around, but Hodgson wasn't there. Where had the man gone? Did he figure out who Kennicott was, and had he waited for a chance to slip outside unseen?

Britt was on the dance floor now, looking as if she was having fun. Lydia was talking to a group of women, but Kennicott could see her attention was directed more to the hallway that led to the back lawn. Kennicott made his way there. At the last moment he saw Hodgson running back in from outside, wiping his hands with a pair of napkins. Before Hodgson looked up, Kennicott ducked into the men's washroom. It was a massive room with a high ceiling, big mirrors, stone floors, and marble countertops.

He began washing his hands under one of the gold-plated taps. A few seconds later Hodgson rushed in and went straight for a stall. He barely noticed Kennicott.

Kennicott watched Hodgson's feet through the mirror. They never turned around. Hodgson wasn't sitting on the toilet. Kennicott heard the toilet flush and, still watching Hodgson's feet through the mirror, he went to the paper dispenser to dry his hands. Hodgson threw open the stall door and walked right out of the bathroom. The napkins in his hand were gone.

Kennicott waited until the bathroom door closed, then another minute to make sure Hodgson didn't come back, before he went into the stall. There were traces of blood on the toilet paper roll. He took some paper towels out of the dispenser, returned to the stall, and carefully folded in the stained pieces of toilet paper.

He took out his cell phone and called Sheppard.

"Hey, Janice," she said, as if she were talking to a friend. "What's happening later? I'm free in a while."

She's a good cop, Kennicott thought. Quick on her feet.

"I need you to meet me outside the men's washroom in the back hallway ASAP."

"Cool," she said. "I've heard that bar is great."

He stood outside the men's room and less than a minute later she sped down the hallway. She loved to drive fast and it seemed she liked to walk fast too. He gave her the wrapped-up tissue.

"Find a plastic bag and seal it, tape over the seal and photograph it. For continuity, you need to keep this on your person at all times and bring it to the homicide department lab when you're done."

"Got it," she said. No fuss.

"Walk around the property, let me know if you see anything. Hodgson was outside and came back inside bleeding."

"I'm on it." She turned and zipped out the door.

Back in the ballroom, the kids were dancing and the hip guy who was leading them was handing out prizes to their outstretched arms. Hodgson and his wife were in intense discussions with the party planner. She handed Hodgson a microphone.

Without warning the music stopped. The dancers froze in position.

"Now, folks," Hodgson said to the quieted crowd, "here she is, the one and only champion, Britt! Come on everyone, clap your hands!"

The party planner signalled the DJ, and he started playing the song "We Are the Champions." People began to clap. The lights went out in the room, then a spotlight came on focused on Britt. She must have snuck out of the room a few minutes before, because now she was being brought back into the hall, carried by four strong men on a chair made entirely of welded-together golf clubs.

"Everyone join us on the dance floor!" Hodgson called out.

Most of the guests left their seats and rushed up. In the dimmed light, Kennicott could see Parish sitting by the window alone at her table. Downing another glass of wine.

Britt was brought into the centre of the dance floor, packed now with people singing along to the music. Kennicott heard a loud bang and was confused. Then he saw what it was. A huge cannon-like machine had been rolled in, and had shot a massive wave of blue, red, and gold confetti over the partygoers.

Britt seemed uneasy with all the hoopla. But the spotlight switched to Hodgson, and Kennicott could see he was in his glory.

"You'll be picking the confetti out of your hair and clothes for days, but don't worry, it's all recycled paper," he shouted to the people around him, who were pulling handfuls of confetti off themselves. Waiters appeared with big green garbage bags.

"Wasn't that fun!" Hodgson roared.

"Yes!" the crowd roared back.

"And now, everyone, look toward the head table for our special video presentation."

A gigantic screen descended behind the head table as the spotlight dimmed and the room went black. Perfectly timed, the video started to play. The opening shots, taken with a handheld camera, were of Britt, just a toddler, swinging a golf club with her dad. A title came up: *Move Over Tiger, Here Comes Britt.*

A witty fake news reporter came on screen, and for the next fifteen minutes a sleekly produced mock-documentary video traced Britt's golf career. Included were interviews with her various coaches—she'd had four already—and older members of the golf club, and clips from home-made footage of Britt swinging the club, sinking putts, and winning tournaments.

Kennicott watched transfixed by the overindulgence. About halfway through, it occurred to him that Melissa had been left out of her daughter's story again. Cruel, he thought, as if Britt's mother had been erased as easily as chalk on a blackboard.

As the video was coming to the end, Kennicott realized he had lost track of Hodgson in the darkness. Was he still in the crowded room, or had he slipped outside again? It was impossible to tell. There was nothing Kennicott could do but wait for the lights to come back on.

Damn it.

29

There aren't many sadder places in the city than a late-night donut shop in a rundown part of town, Greene thought as he strolled into Coffee Time on Sherbourne Street. It was twelve minutes before ten. A predictable group of urban wanderers and lonely misfits were here. In one corner, a pair of prostitutes wearing excessive amounts of makeup, taking a break from their night shift, were pouring copious amounts of sugar into their paper coffee cups. Near the counter an androgynous-looking young woman in army fatigues, a red bandanna tied around her neck, was sitting with an older guy who wore a short-sleeved shirt, his arms full of tattoos. Their faces half hidden under baseball caps, they were munching on stale-looking sandwiches and tapping away on their cell phones. An old man wearing a worn-out felt hat and skinny black tie sat alone at a table by the window bent over a crossword puzzle book. Behind the counter a tired-looking young woman in a sari was doing her homework between serving customers.

Keswick said his daughter came in at exactly ten o'clock. She'd known Greene for years and Keswick was worried that she'd bolt as soon as she saw him. That's why Greene had devised this plan.

He went to the counter, ordered a tea and a donut, and took it back to a table in front of the west window, one away from the empty table in the corner. He'd brought a *Toronto Sun* with him, opened it up to cover his face, and began to read the sports section.

He started with three different articles about the Toronto Maple Leafs: there were "serious" questions about the backup goalie and the defense, the lack of secondary scoring was a "major concern," the power play was radically "underperforming." Bottom line, one of the columnists opined, was that the team still hadn't developed its own "identity."

Greene heard the front door open. He felt a gust of cold wind blow onto his back. A moment later he heard Keswick as he talked to the server behind the counter. He peeked out from behind his newspaper to watch.

"Amaya, how's my favourite student doing this evening?"

"I am well, thank you, sir," Amaya said. "Do you wish to have your usual order? One medium black coffee, one large with triple sugar and triple cream?"

"Yes, Professor."

"I am not professor, only student, sir," she said.

"Also a maple donut tonight," he said.

"Certainly, sir. Will you be purchasing coffee cards?"

"Five-dollar ones, please. I'll take eight this time."

"Your total will be forty-six dollars and twenty-six cents."

He counted out five ten-dollar bills on the counter and passed them to her. "Study hard. I'll vote for you to become prime minister. And keep the change."

"Yes, sir," she said. "Thank you, sir. Have a seat and I'll bring your order to your table."

Greene put his newspaper up, covering his face. Now he was reading about the Toronto Raptors. The team was fighting through an early season rash of injuries. He heard Keswick's heavy footsteps pass by him and stop at the table in the corner, then heard him pull out a chair and plunk himself down. A few seconds later he heard Amaya's light footsteps and the sound of two cups being put down on the table.

"You're an angel sent from above," Keswick said.

"Thank you, sir," Amaya said. "I see your daughter outside now."

Greene heard Amaya walk away.

Keswick whispered to Greene, "Here she comes, Ari."

Greene felt the wind again as the door opened and shut, then rapid footsteps leading to Keswick's table.

"Coffee's still hot," Keswick said.

"Good. Three sugars, right? Triple cream?"

Greene hadn't heard Daphne's voice for many years. It was deeper and coarser than he remembered.

"And I got you a donut. Maple," Keswick said.

Greene heard a slurping sound. "Damn it!" she said. "Coffee in this shithole place is too fuckin' hot."

"How are you?" Keswick asked his daughter.

"How do you think? There's a fuckin' killer on the loose in case you haven't heard. Everyone is freaked. I mean totally freaked. Friggin' cops don't give a shit."

Greene heard the sound of her chewing on the donut.

"Jeez, this thing is stale."

"You're welcome," Keswick said, lacing his voice with sarcasm for the first time.

"Yeah, thanks," she said.

"Where are you staying?"

"Dad, stop it."

"Are you safe?"

Greene heard her take another sip of coffee. "Fucking hell," she shouted. Greene heard her chair scratch across the hard tile floor. Under his newspaper he saw her stand and stomp away from the table. He thought she was going to leave. He was about to get out of his seat when he realized she was headed toward the counter.

He peered out of the side of his newspaper to watch her.

Behind the counter Amaya looked up in surprise.

"Hey, you got some ice?" Daphne demanded.

The low murmur of chatter from the other people in the restaurant stopped.

"Certainly, ma'am," Amaya said. The sound of her scooping ice into a paper cup reverberated around the room.

She held the cup out, and Daphne grabbed it out of her hand. "Coffee shouldn't be so friggin' hot," she said.

Greene pulled his newspaper up before Daphne marched back to her seat.

"Just this one time," she said to her father, "you gotta give me some cash. You keep saying you want me off the friggin' street. I can't exactly rent a room with a handful of coffee cards."

Greene heard Keswick exhale.

"Come on," she said. "I promise, Dad, this time the money's not going to go into my arm. Really. I found a place in a rooming house. Twenty bucks a night."

"I can't," Keswick said.

"You mean won't."

"I know someone who will."

"Who? Who?"

Greene put his newspaper down and stood. In two quick steps he was behind Daphne, effectively cutting off her exit route.

"Hi, Daphne," he said.

She whirled around. Stared up at him and then whipped her head back at her father.

"You set me up with the cops."

Keswick shook his head. "No, no, no. Ari just wants to—"

"I can't believe it. You frickin' set up your own daughter!" she yelled.

"Keep your voice down," Greene said. "I'm not arresting you."

She looked around the coffee shop. He followed her eyes. The pair of prostitutes had gone, but the man with the tattoos and the younger woman hadn't moved. The old man with the crossword book was still at it.

Daphne shook her head, looked away, and started dumping ice cubes into her coffee, one at a time, making a plopping sound. She stared back at Greene.

"Hello, Detective Greene."

"Hi, Daphne. It's been a while."

"Yeah." She took a sip of her coffee then dropped in another ice cube. "I meant to say thank you for helping me with that charge. Really I did."

"I need to talk to you."

"About the murders in the Humber?"

He nodded. Best to use his silence, get her to fill the void and start to talk.

"I don't know anything about them," she said.

He kept staring down at her.

"People are like totally freaked out," she said.

He moved his feet wider. Signalling to her that he wasn't going anywhere, and neither was she.

"Almost no one's left over there. Everyone's moving east to the Don."

Greene reached back for a chair, brought it forward, and pulled it up close beside her. He sat and looked at her straight on.

"Daphne. People talk to you."

She dropped two more ice cubes in her coffee. *Plop. Plop.*

"The two victims, did you know them?"

"Anybody who's been on the street for any kind of time knew them. Nurse Deb had a stack of prescription pads, and Doc would write out scripts for legit painkillers and medical crap. Never oxys or any of that shit. We called them the Hospital Ward. They were always trying to get people off drugs."

Greene remembered that Rene LeBlanc had been a doctor. Deborah Lemon had been a nurse.

"The rooming house needs a twenty-buck deposit. Then twenty a night."

Greene took out his wallet. Peeled off two twenty-dollar bills and held them tight in his fist. "Keep your eyes and ears open for me," he said.

She stared at the money.

"And do what?"

"Tell me what you hear. See. That's all."

"I'm not a rat."

He could see her hands twitching. He knew she wanted to grab the twenty-dollar bills and make a run for it.

"It's not ratting when there's a killer on the loose."

She turned back to her father.

"Dad, you got some coffee cards? I need to eat."

Keswick held out two five-dollar cards.

"That's it?" she demanded.

"I'll give the other thirty dollars' worth to Detective Greene," he said.

Greene braced himself for another outbreak from her. Instead, her shoulders slumped and her whole demeanour softened. "Where's your phone?" she asked her father, her voice now gentle as a child's.

Keswick pulled out his cell phone. Greene could see he'd already cued up the photos. She took the phone in both hands and stared at the picture of an adorable little girl playing with a paint set. She scrolled through to the next one. The third.

"She's starting to draw," she said.

"Just like you did," Keswick said.

"Look," she said, pointing. "My doll! You kept it?"

"Your mother sewed it back together. Go to the next one and watch the video."

Daphne pressed the screen, and a video started to play. Greene heard the innocent sound of a child's voice, which seemed so out of place amidst the dull greyness of the coffee shop.

"I want colour fishy," the little girl said, picking up a red crayon and filling in the outline of a fish's body with large erratic strokes.

"And what colour is the water?" an older woman's voice asked from off screen.

"Is blue," the child said. She reached for a green crayon.

"No!" Daphne shouted at the screen.

"No, dear," the gentle older woman's voice said. "That's green. Here," she said, picking up a blue crayon. "This is blue."

"Blue, blue," the child said.

The video ended abruptly, before she could get the crayon in her tiny hands.

Just as quickly as Daphne's mood had softened, it hardened again. She slammed the phone face-down on the table and grabbed the two coffee cards out of her father's hands.

She swung back to Greene. He'd loosened his grip on the bills. She tugged them out of his hand, stuffed them down the front of her shirt, and stood up fast. Before he could get to his feet, she made a beeline for the door. Greene felt a puff of cold air as it flew open and shut behind her.

"That's my girl," Keswick said. "Thanks for trying, Ari. But I'm still worried sick. I doubt she'll show up tomorrow. She'll probably disappear again, and we'll never know where she is.

"You don't have to worry," Greene said. "We've got that covered."

Keswick gave Greene a curious look.

"How?"

"Remember those two people who were eating sandwiches at the table near the counter?" he said, pointing to the now-empty table.

"Wearing baseball caps? The old guy with the tattoos with the younger woman?"

"They're following her."

"Following her?" He looked alarmed.

Greene grinned. "The older guy is a street contact I've worked with for years, and the young one's an undercover cop. They'll keep an eye on her."

30

Even though it was a cold, rainy night, Roshan was thankful for the work. When the members of the golf club heard about his accident, they'd put together a collection to get him an Uber account for one month for him to get to and from the golf club. Despite Babita's protest, he'd insisted on coming to take the night shift. Since his leg was still sore, he got to drive the security golf cart. Two other guards would have to walk the perimeter. All were equipped with walkie-talkies and high-powered flashlights.

He'd brought a blanket from home and wrapped it around his legs to try to keep warm. He wore a bright headlamp that let him see from side to side by simply turning his head. He had a set route that took an hour to complete. The sky was cloudy, brightened by a three-quarters moon that had crested the trees. First he went through the parking lot to make sure the cars were not damaged before he drove through the front nine holes, returned through the parking lot, then drove along the path in back of the club and around the back nine holes.

When he'd started, the parking lot was full of cars and the party was still going. He said hello to the young people who did the valet parking. Most of them were the members' kids and would make much more money in tips for a few hours of easy work than Roshan and his fellow guards would earn for being out here all night.

By the time he finished his second trip the party was over, everyone had cleared out, and the parking lot was empty. The rain had stopped and the temperature had plummeted, turning the pools of water on the golf cart pathways to ice.

Babita had prepared a thermos of hot coffee for him. He parked in front of the clubhouse and took a fifteen-minute break so he could have a drink and warm up. The air was still and clouds had covered the moon. His knee was beginning to ache but he wasn't going to tell Babita about it.

He started on his third round. Because the lights inside the club ballroom were turned off, now the path in front of it was dark. Roshan didn't mind. He knew the route well and he enjoyed the quiet.

He was far down the path when he spotted something large lying across it, in his way. He yanked the steering wheel to pull his cart onto the lawn just in time and slammed on the brakes.

He swung himself out of the driver's seat and hobbled over to the path. Oh no, he thought, as the moon peeked out from behind a cloud, casting light down on the deserted lawn, and he saw what was there. A body. Lying face-down. He could tell it was a woman because of her long hair. The light from his headlight illuminated blood that had poured out of the top of her head, staining the path.

He knew how to do CPR. Perhaps she was still alive. He knelt down and tried to roll the woman over. She was heavy, and he couldn't do it.

Should he go back to the golf cart and radio for help? But that would waste time. He had to try again. He pulled her up, using all his might, and rolled her over onto her back. Her head flopped over to the side. Lifeless. A golf ball fell out of her mouth and bounced down the hill, disappearing in the darkness.

Her eyeballs had rolled up into her head. She wasn't breathing. He felt for her pulse but there was none. He took a close look at her face in the moonlight.

"Oh no, oh no," he moaned. It was her. The strange woman who'd come to his rescue when he fell down into the valley.

"Help!" he cried as he scrambled to his feet and limped back to his cart. He grabbed his walkie-talkie. "Help!" he shouted. "I found a dead woman on the ground!"

TUESDAY MORNING

31

Kennicott jumped out of his car as soon as he came to a stop in the golf-club parking lot. Three police cruisers were parked in front of him, and he strode past them toward the back lawn. Greene had taught him that unless the situation was urgent, a homicide detective never runs.

A crowd of officers was down the hill surrounding Detective Ho, who was setting up a tent over the roped-off crime scene. A golf cart was parked at an awkward angle off to the side of the path. Kennicott spotted Officer Sheppard standing near a security guard who was seated by the back wall of the main building wrapped in a heat blanket, his head down.

Sheppard saw Kennicott and rushed over. "Call came in at two forty-six," she said, flipping open her notebook. "No identification on the dead woman."

Kennicott pointed to the guard by the wall. "He find the body?"

"It's Mr. Roshan. He came back to work last night and saw her when he was driving down the path."

"Oh my. Poor man. Come with me."

Roshan looked up as they approached. He'd been crying.

"Hello, Mr. Roshan," Kennicott said.

"Detective Kennicott," he said.

"Are you okay?" Kennicott said, kneeling to be at his eye level.

"I found another poor dead woman. Why is Allah doing this to me?"

"I don't know," Kennicott said. "Please, can you tell us what happened?"

"It was terrible. I was driving my cart and I saw her at the last moment. I pulled over to avoid hitting her. I didn't know if she was still alive."

"What did you do?"

"I rushed to her and turned her over. It took two attempts as she was heavy."

Roshan was shaken. Kennicott knew he had to gently tease the story out of him. "And then?"

"When I turned her over, a golf ball fell out of her mouth."

"A golf ball? Where is it?"

He pointed down into the darkness toward the river. "It rolled down there and disappeared. It was more important to try to help the woman."

Kennicott nodded. He didn't want to interrupt him.

"I tried to resuscitate her, but unfortunately she was deceased. I recognized her, Detective. Please, she is the woman who helped me in the valley when I'd tumbled down off my bicycle yesterday morning. The woman who gave my wife Babita her coat."

Roshan began to shiver. He looked at Kennicott, his dark eyes filling with tears again.

"Are you sure it is her?"

"Sadly, yes."

Kennicott put his hand on Roshan's thigh and turned to Sheppard.

"Get Mr. Roshan into a warm cruiser and take him to Police Headquarters to give a videotaped statement."

"Right away," Sheppard said.

"And Officer Sheppard," he said, "I want you to take the statement."

Sheppard nodded. He could see she wanted to say "Thank you" but realized it was the wrong thing to do in front of a witness.

"Yes, sir," she said.

Kennicott walked over to the tent and knelt beside the body. "Preliminary impressions?" he asked Ho.

"It looks as if she was attacked from behind, like the other two homeless victims. Same smashed Smirnoff vodka bottle."

Ho lifted one of her hands. Her long fingernails were perfectly painted a bright red colour.

"Nice manicure job," Ho said. "I should get the name of the shop she used for my wife."

"She was once a Bay Street lawyer," Kennicott said.

Ho turned her fingers over. "Look. There's material under the nails. Blood on her fingers too."

"Defensive wounds?"

"See what comes up under the microscope at the autopsy."

Kennicott took one last look at Copeland. The next time he saw her, the dead woman's body would be unceremoniously cut open, laid bare on a stainless-steel surgical table.

He'd read about Copeland after he'd had coffee with her lawyer, Nancy Parish. Sad. She'd been a brilliant lawyer, but her demons had gotten the best of her. Kennicott thought about the cryptic text she'd sent Parish. "*Nance I warnd you, but no one wd listn. The kilingz contnue. No one is imune. There is no justice.*"

He stood and walked away a few steps so he could call Greene. This was tough news to deliver.

"What have we got?" Greene asked without even saying hello.

"Bad. It's Melissa Copeland."

"Oh no." Greene sighed. It was unusual to hear him express emotion this way. "You certain?"

"One hundred per cent."

Silence again. He could imagine Greene, his head spinning. Losing a contact such as Copeland whom he had known, worked with, and supported for years was a heavy blow. And now they had a third murder on their hands.

"Same MO?" Greene asked at last.

"Looks like it. Vodka bottle. Bash to the head."

"Golf ball?"

"Fell out of her mouth and rolled down the hill."

"I have to make some calls," Greene said. "I'll be there soon."

"Ari," Kennicott said. "I'm sorry."

"Thanks. And Daniel?"

"Yes."

"We have to stop this."

32

Although phone calls in the middle of the night were the bane of a criminal lawyer's existence, everyone who plied the trade knew they were part of the deal. Clients didn't usually get arrested during business hours. The phone calls came in at two, three, four in the morning. The first voice on the other end of the line was always a tired-sounding police officer, who started the conversations the same way: "Ms. Parish, it's Detective X. Your client Y is here at the station and would like to speak to you."

While she scrambled out of bed to find a pen and paper, Parish would hear the shuffling sound on the other end of the line as the phone changed hands. Then a door being closed as the officer left the prisoner alone in the soundproof phone room. Then came the moment of suspense as she waited to hear the frightened voice on the tinny police-station phone.

Was this an old client or someone she'd never talked to before? Were they being charged with assault? Theft? Fraud? Drugs? DUI? Robbery? Murder? It could be anything.

But this time, as soon as the first ring of the phone startled her out of her sleep, Parish knew she was in no condition to deal with a late-night call from a cop. Not after what she'd done last night after she left the party.

Why had she done it? Maybe it was because she needed to release the built-up tension after her crazy day in court with Melissa. It could have been because she'd been stuck at that ridiculous party and felt like a total outsider. Or she could blame it on all the booze she'd drunk.

As the party was winding down, she'd stumbled out of the ballroom to the front steps, where the car jockeys were hanging out. She looked around for Young Jack.

"Remember me? Lucky number seventy-seven," she said, when she spotted him. She was unsteady on her high-heel shoes and had to put her hand on his arm to keep from falling.

"The Toyota. Who could forget?" he asked, grinning away.

He really had a cute smile. She fished around in her little purse searching for her parking ticket.

"Don't worry about the ticket," he said. "I'll get your car."

"No." She tightened her grip on his arm. Maybe a little too firmly. "I'm not going to drive. No way. Hey, I'm a criminal lawyer." Was she slurring her words a little? Maybe a lot? "I want you to call me a cab."

"Then you'll have to drive all the way back out here tomorrow to get your car." He had a cute dimple when he smiled. Such nice white teeth. She was still squeezing his arm, feeling his firm muscles.

"Or the day after that," she said, giggling. "Given how much champagne and red wine I drank."

"Look. It's not busy. I can drive you home."

Huh, she laughed to herself. Maybe Zelda was right about her great hair. What the hell. It's November. It's cold. It's dark. Everyone else at this ridiculous party had someone to go home with.

The temperature was dropping, and the rain was turning to snow. He opened an umbrella, and they both held on to it as they walked through the parking lot. Her Toyota was all by itself at the dark, far corner. Most of the rich people's fancy cars were gone. No one was around. She wasn't very steady on her feet, and the pavement was wet. She let go of the umbrella and held on to his arm. They started kissing as soon as they got in the car. They kissed at every stoplight on the way back to her place. Upstairs in her bedroom she peeled off her cocktail dress and tossed it on the floor. She was naked before Jack could even get fully undressed, and she did the rest for him.

He'd left a while ago. He said his dad would worry about him if he didn't come home and that he had a math tutor coming to the house the next morning. She had a vague memory of him saying he was going to get her contact info from the guest list and would be in touch.

Her phone rang a third time. She didn't feel like answering it. Her head was pounding.

It rang again. Okay, okay, she would answer the damn thing.

"Nancy Parish," she said, groping for the light switch on the bedside table lamp and not finding it.

"Ms. Parish, it's Detective Ari Greene."

Damn it, she was half drunk still.

"Sorry to wake you," he said.

She waved her hand around in the darkness until her fingers hit the base of her bedside lamp. Where was the damn light switch?

"It's okay," she said. "What time is it?"

"Three twenty-three a.m."

Three twenty-three a.m. Cop talk.

Wait, a call from a homicide detective this hour of the night could only mean one thing: someone must have been charged with murder. Was it one of her old clients or a new one? She sat up. Focus, Parish told herself.

"Give me a second," she said.

She found the switch, and it took her two tries to click it on. The light burst in her face. She squinted. She threw back the sheets and swung her legs over the edge of her bed onto the bare hardwood floor. It was cool, and her feet tingled.

"I've just got to find a pen and paper," she said.

For years she'd tried to discipline herself to keep a pad and pen by her bed. Every few weeks she'd set it up, but then she'd need the pen for something else, or she'd use the pad of paper and forget to put it back. Or not bother. Or not want to bother.

"Take your time," Greene said. Nothing more.

Her partner, Ted DiPaulo, had defended Greene successfully when he was falsely accused of murdering his lover, so she'd seen the detective around the office many times. Greene was a quiet man, but something in the tone of his voice even with his few words gave her pause. To hell with the pen and paper.

"Detective," she said.

"Yes."

"What's this about?"

"Melissa."

That was a relief. He was calling to tell her that Melissa had been found. Thank goodness she was safe. Parish didn't need a pen and paper. She needed two aspirins and a glass of water.

"Thanks for calling," she said. "Kennicott told me that you've been secretly taking care of her for years. Where did they find her?"

"Nancy," Greene said, "I'm sorry."

Sorry? What was he sorry about?

She felt a chill. Oh no. Greene had called her Nancy, not Ms. Parish. To soften the blow. He was a homicide detective. She could hear the horrible words in her head before he said them to her on the phone.

"Melissa's been killed."

"Melissa? Killed?"

"Murdered."

"Murdered." Parish gasped. "Murdered?"

"At the Humber River Golf Club. Night watchman found her."

"I was there tonight. So was Kennicott. Britt, her daughter, and . . ."

"I know."

"How did this happen?"

"I can't say right now."

"When was she . . ."

"She was found a short while ago."

No. No. No. This couldn't be. How? Why? Parish had too many questions. She tried to catch her breath. Her feet on the floor were growing cold. The alcohol zapped out of her system, and she was to-tally alert. Stone sober.

"I mean do you know when she was . . . ?" Parish didn't want to say the word.

"We'll have to wait for the pathologist."

"Britt? Does she know?"

"You're my first call. Now we have to go see Britt's father."

"Karl," she said. "And Lydia."

Parish pulled her feet back off the floor and curled them under her thighs. They felt frigid against her skin. She squeezed the phone. Greene wasn't saying anything more. She had this absurd thought that at least now she didn't have to worry about Melissa getting ar-rested again and going back in front of Judge Tator. She let out a low sigh.

"Thank you, Detective." He'd called her Nancy, but she couldn't call him by his first name.

"I'll be at Police Headquarters later in the day," he said.

The implication was clear. He had things to talk to her about, but not over the phone.

"I can come to you," she said.

"Any information you have that can be of assistance would be most helpful. I can send a car to pick you up."

"No, thanks." She wanted to be alone. The thought of having to talk to or deal with anyone else right now was too much.

"Nancy," he said. Using her name again.

"Yes."

"You did everything you could for Melissa."

"But not enough." Her feet were warming against her skin. She could tell Greene wanted to get off the phone. He must have a million things to do. But he was kind enough not to rush her.

"I have to make some calls," he said gently.

"I know."

"You okay?"

"No."

"How could you be?"

"Thanks, Ari," she said, his first name slipping out into the darkness like a wisp of smoke through a crack in a window. Searching for fresh air. And contact with the outside world.

33

Kennicott peered down the paved pathway. The moon had slipped behind the clouds and it was too dark to see very far. He took out his cell phone and clicked on its flashlight, and it cast a bright but narrow beam. He started to walk along the pathway, which took a sharp turn to the right, running parallel to the river below.

He swept the light back and forth in front of him, making sure before every step that he was not disturbing any potential evidence. The pavement was clean and smooth. Thick grass on both edges of the path formed a low barrier. Had the golf ball built up enough momentum as it rolled down hill to slip over onto the lawn, or had it stayed on the path, like a hockey puck bouncing off the side boards? It was hard to tell.

Even in the darkness, illuminated only by his thin cell-phone light, Kennicott could tell that the landscaping here was pristine. It was as if the wealthy golf-club members were determined to conquer every last bit of the natural setting, in stark contrast to what lay across the river, where the forest, and the homeless people, were overgrown, unkempt, and wild.

It would be easier to wait and try to find the ball once the sun came up. That would be the prudent thing to do. But Kennicott didn't want to wait. He continued down the path, careful mini-step by careful mini-step, counting them as he walked. On his tenth step, where the path turned, he spotted a subtle indent on the edge of the grass and the faint outline of the route the ball had taken across the manicured lawn. Bending down with his light, he plodded parallel to the line in the grass, like a tracker in the desert following the faint footsteps of his prey.

The hill grew steeper as it descended toward the river. He imagined how the ball would have accelerated into a free fall. Another twenty steps and the grass gave way to a row of bushes. He scanned the edge of the foliage hoping that a low branch had stopped the ball. No such luck.

What now? He could mark this spot and come back at first light. Instead he got on his hands and knees. He inched his way forward, the way he'd done as a kid at the family cottage, playing catch with his older brother, Michael, when he'd searched the thick bushes at the back of their property for a baseball that had flown over his outstretched mitt.

He started to sweat. The branches were thick and scratched his hands. The earth was cold and wet. Muddy. He could hear the river close by.

Holding the phone in one hand, he dragged himself forward with the other. He could hardly move. He put the phone in his mouth, lifted his head and shone the light in front of him so he could use both hands.

This must look ridiculous, he thought, laughing to himself. He'd give it another minute, then forget it. He shifted forward. His head hit a branch and the phone tumbled out of his mouth and landed face-down on the earth, obliterating the light and leaving him in total darkness.

"Idiot," he hissed. He padded his fingers around on the ground, getting them dirtier and dirtier until he found the phone. He flipped it over. A faint ray of light was visible through its now-muddy surface. He wiped it clean with his forefinger, and a strong beam of light hit him in the eyes, blinding him for a second.

Damn. He pointed the phone toward the ground and waited for his eyes to readjust. Enough. It was time to cut his losses. He moved to get up, and flickered the light in front of him one last time.

The golf ball.

It was nestled in the crook of a branch. If it had gone two or three inches farther, it would have popped over the side and tumbled into the river below. Even now, a gust of wind could push it off into the water.

He reached back into his pants pocket, pulled out a latex glove, and put it on. Propping himself up on his elbow, he tiptoed his fingers to the base of the branch.

His elbow slipped, and his hand knocked into the bush. He saw the golf ball teeter on its precarious perch, like a basketball on the rim of the basket. There was only one thing to do. He lunged forward, the branches scraping at his face, and grabbed the ball. It was small and slippery, but he held on to it.

He flopped on his back and exhaled. The air was still. He brought the golf ball into the light and turned it to read the label. It was the same as the others, with the club logo and the initials K.L.H.

He clicked off the light, and was instantly enveloped in total darkness. He put his hands across his chest and felt his heartbeat begin to slow down. There was a faint smell of rotting leaves, and all he could hear was the sound of the rushing water in the unseen river tumbling over the rocks below.

34

"Alison," Greene said in a loud voice as he rapped his knuckles hard on her bedroom door. He rarely came down the internal staircase in the house to her apartment, which had a bedroom, living room, and bathroom. And he'd never done this in the middle of the night as he was doing now.

"Alison, I hate to wake you up, but I think you'll want to hear this," he said, knocking again.

He stopped and listened. Maybe she wasn't home. She often worked the night shift, and he made a point of not monitoring her movements. A few months ago, when she'd had a boyfriend, Greene never inquired if she was home at night or if he stayed over with her.

Some nights when he came home late, Greene would see the boyfriend's bicycle parked next to Alison's in the bike rack beside the separate entrance to her place. But he never said a word.

"Alison?" he tried one more time.

"Dad," he heard her say, her voice groggy. It had taken her months to start calling him Dad. When they'd first met in England, she'd avoided calling him by any name at all. Then, for a long time, once she came back with him to Canada, she called him Ari. He was happy with that. Being Dad was a bonus. A gift that secretly thrilled him, which he never took for granted.

"Sorry to wake you," he said. "There's been another murder."

More shuffling before she spoke again. Then it hit him. Maybe she wasn't alone. He felt foolish.

"In the Humber Valley?" she asked through the door.

"Yes. On the golf course this time. Another homeless woman. It came in a few minutes ago."

"Thanks," she said.

"I'm going upstairs to make you some tea."

He stomped hard as he ascended the stairs and shut the door to the downstairs with force. Signalling to her that the coast was clear for whoever had spent the night with her, if someone had, and they could exit without being seen if they wanted to.

In the kitchen he filled the stovetop kettle with cold water and put the kettle on the burner. From the cupboard he took down a teapot, two large mugs, and two tea bags. He knew exactly what the next hours of his life were going to be like, the way actors know before they go on stage how they will deliver their lines, and the reaction they'll get from the audience. He wanted a few minutes of calm before the chaos.

He heard a light tapping sound on the front window over the sink. It had begun to snow. He walked out onto the porch, put his hand on the cold railing, and looked downtown at the snowflakes falling on the forest of shimmering high-rise condos and office towers. It would be falling on the dead body of Melissa Copeland until the forensic officers could cover it with a tent. It would be falling on the makeshift houses of the homeless people living across the river. The wind came up, sending a chill down his spine, but he didn't move. There was the faint smell of wood burning in a neighbour's fireplace. Soon news of this third murder would explode across the city. He looked down at his bare hands and watched the snowflakes gently land and then slowly disappear into his skin.

Back inside the kitchen, the water in the kettle had just started to churn. He waited until the whistle began to blow and pulled it from the flame, cutting the sound off mid-breath.

He estimated it would take maybe fifteen minutes for the rest of the media world to discover what had happened. Fifteen minutes. That was the head start he'd just given Alison on the story. Was it a conflict of interest for him to pass a scoop to her? Or was he just being a good dad?

He poured some hot water into the waiting pot, swirled it around to heat the pot, and then tossed the water into the sink. Then he gently placed the tea bags in one side of it and poured the hot water onto the other side, taking care not to crush the leaves by pouring the water directly on them.

There were so many things out there he couldn't control. But at least he could prepare a cup of tea for his daughter the way her mother used to make it for her.

35

Kennicott turned his light back on and walked carefully through the darkness, toward Ho's lit-up tent, which stood out like a beacon up the hill.

"Find anything?" Ho asked as he approached.

Kennicott showed him the golf ball in his gloved hand.

"Another hole in one," Ho said.

He pulled out a plastic evidence bag. Kennicott dropped the ball inside and watched Ho seal and label it.

"Same initials on it too," Kennicott said.

"I'd heard that Hodgson was a scratch golfer, but three holes in one in a row. Now that's quite something," Ho said. He picked up his camera and started photographing the body from above, the sound of the shutter extra loud in the silence of the night.

Kennicott stood back and watched. Ho stopped every few shots to check his camera to make sure his exposure was right.

"Do you have any idea who she is?" Ho asked, clicking away like a tourist on vacation.

Kennicott bent down by the body again. "Her name is Melissa Copeland. She's Hodgson's ex-wife. Used to be a top Bay Street lawyer, ended up on the street. Their daughter, Britt, is the girl Hodgson just had this big celebration for tonight."

Ho let out a low whistle. "Wow. Hodgson's ex homeless? Murdered at his golf club where he killed another homeless person and was having a party? The press is going to go crazy when they hear about this."

Kennicott scanned Copeland's body. She wore layers and layers of shirts and jackets, and her pants were baggy, tied together with a worn but beautiful leather belt. She had on a pair of old boots and multiple layers of socks. Her hair was long and pulled back.

Ho changed lens on his camera and moved near her head for some close-up shots. "Presumably, she wasn't on tonight's invitation list."

"Good guess. She was on bail to stay away from the whole family."

"You think she tried to break into the party, and he stopped her?"

Forensic officers were supposed to be objective. Gather evidence and do no more. But that never stopped Ho from speculating.

"That would give Hodgson motive," Ho said. "He had opportunity."

Kennicott gave Ho a long look. They both knew that a few years earlier Kennicott had arrested Greene for murder. Greene had had opportunity and perhaps motive too. The only problem was that it turned out that Greene was innocent. Kennicott was determined to never make that mistake again. To never jump to conclusions.

Ho wasn't finished hypothesizing. "Hodgson's beaten the rap once, but maybe this time . . ."

Kennicott shook his head.

Ho checked his camera again, then put it back in its case.

"You got everything?" Kennicott asked.

"Done. I videotaped the whole scene when you went golf-ball hunting."

That meant now Kennicott could touch the corpse. He put a glove on his other hand and moved a wisp of hair across Copeland's forehead.

"I want to check her pockets," Kennicott said. He remembered how she'd secreted her business card with Greene's number on the back deep in a hidden pocket of her Max Mara coat. Taking his time, he went through each pant pocket, then the pockets of the layers of shirts she was wearing. He unlaced her boots. They were Chanel and must have cost hundreds of dollars, but now the leather was fraying, the heels ground down.

With effort he pulled them off. Rigor mortis had not yet set in. A foul smell erupted from her feet.

"Agh," Ho said.

Kennicott ignored him. He put his hand in the boots and fished around. Nothing. Then he peeled off her socks. She had two layers on one foot, three on the other. Oddly, her toenails were perfectly manicured as well.

"Very nice," Ho said. "My wife would be impressed."

Kennicott turned every sock inside out. Still nothing. He heard footsteps approach, turned around, and saw Greene walking up.

Without saying a word, Ho handed him a pair of latex gloves. Ho's face was serious now, no hint of his usual sarcastic banter.

Greene took his time looking over Copeland's body. Kennicott showed him the evidence bag with the golf ball, and Ho showed him the material under her fingernails.

"Looks as if she put up a fight," Kennicott said.

"She would have," Greene said.

He knelt down to get a closer look. He reached down to the bottom of her pants. They were too long and she'd folded them up. Greene unrolled the cuffs on the left pant leg. Nothing. He did the same with the right. Nothing in the first two folds, but in the third he spotted a thin piece of paper that looked as if it had been deliberately tucked in there.

Ho grabbed his camera.

"Make sure you get good pictures of it in situ," Greene said. "Then bag it."

"What is it?" Ho said, already clicking away.

"It's a piece of confetti in one of the golf club colours," Kennicott said. "When Hodgson's daughter, Britt, was brought into the party, they shot thousands of pieces over the crowd."

"While Hodgson was there?" Greene asked.

"He was," Kennicott said. "Right in the middle of it."

36

Alison flipped open her laptop and checked online. Good. There was nothing in the news yet about another murder in the Humber Valley. Her dad was giving her a scoop, but she had to talk to him first before she phoned it in to Persaud.

She smiled to herself. It was a good thing that Burns hadn't taken her up on her invitation to come back home with her. Last night, there had been that moment on the Danforth Bridge after their first kiss when everything seemed to hang in the air. Neither of them spoke.

She walked with him in silence into the city. When they got to a quiet park, they held hands. They arrived at her streetcar stop, and there was no one around and only a few cars passed by them. So unlike London. Even though Toronto was a big city, there were pockets that were very quiet.

"I should be getting home," she said.

"Thanks for volunteering."

"I enjoyed it."

She looked over his shoulder and saw the streetcar approaching.

"That's my streetcar," she said.

She looked back at him and their eyes met.

"Well," she said. Wondering if she should invite him over and wondering what he would say if she did.

"Well," he said. He squeezed her hand. She squeezed back.

"Do you want to pop over?" she decided to ask him. "The streetcar won't be crowded, so you can bring your bike on it."

"It's late for you, isn't it?" he said, letting go of her hand. "You said you were up all night."

"And I'm on assignment tomorrow morning. I do have to be up early . . ."

The streetcar was pulling up to the stop.

"It's fine," he said. "I've got things to do . . ."

He was being vague. Does that mean he has things to do with another woman? she wondered. She gave him a quick hug. He kissed her on the cheek.

"Later," she said before getting on board.

There was almost no one on the streetcar. She'd taken a window seat and looked out. Still standing on the sidewalk, he'd waved at her before getting on his bike and riding off.

She closed her laptop, tossed back her bed covers and threw on some clothes. She was glad Burns hadn't come, after all. She hadn't told him that her dad was the head of the homicide squad, the person Burns was publicly criticizing. Besides, she had work to do.

She headed upstairs. Her father had made tea, and she sat down across from him and started to drink while they talked.

"How much can you tell me about this murder?" she asked him.

"A woman was murdered on the golf course, not in the valley. I can't say more."

The tea was nicely warm, not too hot. She took another deep sip. Her father always tried to look cool and objective, but she could see he was upset. How could he not be? Three murders in less than a week.

"Can you tell me her name?"

"Not until we notify the next of kin."

He took a pad of paper and wrote something on it, folded it. "I'm leaving in a minute. Look at this when I'm gone. You're going to want to do some background research on the victim by yourself. Only you, no one else. Everything you need to know about her will be online. You can't broadcast her name until I give you the heads-up."

He passed the paper over to her.

"Thanks, I'll wait. Can you tell me when it happened?"

He shook his head. "Some time last night, that's all I have right now."

"Dad, off the record, do you have a suspect?"

"Off the record? Maybe."

"There's a serial killer on the loose, isn't there?"

"No matter what I say, we both know that's going to be the headline news today."

She got up, went over to him, and held his hand.

"Three people dead," he whispered.

She gave him a long hug. "You'll catch the killer. I know you will." She kissed him on the cheek. That got a smile out of him.

"I've got to go," he said.

Back in her bedroom, Alison was about to call Persaud at the TV station when her phone pinged with a text. It was from Burns. "Nice to see you last night. Hope we can 'volunteer' together again."

She grinned at his gentle flirting. She had to call Persaud. But it would only take a second to text him back.

Her phone pinged again. A second text from Burns. One word. "Soon."

She hit the reply button and wrote: "Good idea. Busy day ahead." She paused. Should she tell him about the new murder? Even before she told Persaud? She pushed send.

She waited a few seconds to see if he'd reply. He did.

"Busy. What's happening?" he texted back.

"Third victim. Another woman. Horrible," she typed. She stopped and looked at the words. Maybe she wasn't being one hundred per cent professional, but this was terrible, and she wanted to share it with someone who really cared. She pushed send.

Before he could text her back, she called Persaud.

37

There were no gated communities in Toronto, but if there ever were a street that could be gated one day, then Hodgson's would be a prime candidate, Kennicott thought as he drove with Greene up to the alderman's faux-mansion. Kennicott had already briefed him on Hodgson's movements at the party, including the two times he'd lost sight of him.

"How much are you going to tell Hodgson?" he asked Greene.

"Keep it simple. His ex-wife is dead. We're investigating this as a possible homicide. He'll need to tell his daughter."

"Will you tell him where the body was found?"

"No. Let's see if he acknowledges that he went outside to the back lawn during the party."

The implication of what Greene was saying was clear. If Hodgson denied that he'd been outside, then they'd almost certainly caught him in a lie. But it was tricky. If Greene believed Hodgson was a suspect, then Greene had an obligation to read him his rights to counsel. This was not something you would do when you were telling someone their ex-wife, the mother of their daughter, is dead.

So almost anything Hodgson said now would never be admissible in court. Still it would help to know if Hodgson was lying. And to see him doing it.

They walked up the granite steps of the house to the ornate front door. Greene pulled out his cell phone, put the phone on speaker, and let it ring. On the fourth ring a male voice came on the line.

"Hello." The voice sounded as if the man had been woken up from a deep sleep.

"Mr. Hodgson," Greene said.

"Greene. Your number came up on my call display. Why the hell are you calling me? What time is it?"

"It's four thirty-five. I'm here with Detective Daniel Kennicott. I'm afraid we have to talk to you immediately."

"What the—"

"We're standing at your front door."

"Why didn't you call my lawyer? What are you doing here at this time of the night? Do you have a warrant?"

"We don't need a warrant. We're here to tell you about something that has happened."

There was silence on the line for a few seconds. Then Kennicott heard a woman's voice say, "What's going on?"

Then the sound was muffled. Hodgson must have put his thumb over the speaker. He came back on the line.

"I'll be down in a few minutes."

"Okay," Greene said, and hung up.

Kennicott looked at him. "What do you think?"

"He sounded genuinely surprised, for what that's worth," Greene said.

They both knew that meant little. Cold-blooded killers could appear perfectly innocent, and perfectly innocent people could appear to be cold-blooded killers. And at some later date when they were testifying at a trial, a defence lawyer would try to pounce on their first impressions as evidence of their client's innocence.

The cross examination in front of the jury could go something like this:

"You will agree with me, Detective, my client sounded surprised, shocked, didn't he, when you told him this devastating news?"

To which Greene had taught Kennicott to reply by turning to the jury and saying: *"Yes, that is how he seemed to react, but in my experience this could equally be the reaction of a pathological liar and killer who was in self-denial or is simply a good actor."*

It took almost ten minutes for Hodgson and his wife, Lydia, to open the door. They were both dressed, Lydia in stylish jeans and a bulky sweater, Hodgson in sweatpants, his head covered by a hooded sweatshirt pulled tight over a baseball cap. Both the sweatshirt and the cap were adorned with the Humber River Golf Club logo. Clearly they'd changed out of whatever they'd worn in bed.

Hodgson stood in the doorway, his arms firmly across his chest.

"Can we come inside, or do you prefer to speak out here?" Greene asked.

Lydia, who was standing nearest the door, reached to open it further. She said, "Karl, maybe we should—"

"Here is fine," Hodgson said, waving her off with a flick of his hand. "Detectives, what do you want to tell us?"

Kennicott looked at Greene.

His focus was entirely on Hodgson. "Sadly, we have to inform you of tragic news." His voice calm. "I'm sorry, Mr. Hodgson, your ex-wife, Melissa Copeland, has been found murdered."

Hodgson uncrossed his arms and thrust his hands to the top of his head.

"What?"

"Oh no," Lydia said. "Mel."

"I know you two were close friends from childhood," Greene said, turning to Lydia.

"Where, when?" Hodgson asked.

Kennicott had to admit, they both did seem genuinely upset and shocked.

"I can't say yet," Greene said. "We needed to inform you right away. You'll want to tell her daughter."

Kennicott took note of how Greene used language. "Tell *her* daughter." Melissa's daughter.

"Britt," Lydia said. "This is terrible for her."

That surprised Kennicott, coming from this couple who had fought for years to keep Melissa from seeing Britt.

"I suggest," Greene said, "that you tell her soon. I'm afraid with everything that is going on, this will be all over the media."

"My God," Lydia said.

"Don't be surprised if there are TV vans parked outside your home this morning," Kennicott said.

"Not again," Lydia said.

He realized she was referring to the media frenzy that had surrounded Hodgson's murder trial.

"I'd advise you to make no comment to the press," Greene said.

Hodgson frowned. "Thanks for that, Greene. You know it's going to be a circus."

He took his hands from his head, wrapped his arm around his wife's shoulder, and pulled her to him. His tone softened. "It's going to be hell for Britt. Losing her mother, and then the media. I bet the bastards camp right outside our door. What can we do?"

"Nothing right now," Greene said, then he asked casually, "When was the last time you saw Melissa?"

Smart. Now Greene was calling her "Melissa," no longer "your ex-wife."

Kennicott watched Hodgson carefully. He got a quizzical look on his face. He turned and looked at Lydia before answering.

"It was what, three, four months ago when Britt was in the school production of *Peter Pan*. I ducked out of a city council meeting early. You remember, I got there just before the end of the first act. Britt played Captain Hook."

Lydia nodded. "It was in May, May twenty-eighth, dear."

Hodgson turned back to Greene. "We worked out a deal in advance through the lawyers so that Melissa could come to see the show if she stayed in the back three rows."

"Did you talk to Melissa then?" Kennicott asked Lydia.

"No. She stayed in back," Lydia said. She started to cry. "I wanted to but all I could do was wave. I can't believe this happened to Mel."

"Lydia and Melissa met in kindergarten, for goodness' sake," Hodgson said. "They had nicknames for each other. Mel and Lyd."

Greene turned to Lydia. "I'm sorry," he said.

He turned back to Hodgson. "We'll be in touch later."

"That's all?" Hodgson looked taken aback that they were leaving. This often happened. Once you'd delivered horrible news to a family, they were paralysed. Didn't want the police to leave too quickly, didn't want the finality of that moment.

"I'm afraid that's all for now," Kennicott said.

The couple looked at each other. They seemed lost. "Okay," Hodgson said. Without saying another word, he slowly shut the door.

Back in the car, Greene said to Kennicott, "Well?"

"I have to admit they looked as if they were surprised and upset."

Greene eyed Kennicott.

"Looked as if," Greene said. "Did you notice, the only time he hesitated in his answers was when I asked him about the last time he'd seen his ex-wife?"

38

P arish didn't know what to do with herself. She'd taken a shower and even though she hardly ever cried, she cried. She lost track of time wandering around her house, trying to get organized. What the hell should she wear? Was it cold or warm? Where were her keys?

By the time she got herself together, the sky was brightening. She drove slowly, realizing she was in a fragile state. As she crossed the Danforth Bridge, the sun burst over the horizon, gleaming off the downtown office towers, splaying across her windshield. It was beautiful. There were some good things in life, weren't there?

Thankfully there was no one else in the office. Ted DiPaulo had a trial out of town this morning. Although she would have loved to talk to her partner of more than ten years, she didn't have the energy to break the news to him. It could wait. She appreciated the silence.

Was there anything in all of Melissa's endless emails and texts and letters and voice mails that could somehow help the police? Plus, she had stacks of legal files and interview notes from all her cases. Melissa was paranoid but brilliant. Did she leave some kind of clue?

Parish opened her briefcase and pulled out her trial binders. They felt heavy, like weights at a gym. She dumped them on her desk and stared at them. She went to her filing cabinet and pulled out all of Melissa's other files and piled them up, one on top of the other.

She stared at all the paper. She didn't want to face this.

There was a noise down the hallway. Footsteps coming her way. Who could it be? Ted was the only other person with a key.

"Ted?" she called out.

More footsteps. Closer now. No answer.

"Ted?"

The footsteps slowed.

She looked back at Melissa's files. Was there something in them? Is that why she had been killed? She stepped behind her desk, wrestled open the top drawer, and felt around for a pair of scissors. She had them in here, didn't she? Somewhere?

The footsteps stopped.

Where were the scissors? There. She grabbed them.

"How about an extra-hot cappuccino?" a voice she recognized asked from the hallway. It was Ted. He popped his head around the doorframe. "Plus homemade cannoli."

She flushed. Dropped the scissors back in the drawer. "Jesus. You scared the life out of me."

He strode into her office and pushed the binders and files on her desk aside to make room for the coffee and pastry, then turned to her with his arms open.

"I heard," he said.

"How? It's not public yet."

"Ari called me."

She folded herself into his arms.

"He told me to keep an eye on you," DiPaulo said.

"We all thought Melissa was paranoid. Now look what happened. She was right. Someone was out to kill her."

"The wise fool knows best."

Something occurred to her. "Wait, you're supposed to be in court up north this morning."

"I told them I'd be late."

"Thanks."

She slipped out of his arms and pointed to her desk. "Greene wants to talk to me. I'm going to go through everything I've ever received from Melissa to see if there's anything there that could be useful to him."

DiPaulo rubbed his goatee and nodded. This was what Parish

called "Ted the Sage in His Deep Think Mode." He was a brilliant and thoughtful lawyer who cared about the law. It was part of his being, the thing that made him a great advocate.

"Don't forget," he said slowly, "that even when a client dies, they're still covered by solicitor-client privilege."

This was Ted in lecture mode. Parish thought back to how she'd written out one of Melissa's texts for Kennicott. She wondered what Ted would think of that. He might not be happy about it, but right now she didn't want to worry about legal niceties. Melissa was dead.

She picked up the cappuccino and returned to her seat. "Thanks, Ted. You're the best. Good luck in court."

He pointed to her file-filled desk. "Happy hunting. The most important thing to know is that my mother made that cannoli last night," he said on his way out the door.

Parish was starving. She devoured the pastry and gulped down the cappuccino. She needed the sugar and caffeine. For the next few hours she scoured through Melissa's emails and texts. Maybe, she hoped, she'd find something that would be useful for Detective Greene, but they were just Melissa's endless diatribes about her ex-husband and her specious conspiracy theories about drug companies trying to kill the homeless.

She stood, stretched, and paced around her office, around and around like a dog circling its bed. On her third lap she spotted Melissa's bag of old clothes on the chair in the corner. For no reason other than for something to do, she tugged it open.

How depressing. When Melissa was a successful lawyer at the top of her game she had a gorgeous wardrobe. Every spring she and Karl would jet off to Paris to see the fashion shows. She was great at making contacts, and in a few years she was the lawyer for all the big-name designers who wanted to do business in Canada. Chanel, Armani, Chloé. You name it. She always had the latest jacket, skirt, shoes, purse, scarf, and accessories, all with the right names on them.

Parish pulled each item out of the bag one at a time and laid them on the floor. It was amazing, so much time and energy spent picking out these clothes, so much importance once placed upon them, and now they looked like nothing more than worthless rags.

Before Parish even finished emptying the bag, a flash of anger rolled through her. "Damn it!" she cried out, even though no one would hear her. "Such a waste, such a goddam waste!"

She closed the bag, raised it high above her head, and whacked it down on her desk as hard as she could. To her astonishment, she heard a loud smack.

What the hell was at the bottom of the bag? She tore it back open, tossing the rest of the designer-label rags onto the floor until she felt something solid and pulled it out.

It was a hardbound notebook. A typed label affixed to the front cover read, "JUST IN CASE: Nance Read This When They Kill Me. By Melissa Copeland."

Parish sank to the floor, sitting on a pile of Melissa's clothes and staring at the book. She thought back to yesterday morning, when Melissa tossed the bag in the corner. "Keep my stuff," she'd said. "You never know when it might come in handy."

Parish turned to the first page and started to read, whispering over and over and over again to herself, "Melissa. Oh, Melissa."

39

"In an exclusive report, *T.O. TV News* has learned that a third homeless person in less than a week has been murdered in the Humber Valley," Alison said, looking straight into the camera. "The victim this time was Ms. Melissa Copeland, the ex-wife of well-known city councillor Karl Hodgson. Her body was found on the grounds of the Humber River Golf Club, where three years ago Hodgson killed a homeless man who had tried to rob him."

The legal department at the TV station had carefully vetted Alison's script. It was true that Hodgson had killed a homeless man, but the lawyers cut out any reference to the fact that he'd been tried for murder.

She was standing on the sidewalk in front of Hodgson's enormous house. Now, as she'd rehearsed a few minutes earlier with Krevolin, she turned and pointed while he followed her arm with his camera.

Alison kept speaking: "After Hodgson divorced Melissa Copeland, he obtained a court order to prevent her from coming back to her home or from seeing her daughter. Sadly, Melissa, once a top lawyer at one of Toronto's largest firms, ended up on the street. Homeless."

Krevolin panned the camera back to her. Alison put on her most serious face.

"Three homeless people murdered in the Humber Valley, just blocks away from where I'm standing. Right now, people in this neighbourhood, and the estimated ten thousand homeless people across the city, are living in fear. Reporting live, on scene, this is Alison Greene."

She stared directly into the camera and waited for the red light to go off. The approved script read "the city's homeless," but she'd added the phrase "estimated ten thousand" on her own. If she was going to do her job, which meant she was going to have to exploit this situation, she was going to make sure she made a statement.

"Well done," Krevolin said, pulling the camera off his shoulder.

Alison unpinned the mic on her shirt. "It feels dirty."

After her dad gave her this scoop, even though it was the middle of the night, Alison had called her boss and told her what had happened.

"Hodgson's ex-wife? Murdered?" Persaud had asked, immediately alert. "At his golf club? Are you sure?"

"Yes. My source is totally reliable."

"Wow. And you say she was a lawyer who became homeless? This story's going to go viral."

"I'll get Krevolin and rush over to the golf club for a live hit."

"Absolutely not," Persaud said. "You've got this amazing scoop. Hodgson's ex, homeless while he lives in a mansion. The big house—that's what people want to see. This is TV. Images tell the story."

"But what about their daughter? She's only eleven." Alison knew how it felt to suddenly lose your mother and could imagine the horror Britt was about to go through.

"Like it or not, she's part of the story."

"But her mum was just murdered. She'll have to wake up to that terrible news. It will be awful enough. She doesn't need our van parked outside her front door."

"Alison," Persaud said, "this news is going to get out in the next hour if not sooner, and the other stations will descend on that house like a pack of hungry wolves. Do you want to be there first, or do you want to be stuck in the crowd?"

Alison sighed.

"Listen to me," Persaud said in a stern voice. "I took a chance on you last year because I thought you were going to be a fearless journalist. Sometimes you have to do the dirty stuff."

Alison knew she was right. A year earlier she was a journalism school dropout who had stumbled upon the high-profile murder of one of the city's top condominium developers. Persaud believed in her enough to let her run with the story, and Alison did such good work, it had led to this job.

"Okay," she said, "but I'm not mentioning their daughter's name. That's where I draw the line."

"Agreed," Persaud had said before she'd hung up.

Alison looked back at the Hodgsons' home. She had to admit, filming here made the story. All the curtains were drawn across the many windows. She hated to think of what was going on inside and the emotions of Britt, who just last night was the star of a party held in her honour.

"Time to go," she said, helping Krevolin pack up his gear. "I don't want that little girl to look out her window and see us parked right outside."

"Noble of you, but it won't matter." He pointed down the street.

Alison saw two other TV station trucks zipping up the road. Behind them were a bunch of cars with radio station logos plastered all over them.

"Here come the hairy hordes," Krevolin said.

Alison grabbed one of Krevolin's bags. "Let's get the hell out of here," she said. "Pronto."

She stepped in the TV van, and her phone buzzed. An incoming text. It was from Burns.

"Well done!"

"Thanks," she typed back.

"The ten thousand homeless. Right on."

She nodded. She had come up with an idea for a story and was determined to do it. He could help her.

"I want to do a story on homeless women in the city. When can we meet?"

"In an hour."

"Where?"

"Fahrenheit. I'll take you to a nearby women's drop-in centre."

"I can't wait."

40

Years ago, when Greene started on the force, the coroner's office was housed in an old, wood-panelled, Victorian-era building with high ceilings and stone walls. Despite the grim tasks being done inside, there had been a friendly informality about the place. Back then Toronto was a much smaller city, there were hardly any guns around, and most of the murders were crimes of passion. The receptionists, the support staff, the pathologists, even the cleaners—everyone knew each other, everyone worked together. There were no identification cards or even sign-in sheets. He would walk in, wave at the receptionist, and go inside. No problem.

Now the city was three times bigger and the murder rate had grown with it. The coroner's building had moved to a concrete, ultra-modern facility. Greene hadn't been here since they'd installed a sterile security system that started with a bored-looking young man behind a bulletproof-glass window, tapping on his cell phone. He took his time before he peered up at Greene, then hit a switch on his desk. His tinny, mechanical-sounding voice came through a small square speaker at the top of the glass.

"Purpose of your visit," he said.

"My name is Detective Ari Greene. I'm here to observe an autopsy."

Why else would he be here? Greene thought. And why a bulletproof window? Did a faceless bureaucrat think some gang members were going to try to blast their way inside to kill someone who was already dead? He fished out his identity card from his wallet and put it up to the glass.

"I spoke to Mr. Krangle. Take a look, my name should be on your list."

Krangle was the manager who'd been in charge of the Coroner's Office for years. He ran the place with an iron fist in a velvet glove, cajoling, bargaining with, and forcing his team of pathologists —whom he liked to call "physician prima donnas"—when he had to get them to come in on short notice to perform urgent autopsies in the middle of the night or on holiday weekends.

Krangle, who spoke in short sentences, had been all business when they'd talked earlier.

"What do you need?" he'd asked Greene.

"It looks as if we have another homeless person murdered. No time to waste."

"I've got a tremendous new pathologist. She's very keen. I'll get her in ASAP."

The young man behind the glass pulled out a clipboard and flipped through a few typed pages.

"Identification on the tray," his tin voice said. He didn't bother to look up at Greene.

Greene glanced around but didn't see a tray.

"Below the counter," the tin voice said.

Greene found the metal tray, pulled it out, put his ID in, and pushed it forward. Tin Voice finished tapping on his phone, then picked up the ID, glanced at it, put a small clipboard, a guest tag, and the ID back in the tray, and shoved it back to Greene.

"Sign in and wear the ID," he said, already back on his phone.

Greene took his card, clipped on the ID, signed the sheet, sent it back, then had to wait at a locked door for Tin Voice to stop tapping and hit the switch. There was a high-pitched buzzing sound, and Greene pulled the entrance door open.

The cadavers must sleep soundly here now, he thought, knowing there is such a high level of security.

As soon as he made his way inside, he saw Krangle.

"Ari," the man called, a warm smile lighting up his face.

Krangle was a squat man with a bald head that seemed to shine in the light. He rushed up to Greene and took his hand.

"Been too long."

"Nice to see you again," Greene said.

"Sorry for all you went through."

"Life happens."

Krangle was still holding his hand. "We're all glad you're back."

Since his arrest and trial and acquittal, every time he encountered someone from his earlier police days, there was the same type of conversation. He'd gotten good at changing the subject.

"Everyone except your young receptionist."

Krangle's dark eyebrows shot up. "Millennials," he said, as if it were a punch line in a bad joke. "They live on their phones."

"Who's the new pathologist?" Greene asked.

Krangle smiled again.

"Dr. Juliana Ramos. She's new. Top-notch. Did the other two homeless. Insisted on doing this. Didn't want to wait. She's almost done. You'll like her."

Greene followed Krangle down the hallway. The walls were filled with framed black-and-white photographs of the old stone coroner's building. Funny how they tore down buildings in the city, then glorified them when they were gone.

Inside the operating theatre, Dr. Ramos was dressed in white scrubs, gloves, and a hair net, with a mic around her neck. She dictated as she worked on the opened body of Melissa Copeland. An assistant stood behind, peering over her shoulder.

Greene stepped closer, gingerly, and watched. Ramos's movements were agile and precise. She looked up and noticed him.

For some reason he'd assumed she'd be young, but she was older than he'd expected her to be, closer to his age. With a smooth, intelligent face, high cheekbones, and piercing black eyes.

"You must be the detective." She had a charming accent that he couldn't quite place. Maybe Spanish?

"Ari Greene. I appreciate you coming in on such short notice."

"The work must get done," she said, all business.

Over her shoulder Greene saw Krangle wink at him. Greene frowned.

"Preliminary findings?" he asked her.

"Appears to be similar to the other two homeless people murdered this week. Crushing blow to the back of the head, not consistent with a vodka bottle being used but a heavier blunt object. Except one thing."

Without ceremony she pulled Copeland's limp wrist up and showed Greene her fingernails. "Skin under the fingernails and bits of glass." She picked up Copeland's other wrist. "Both hands."

Their eyes met.

"This woman fought hard," she said.

It was grim to see such stark, sad evidence of Melissa's struggle in the last seconds of her life. He could see Ramos was sympathetic.

"We need to send samples out for DNA comparison right away," he said.

She shook her head and gave Greene a mildly condescending frown.

"Detective . . ."

"Greene."

"This was the first thing I looked for. I sent the samples out for urgent results, which I am told in this jurisdiction takes at least three days."

She was confident but not cocky. Professional.

She turned to her assistant, who handed her a nearby iPad.

Greene expected her to show it to him. Instead she said, "Detective, I am done with my work here, my assistant can finish up. Please, come with me."

She efficiently took off her scrubs, folded them into the laundry bin, then walked quickly through the autopsy suite.

"You work fast," he said, keeping up with her.

"Why waste time?"

They came to a small anteroom off to the side. There was a single metal locker there that looked old and out of place. A handwritten label with the name "Ramos" was slipped into the label slot on the door.

She pulled off her gloves and her gown with practiced efficiency. Underneath she wore a trim pair of black jeans that looked as if they had been ironed, a crisp white shirt, and a turquoise necklace that looked like some ancient Aztec design.

She kicked the locker. He noticed for the first time she was wearing brown leather laced-up boots.

"Apparently, I am the only female pathologist in Toronto," she said. "They gave me this room to change in."

"At least you deserve a typed label," he said.

"It's on my list, Detective, but I've been kept busy since I arrived."

"When was that?"

"Two weeks ago."

She pulled off the hair net. A tumble of straight jet-black hair cascaded down her back.

"Had you ever been to Toronto before?" he asked her.

"Never been to North America before. They flew me in for the interview on a Friday."

"Flew you in from where?"

"Uruguay. They needed someone thanks to the recent spike in crime here. They asked me if they offered me the job, when could I start? I said Monday. I went home, packed up, and here I am."

"Decisive."

"Always." She ran her fingers through her hair and grinned. She had perfect white teeth, and Greene realized she was wearing bright-red lipstick.

"Then you don't know Toronto very well."

"Not at all. I've hardly had time to unpack." She looked straight at Greene. "I hope to find someone who can show me where I can get a good cup of coffee."

He smiled back. "I know a good place, but I'm not a coffee drinker."

She laughed. "A police detective who doesn't drink coffee. That is very strange."

She pulled up her iPad. "I wanted to show you this out of earshot of anyone else. I lifted a fingerprint from the victim's neck. I was able to get a match in minutes. I believe you will be interested in the results."

Ramos's face was now blank. She wasn't going to give anything away.

He took the iPad from her and read the name displayed there. He looked back at her.

Her face cracked into a hint of a smile. "I looked this name up on the internet, Detective," she said. "You have charged this man with murder one time already, no?"

41

Always one step behind. That's how this whole investigation felt to Kennicott right now. He'd underestimated the first murder of a homeless man, and so had the media. The story had hardly made a blip in the press. The second one had set off alarm bells. The media coverage exploded, fuelled by the protests outside Police Headquarters. That got Greene assigned to the case and the mayor involved. But now there had been three homicides right under Kennicott's nose. Add to that a huge protest planned for some still-unknown location tomorrow, and now the mayor and the premier and even the prime minister were chiming in on the plight of the homeless and making noises about showing up to speak to the crowd.

Kennicott and Greene were under the gun in a way they'd never been before. And Kennicott was kicking himself. He'd been undercover as a waiter at Britt's party but had lost track of Hodgson. Wasn't it predictable that Melissa would show up at the celebration for her daughter? Shouldn't he have had someone out patrolling the grounds full-time?

As usual, it all seemed obvious, in hindsight.

He'd gone back and talked to Marvin Lemon, the frustrated, grieving husband of Nurse Deb. Kennicott asked him about the fight he'd had with her on that horrible night he'd locked her out of the house.

"She was ranting," he said.

"What was she saying?" Kennicott asked.

"Nothing logical. She'd become totally paranoid. Screaming at me that the drug companies were after her, that people were out to kill her. Maybe she wasn't so crazy after all."

"Did you know that she had cancer?" Kennicott asked.

"I never knew how bad it was. She was totally emaciated. Her old friends at the hospital begged her to go for treatment. Good luck with that."

What could he do next? Work smarter, work harder. He'd tracked down the videographer and got copies of all his tape from the party, and this morning he'd spent hours in the video room at the homicide bureau going over it.

He'd fast-forwarded past the guests arriving, the kids dancing, the food being served, and stopped at the point where Hodgson made his speech on the dance floor. Where had he gone, when Kennicott had been serving the tables and before Kennicott saw him come back inside? Was there any footage of that? No luck. The only thing that had been filmed was the kids getting back to dancing, and the guests playing the various golf games around the perimeter of the room.

Kennicott skipped ahead to later in the party, after the dinner, when Britt was carried back inside on the golf-club chair like a champion. He wanted to see what happened when the confetti cannon went off, before the lights went out and the *Move Over Tiger, Here Comes Britt* tribute video was played.

There was Hodgson, clear as day, right in the middle of things. Laughing along with others in the chaos as the confetti rained down on everyone. Then he was mugging for the camera, picking confetti out of his hair and from his jacket as he talked to the crowd.

If Hodgson were ever put on trial for the murder of his ex-wife, this image of him smothered in the sticky confetti could be compelling circumstantial evidence against him. Kennicott could imagine the prosecutor telling the jury that this was proof that, while the video was playing, Hodgson had snuck outside to confront Melissa. And as one of her last acts, she had bravely hidden the piece of confetti in the folds of her pants as proof her ex-husband had confronted her. And killed her.

Next the lights went dark when the tribute video to Britt started to play. Did Hodgson use the cover of darkness to go back outside? Unfortunately, it wasn't clear. Kennicott was hoping that when the lights came back on in the room, the video might show he was no longer on the dance floor. Instead there he was in the crowd, making it seem as if he had never left. And perhaps he hadn't.

At a trial, as inculpatory as the piece of confetti might be, this evidence would have the exact opposite effect. A good defence lawyer would use it to show there was nothing to prove Hodgson left the hall after the confetti came down. So the piece on Melissa couldn't be traced back to him.

Kennicott patiently went through the rest of the tape and recorded each time Hodgson was on camera and when he wasn't. It was a slow process, and when he was done he made a chart and tallied up seven gaps when Hodgson was off screen, the longest being eleven minutes and sixteen seconds.

Was it enough time for him to encounter Melissa outside and kill her, while leaving a telltale piece of confetti on her body? And if Melissa was threatening to crash Hodgson's special party for Britt, that would certainly give him motive. It was suspicious, but was it enough for them to arrest him?

Kennicott turned off the video machine. Although Greene was just down the hall, he decided to write him a confidential email and include his time chart. Sometimes it was best to put your thoughts on paper first. It was the ex-lawyer in him.

When he finished writing, he only felt more frustrated. The only thing he was certain of was that, despite his best efforts, he was still one step behind.

42

As she walked past the window of the Fahrenheit Café, Alison spotted Burns perched on a stool in the same corner where they'd met yesterday. He gave her a quick wave and headed toward the door.

She waited for him to come outside. This was always awkward. The first meeting after the first kiss. How should they greet each other? Would they pretend their kiss had never happened? Would they give each other a quick, "just friends" peck on the cheek? On the lips? Or would it be a long, real kiss and tender embrace?

And what did she want? A real kiss? A warm hug? Maybe nothing and forget all about it? Alison wasn't sure.

She watched him walk out and smile. What should she do? Before she had time to move, he came right up and reached out his arms. That made it easy. She reached out too, and they hugged. It felt good, the warmth of his body, the strength of his embrace.

"Your report this morning was terrific," he said.

"You really think so?" she asked.

They pulled away from each other at the same time, as if they had a silent agreement that their coupling would be longer than just a friendly hug, but not as long as a real lovers' embrace.

"Like I said in my text. It's great you're using the shocking statistics. Getting the message out. You seem to really care."

"Seem?"

He laughed. "I can tell you care. It comes across. Coffee?" He pointed back through the window. There was a long line up at the counter.

"No. Good news. My boss gave me the go-ahead to do this story if I can find a woman who will let me interview her on camera. I'm doing this on my own time. Where is the women's drop-in place you told me about?"

"It's not far." He unlocked his bike and walked with it on one side, while he put his other hand on her shoulder.

Alison didn't know this neighbourhood. The streets were filled with new condominiums, trendy-looking boutique shops, and high-end restaurants. They crossed over to Adelaide, a soulless one-way street heading downtown. It was backed up with expensive cars filled with well-dressed, impatient-looking drivers, most talking to someone on their headphones on their way to work, and hearty cyclists rolling by in the bike lane. Burns stopped in front of a nondescript brick building on the south side and locked his bike to a pole.

A woman wearing a pair of pink plastic clogs and a thin green raincoat was walking back and forth in front of the door, bobbing her head up and down, talking to herself in a rapid, high-pitched voice.

"Yes, yes, go in," she said, and turned, "no, well, maybe," turned again, "cold, it's cold," and turned yet again, "but, but, but."

"Good afternoon, Wendy," Burns said, as casually as if he were greeting a colleague at work.

"Doctor, doctor," Wendy said, walking faster, turning in shorter and shorter circles.

"You coming in today?" he asked. "A nice cup of tea, a bowl of soup to warm you up?"

"Yes, no, maybe, no."

Saying that, she rushed down the street and turned down a corner.

"When she's on her meds, Wendy is one of the country's top Scrabble players," he said.

They turned back to the building. A white sheet of paper was taped to the glass entrance door. The typewritten sign read

Physical Violence of
Any kind will result in a
Service restriction from
The Drop-in

Alison peered inside. She could see groups of tired-looking women sitting on stackable chairs gathered around an eclectic collection of tables. Each woman had at least one, some had two, bulging plastic bags at their feet. A few of them wore white masks. One was in a wheelchair, another had a breathing tube in her nose. She could see from their caved-in cheeks that many had no teeth.

"Welcome to Paradise, Part Two," Burns said.

Alison felt a lump deep in her throat. Despite herself she felt, what? Fear? Embarrassment? A hint of revulsion, which made her feel guilty? A part of her didn't want to go inside. And a part of her hated herself for feeling that way.

"I should warn you," he said. "I find that when their lives fall apart, women are more closed than men. I doubt any of these ladies will want to talk to you on camera."

"I'm pretty good at persuading people," she said.

He pulled open the heavy door. Some of the women looked up, and a few of them smiled at Burns. But most seemed preoccupied, in their own worlds, sipping cups of coffee from chipped mugs or eating sandwiches off white paper plates.

The lighting was harsh. Something else was strange about the place. It took Alison a few seconds to realize what it was. The big room was quiet. All these women in one place, hardly anyone talking.

Alison looked around, careful not to stare at anyone in particular. The only person who made momentary eye contact with her was a woman in the corner by the far wall. She caught Alison's eye before she turned away and stared into space.

Alison slowly made her way over to her. The woman sat alone at a small table with a slim Whole Foods bag by her side. There was a chair across from her.

"Do you mind if I sit down?" Alison asked.

The woman peered up at her. She didn't move, just stared right at Alison. Her eyes were a dark, almost-black brown, matching the colour of her straggly long hair. Both were in sharp contrast to her near-bleached-white skin. Her face was gaunt. She wore layers of loose-fitting clothes that Alison suspected hid an emaciated frame.

She didn't say a word.

"I . . . I don't want to bother you," Alison said.

Perhaps the woman didn't understand English. Alison was about to walk away when the woman spoke.

"Why?" she asked. Her voice was as thin as she was. Those dark eyes of hers didn't leave Alison's face.

"Why what?" Alison asked, sitting across from her.

"Why do you want to sit with me?"

"Perhaps we can talk? I'm a journalist."

"I know," the woman said, still staring. "I've seen you on TV."

"I want to do a story. About a woman who lives . . ."

The woman broke off eye contact.

"I won't use your name. I won't show your face. I promise."

The woman swivelled in her chair, turning away. Alison was sure she had lost her. Any second now she expected her to get up and walk away.

Instead the woman reached down into her bag and pulled out a small notebook with a pen clipped into the wire binding. She placed it with care on the table in front of her, and then, like a well-organized schoolteacher about to start a lesson with her class, opened it to a page marked by a ribbon. It was a diary, and Alison could see that the woman's handwriting was tiny and precise.

"What is your full name and date of birth?" she asked in an officious voice, as if she were a clerk at a government office. Once again she locked her eyes on Alison.

Alison told her. Then her address, her cell phone number, her height and weight. When she'd finished taking her notes, the woman flipped to the back of her notebook and deftly tore out a blank page.

She started to write as she spoke. "This is the contact information for my daughter, Gina. She just had a baby. And my husband, Marcel. This time I've been gone for one hundred twenty-four days. Tell them there's no point in them trying to contact me."

"Okay."

"Then come back and maybe we'll talk. I'll be here."

"I will."

The woman folded the paper exactly down the middle and passed it to Alison. Then she returned to staring into space.

Alison got up and walked away quietly, clutching the piece of paper in her hand the way she used to hold a treasured seashell when her mother would take her to Brighton for afternoons by the sea.

43

"Mr. Hodgson, welcome back to the homicide department," Greene said as he watched Hodgson walk into the reception area accompanied by his lawyer, Phil Cutter.

Hodgson looked haggard. He wasn't wearing his usual high-end golf sportswear but instead was dressed in old running shoes and the same baggy sweatpants, baseball cap, and hooded sweatshirt he'd been wearing when Kennicott and Greene had gone to talk to him earlier. He still had the hood up over his head, Greene assumed to hide his face in case some newspaper photographer saw him walking into Police Headquarters. Greene expected he would pull off the hood now that he was inside the building, but he didn't.

Greene turned to Cutter. He looked calm and collected, sharply dressed in a handmade Italian suit and hand-made leather shoes. His regular uniform.

"Mr. Cutter, lovely to see you again as well," Greene said.

Greene referred to Cutter as "Mr. Cutter," because he knew it annoyed him. In response, Cutter called him "Detective." Cutter was always chummy with people and he called everyone by their first name, except Greene. Greene was sure Cutter would have loved to call him Ari, but he didn't have the nerve to.

"Trust me, Detective," Cutter said, "there's no place in the whole wide world that I'd rather be this morning than right here at the homicide bureau at Toronto Police Headquarters. I'll be sure to write a review on Tripadvisor."

They both laughed.

"It was your idea," Greene said. "Not mine."

Half an hour earlier, Greene had finished reading Kennicott's email about the videotape from the party when his cell phone rang. Greene wasn't surprised to see the lawyer's name pop up on his call display.

"Mr. Cutter, what took you so long?" he said, opening his notebook as he spoke and recording the time. "It's already ten thirty in the morning. I've been expecting your call for hours."

"Nice to talk to you too, Detective," Cutter said.

"I assume you're calling to tell me Mr. Hodgson won't speak to the police again, and that unless I intend to arrest him I should leave him alone, and you want any future communication to go through you."

Greene started writing in his notebook: *Call from Hodgson's lawyer Cutter: re: further contact with client.*

"You can assume that, Detective."

"Message received," Greene said. He kept writing: *Hodgson won't make stmt.* Then he said, "I'll be in touch if we do decide to arrest—"

"But your assumption would be wrong," Cutter said, cutting in. "Mr. Hodgson has instructed me that he would like to come to Police Headquarters to give a full statement."

"I see," Greene said, trying not to sound surprised. He never crossed anything out in his notebook. He wrote: *Correction. Hodgson does wish to make stmt.* "When would he like to do that?"

"Right now. My client is here with me at the Starbucks down the street. We can be there in five minutes."

Greene looked at Kennicott's email on his computer screen. It was a good thing he was in the building. They needed some time to prepare for this. In his notebook he added the words: *this morning.*

"I have to set up an interview room," Greene said. "Detective Kennicott will join us."

"I have one condition," Cutter added. "And don't write this down in your notes."

Greene lifted his pen. "Let's hear it."

"You can tape this, but no video. Deal?"

Greene was pretty sure he knew why Cutter was asking for this. "Deal," he said. "Mr. Cutter, buy your client another latte and come over in half an hour."

Cutter chuckled and hung up.

Greene walked over to the video room. Kennicott was slouched down in a deep chair staring at photographs from the party on a monitor. He looked exhausted.

"Good work on your report," Greene said.

"I could have done better. I should never have lost sight of Hodgson."

"Only so much you can do when you're at a big event like that where someone doesn't want to be seen. I have news. Cutter just called. He wants to bring Hodgson in to make a statement."

Kennicott sat bolt upright in his chair. "You're kidding."

Greene shook his head. "They're going to be here in half an hour."

"You don't think Hodgson's coming here to confess, do you?"

"You never know. Turn off the video, that's part of the deal."

For the next twenty minutes they planned their strategy. How to arrange the seating in the interview room. Who would lead the questioning. What things to look for in Hodgson's behaviour and reactions. How to respond to various scenarios Hodgson might present.

"If Hodgson says the only time he went outside was the time when I saw him in the washroom, then he's lying," Kennicott said. "That was before the confetti shower."

Greene nodded. "Bring your time chart with you."

When Hodgson and Cutter arrived, the detectives were ready to go. On Greene's instructions, Kennicott set up the interview room so Cutter and Hodgson sat on the side of the table farthest from the door. Even though Hodgson had come voluntarily and could terminate the interview at any time, Greene didn't want to make it too easy for him to leave.

Greene sat directly across from Hodgson, and Kennicott faced

Cutter. Greene had put his briefcase on the end of the table. He opened it and pulled out his notebook and a pen. He clicked his pen. Kennicott took out his notebook too and then placed a handheld tape recorder in the centre of the table and turned it on.

Kennicott stated the time and location and identified everyone in the room, clicked off the recorder, rewound it and played it back to make sure it was working, then turned the recorder back on.

Greene kept his eyes on Hodgson, waiting to see if he would break out into a sweat. But he appeared to be uncharacteristically calm under his hood. And like a well-coached witness, he was staring with laser-like concentration at Greene.

"Mr. Hodgson, your lawyer, Mr. Cutter, informs me that you wish to make a statement."

"I do."

"Go ahead."

"I have come to confess," Hodgson said, with no emotion in his voice.

Greene glanced at Kennicott, then back at Hodgson. The room became still and silent.

"I'm guilty."

44

P arish felt paralyzed with fear, anger, confusion.

She'd lost track of how long she'd been sitting on the floor of her office reading Melissa's notebook. The way she used to sit on the floor of her bedroom when she was a young girl and read Nancy Drew mystery books one after another for hours and hours.

Everything Melissa had written to Parish in the last few years—all her texts and email letters—had been disjointed and paranoid, but here in her secret book Parish could see the work of the brilliant lawyer Melissa had once been.

She'd done an exhaustive study of the problem of homelessness in the city. It started back in the 1960s when the federal government poured money into housing projects both downtown and in the suburbs, creating ghettoized communities that featured circular roads that kept through traffic out and the poor people in. No surprise, in time they became major crime centres. And even worse, over the years as the buildings decayed, there was never substantial funding to keep them in good repair.

Next Melissa outlined in detail the lack of basic facilities for poor people in the city: transportation, parks, and decent schools. Then she charted the city's rapid expansion in the next decades, the influx of immigrants from all over the world, and indigenous Canadians drawn to Toronto. And how, at the same time, the federal government retreated from its commitment to public housing and the provincial government downloaded the cost of housing and welfare onto the city. The drip, drip, drip of decay.

In the next chapters she wrote about the closing of mental-health facilities and the broken promise of providing services for the most needy and mentally ill in the community. Then came the drugs. The crack cocaine, the heroin, and finally the fentanyl, all while the public housing, which had been poorly built decades earlier, was falling apart as the waiting list for apartments grew exponentially longer. And now the massive building boom and skyrocketing rents were forcing anyone marginal who ran into some bad luck out onto the street.

Parish was transfixed. Melissa had written this all out by hand, in her meticulous handwriting. She must have done hours and hours of research.

The next section was an extensive review of the homeless problem in other countries. The overrun streets of San Francisco. The tent city outside the Prado Museum in Madrid. And a long section on Finland, the only European country that had had success with the problem. Why? Because as soon as someone was identified as homeless, that person was provided with a decent place to live and support

There was a chart. Melissa loved charts. This one analyzed the true cost of homelessness. An emergency hospital visit even for a simple matter cost the government a thousand dollars. She had stats on the cost of running shelters, social workers, food, criminal charges for petty crimes. To say nothing of the human cost. It went on and on for pages, building a brilliant argument that putting money into housing, instead of relief and support programs, was a large long-term financial saving.

As Parish got near the end of the book, Melissa's handwriting changed. Her penmanship was no longer precise and clean but erratic. A new chapter was headed: "Who Profits?: Homelessness is a Money-Making Machine!"

She pointed her finger at the social workers and shelter workers who had good jobs, at the drug counsellors and therapists who had a constant supply of patients, and at the doctors who ran homeless drug addicts through their offices on ten-minute weekly visits. But most of her anger was directed at the pharmaceutical companies. They had an endless lineup of customers who needed their product and governments only too happy to pay their bills to keep the homeless out of sight.

"Everyone wins, everyone makes money!!!" she'd written. "Except the people who needed help!!!!"

Parish turned the page. Melissa had written a new heading in capital letters. "TWO MURDERS: J'ACCUSE" It was dated yesterday.

Parish read on transfixed. Melissa had laid out in precise detail, as if it were a well-argued lawyer's brief, the case against the person who she claimed was the killer. Her conclusion was devastating.

Parish exhaled and slammed the book shut.

She didn't believe it. Or didn't want to believe it. Really, could it be?

45

Greene kept his eyes fixed on Hodgson. He looked much too relaxed for a man about to confess to murder. Perhaps three murders.

"Your suspicion about me was right, Detective Greene," Hodgson said. "I was the one who struck Jember Roshan on Sunday morning when he was riding his bike to work at the club. It was dark, and I didn't see him. I had no idea I'd hit him until you came to my office and showed me the picture of the damage to my car."

Hodgson never looked at Cutter for direction but kept his eyes trained on Greene. He didn't have a hint of his usual arrogance or bravado. And his hood was still up, as if he were hiding his real personality underneath it.

Greene felt like he was playing along in a drama that Hodgson and Cutter had scripted out for themselves without telling him his part.

"I'll make arrangements with Mr. Roshan to reimburse him for the damage to his bicycle," Hodgson said.

"I'm sure he'll appreciate that."

"And I'll pay for any physical therapy he needs."

"And I'll pass your confession along to the division that handles traffic violations," Greene said, "and let them decide if there will be charges."

They were sparring, like boxers waiting for the opponent to make the first move so they could counterpunch. Everyone in the room knew that Hodgson hadn't come in with his lawyer early this morning to talk about a possible highway traffic act violation.

Greene reached for his tape recorder. "If that is all, I'll conclude this interview."

"There's one more thing," Hodgson said.

Greene let his hand hover over the recorder.

"I lied to you and Detective Kennicott early this morning when you came to my house and informed me that my ex-wife Melissa had been murdered," Hodgson said.

"You did?" Greene said, keeping his voice level. He resisted the urge to look at Kennicott. "For the record, at four thirty-five a.m. this morning, Detective Kennicott and I attended at your home and informed you that Melissa was dead. And at that time, you told us the last time you had seen her was many months ago at your daughter's school play in May of this year. Do you agree?"

"No."

Greene looked over at Kennicott.

"Detective Kennicott," he said. "Can you confirm that we had that discussion with Mr. Hodgson?"

"Yes, we did," Kennicott said.

Greene was getting angry. He looked back at Cutter. "Counsel, we're not here to play games. We're investigating three murders in the past week. If your client has information for us, we'd like to hear it, otherwise this interview is over."

"Hear him out, Detective," Cutter said. He was nonplussed.

Greene looked at Hodgson. "Let me be clear, you are saying you don't agree that Detective Kennicott and I attended at your home, and that you made that statement?"

"I agree that you both came to my house, and I made that statement."

"You did?"

"One hundred per cent."

"What do you disagree with then?"

Greene glanced at Cutter. The lawyer smiled back at Greene with a smug look on his clean-shaven face that said "Gotcha." There was something more to come, and Greene had no idea what it was.

"You implied that you spoke to me alone at my house," Hodgson said. "I was not alone. You informed me in the presence of my wife, Lydia."

So that was it, Greene thought.

"True. Detective Kennicott and I spoke to you and your wife at the doorway of your home."

"I lied to all of you," Hodgson said. "The truth is that I met Melissa last night outside the dining hall. I didn't want Lydia to know that I had been in touch with my ex. That's why I lied, and that's why I'm here now."

"Unfortunately, my client was not interviewed by the police on his own," Cutter said, finally speaking up. Greene could see he was already formulating his legal argument in case Hodgson was arrested.

"It was not an interview," Greene said. "We were informing him at the earliest possible opportunity."

"Nevertheless it was most unfortunate," Cutter said. "My client has now attended here voluntarily, because he wants to set the record straight at the earliest opportunity."

Greene knew Hodgson well from his trial. Usually the man was hyper and animated, but now he was still. With his hood up, he seemed like a priest about to make his own confession.

Greene had to keep his demeanour calm. He turned back to Hodgson. "How did that come about? Your going outside to meet Melissa?"

"I knew she was going to be there, because I invited her."

"You invited her to the party?"

"Not the party. Not inside. I wanted her to see Britt, and Britt wanted to see her mom. There were a few minutes between the time when Britt snuck out of the party and before the four guys brought her back in on the golf-club chair. I went outside to get Melissa to bring her to the back room. Britt waited for us. Lydia didn't know anything about this. You know Lydia and Melissa have, well, let's just say it's complicated for them."

Interestingly, Hodgson was still referring to Melissa in the present tense.

"Have you told Lydia about this now?"

"After you two left this morning, I told her what had happened. Then we had to wake up Britt and tell her this horrible news."

For the first time Hodgson's calm demeanour changed. He looked upset. Sad.

"What happened when Melissa saw Britt?"

He shook his head. "She never saw her."

"Why not?"

To Greene's surprise, Hodgson thrust his body about halfway across the table. He was a big man, and he quickly filled the space between them. In one swift motion he yanked off his hood, pulled off his baseball cap and unzipped his sweatshirt. He was wearing an unbuttoned polo shirt. He pulled the collar down and turned his head to the left then to the right.

There were long, fresh-looking scratch marks on both sides of his neck.

He sat back down.

"When I met her outside, Melissa was totally out of control. I pleaded with her to calm down. She attacked me."

He pointed to the marks on his neck.

"We tussled. Despite everything, for all those years, Detective Greene, I never once hit Melissa."

"What happened?"

"I backed away. I promised her I'd arrange for her to see Britt next week. I couldn't ruin the party for my daughter, and I didn't want to upset Lydia, so I didn't tell her."

"What about the scratch marks? How did you explain them to Lydia?"

"I didn't. When I went back inside, I went to the bathroom and dried them off as best as I could. I had one of the scarves that we gave out to all the guests, and I used it to cover my neck. Just before Britt was brought back in to the party, I had to tell Britt what happened. She was sad but she understood."

Greene looked over at Kennicott. They both had the same thought. This story explained his fingerprints on Melissa's neck. It would take a few days to get the results back, but she probably had his DNA under her fingernails. Kennicott himself was a witness to Hodgson's spending a lot of time in the bathroom stall. It all fit, perhaps too neatly. Had Hodgson recognized Kennicott and made a point of using him as a partial alibi?

There was one key question left. The timing.

Greene turned to Kennicott. "Detective," he said, "do you have any questions for Mr. Hodgson?"

This was a way of stalling and giving Kennicott a chance to formulate what he wanted to say.

"I do," he said. "Do you know what time you went outside to meet Ms. Copeland?"

"It was supposed to be at nine thirty. I got there a few minutes early."

Kennicott opened the binder in front of him. "We've viewed a copy of the video taken at the party last night. I've gone through it and made a time chart of everything that took place that night."

Greene watched Hodgson's eyes as Kennicott slowly ran his forefinger down the typewritten page. Nice work, taking his time.

Hodgson looked surprised but not concerned.

"At nine twenty people were dancing on the dance floor. You are seen exiting at nine twenty-five and re-entering at nine forty-two."

"Okay," Hodgson said, following Kennicott's finger on the page.

"At nine forty-five Britt is brought in, and the confetti cannon goes off."

"That sounds right. You can check with the party planner, she had this scheduled right down to the minute."

"At nine forty-seven the video starts. You are not seen on camera until after it ends at ten oh-three. Where were you at that time?"

For the first time since he'd come to the police station, Hodgson seemed to falter. He glanced over at Cutter, then down at his hands. He wasn't answering the question.

"Did you go outside again?" Kennicott asked.

Hodgson cast his eyes down. Shook his head. Snuck a look at Cutter.

Cutter nodded, turned to Greene, and pointed at the tape recorder. He brought his finger across his neck, making a cut-it motion.

This was why Cutter had insisted the interview not be videotaped. Greene had anticipated Cutter would do this and told Kennicott in advance to follow his lead. He tapped Kennicott on the shoulder, pointed to the recorder, and Kennicott reached out and turned it off.

Cutter, still pantomiming, pointed to himself, then Greene, then to the door. Greene nodded and stood, as did Cutter. They went into the hallway and Cutter closed the door behind them.

Greene folded his arms across his chest and waited for Cutter to start the conversation.

"Detective, I know you don't trust me as far as you can spit," Cutter said.

Greene kept his arms crossed and started tapping his foot.

"We both know that if Karl walks out now, you don't have enough to arrest him, and you know in your gut that he didn't kill her."

"Then why doesn't he answer the question?"

"He will, but only if you take that recorder off the table."

"Because?"

"Because it's personal. Here's the deal: No recording. No notes. This part of the conversation never happened. Or we walk right now."

Greene kept tapping his foot. It was personal. What could that mean? Then he figured it out. "Lydia?" he said.

"Yeah," Cutter said.

"Tell me," Greene said.

"You'll hear. He was still supporting Melissa."

"Financially, emotionally?"

Cutter put his hands up in the air. "Who are we to judge? The post-man doesn't always ring twice, Ari. You of all people don't want to arrest the wrong man. Do we have a deal?"

"Okay. He needs to answer that last question on tape, then the recorder goes away."

They walked back in. Cutter sat down and whispered in Hodgson's ear. When Hodgson was ready, Greene pointed to the recorder and gave Kennicott a thumbs-up. Kennicott turned the recorder back on.

"No, I didn't go back outside again," Hodgson said. "I stayed inside at my daughter's party."

"Okay, thank you," Greene said. "That concludes this interview."

Kennicott reached over again and turned the recorder off. He handed it to Greene, and Greene put it in his briefcase, along with his notebook. Kennicott threw his notebook in too.

Greene looked back at Hodgson. "Let's hear it," he said.

Hodgson pulled his hood back and took off his baseball cap. "The video about Britt was fifteen minutes and twenty-two seconds long. The room was dark and I slipped outside to talk to Melissa again. There was a spot where we used to sit at night when we first met. Look out over the river and talk about all the great things we wanted to do in our lives. She was sitting there. Crying."

Cutter had bridged his hands and turned his head, looking at Hodgson from the side. Not moving a muscle.

"I sat beside her. I know Melissa better than anyone. When her fury is over, she becomes her old self again. Lydia can never know this, but I've been funnelling money to Mel for years. She's the mother of my daughter. All the times when we were married when she hit me, I never once struck back. I would never have hurt her."

Greene stole a glance at Kennicott. He was watching Hodgson, transfixed.

"We talked. She was still living in the valley and I pleaded with her to leave. Almost everyone else had. She always loved running her fingers through my hair and she started doing it, picking out pieces of confetti. We laughed. She told me that Britt was lucky to have me. She kissed me. I told her I had to get back. We hugged and both cried a little. That's the last time I saw her. I can't believe she's gone."

He stopped.

"You don't want Lydia to know about any of this?" Greene asked him.

"What's the point? People don't understand. Melissa and I had such a good life before she became sick."

For the first time since he'd arrived, Hodgson became animated. Angry.

"She needed help. She didn't need people telling her how noble it was to be homeless. This whole damn support network. All it did was reinforce her illness, give her a built-in excuse to avoid her real problems."

This was the real source of Hodgson's anger at the homeless movement, Greene realized. It was personal. He believed it had betrayed him and the woman he loved.

Hodgson stood, put his baseball cap back on, and flipped his hood back over his head. He turned to Cutter. "I need to go home to see my wife and daughter."

Greene walked them out. Back in the conference room he sat with Kennicott.

"What do you think?" he asked Kennicott.

"Melissa probably put the confetti in the cuff of her pants as a keepsake. What do you think?"

"I think," Greene said, fishing the recorder and the notebooks out of his briefcase, "that Hodgson still wanted to love her, but that he knew it was impossible."

TUESDAY AFTERNOON

46

"**N**ance, have you heard?"

"I'm still in shock."

"It's horrible. Poor Britt. We told her, and she's so upset. Karl is beside himself. We're all shattered."

Parish nodded. She was squeezing her office phone so hard that her fingers hurt. She didn't know what else to say. Lydia had called her, and Parish could hear from her voice that she was crying. It was unlike Lydia to be so emotional, but this was overwhelming.

"Nance, the Three Amigas. We were happy. We loved each other."

"I know," Parish said.

"What happened to us?" Lydia's voice was faint. Parish could hardly hear her.

What had happened to them? They had been young, smart, with the whole world at their feet. Then it all fell apart. Melissa went crazy. Lydia married her friend's husband, and they cut Melissa off from her daughter. That's what happened, Parish thought. But she didn't say it.

"I still don't know," she said.

Really, who was at fault? Karl? For years he'd tried to deal with Melissa's mercurial behaviour. Could he really be blamed for eventually giving up? What about Lydia? Was she to blame for falling in love with him? And how they kept Melissa away from Britt—did they really have any choice, given how erratic she had become?

"I need to see you," Lydia said, her voice stronger now, sounding more the businesslike corporate lawyer Parish knew.

In the background Parish heard a car horn honk. Lydia was talking to someone else: "No don't go that way, turn here."

"Where are you?" Parish asked her.

"In an Uber. I'll be at your office in about five."

Speaking to the driver again, she said, "There, turn at the light."

Then back to talking to Parish: "Almost there. I need to see you."

This was classic Lydia. Emotional one moment, then cool and clinical the next. At the firm, lawyers used to call her "To-Do List Lydia" because she was one of those straightforward people who was always on the go, always eager to put a check mark beside the next task done.

"I'll unlock the front door," Parish said.

She hung up and opened Melissa's book and reread the last page, titled "J'Accuse." It was incredible, wasn't it? Melissa had accused Lydia of murder.

Her reasoning was typically complex and compelling. Was she crazy or was she brilliant?

Melissa argued that with the proliferation of safe injection sites and methadone clinics for drug addicts, the government had created an underclass of people dependent on free drugs. They had no incentive to work or change their lifestyle thanks to all the Good Samaritan types who handed out free sleeping bags, socks, toothbrushes, and the like. Then there were the Law Society lawyers and drop-in centres that gave them free food, and the state shooting them up with free narcotics.

Because the government was more than willing to quietly pay whatever it took to keep the masses stoned and out of sight, the drug companies had stumbled on a gold mine. A guaranteed market with a never-ending supply of return customers, with the taxpayer paying the bill.

Melissa had dug deep into volumes and volumes of the corporate records Lydia's company had filed with the regulators and had discovered that much of their profits were based on the production of methadone for heroin addicts and sterile equipment for safe injection sites. In the last few years, thanks to the burgeoning opioid crisis, they'd created a new income stream by selling the antidote drugs.

The only threat to their unbroken circle of profit was an end to homelessness. Imagine if all these street people were well housed and healthy? And take a closer look at the two people who had been murdered. A doctor and a nurse. Professionals who were helping people get off the needle. They knew what was really going on with these corrupt drug companies and were a threat to expose them.

Lydia was the murderer. She had to eliminate them.

It sounded crazy, Parish thought. Like every bogus conspiracy theorist, Melissa had worked backwards, saying, "Follow the money." Look at the person who benefits from a murder and assume they are responsible. It was the kind of motive-only thinking that leads to "Lyndon Johnson wanted to be president, so he had Jack Kennedy killed."

It couldn't possibly be true, though, could it? A voice in the back of her head whispered to her that Melissa was killed at the golf club while Lydia was there at the party. Think. During the video about Britt, she could have slipped outside and . . .

Parish closed the book, pulled out her bottom desk drawer, and slid it inside. DiPaulo had reminded her that alive or dead, Melissa was still her client. Her instructions to Parish from the grave were clear: prove that Lydia is the killer. And implicitly now, prove that Lydia killed me.

Parish took her cell phone, pushed the record button, and popped it in her pocket.

She walked down the hallway toward the front door, a cascade of emotions coursing through her. Anger, confusion, betrayal.

She opened the front door and Lydia stood there. Her eyes blotchy.

"Nance," she said.

"Lyd."

Lydia fell into her arms, heaving.

47

"This is my mom's photo album. Here she is with my grandmother when they first came to Canada from Holland. This is her high school graduation picture. This was her favourite wedding picture, then there are a bunch with her and me when I was a baby."

Gina Frankel was seated in the window seat, in the ground-floor living room of her well-appointed home. Her two-month-old baby girl was bundled up in a tiny Hudson Bay blanket and tucked in beside her.

"And this picture is when . . ."

She stopped. Shook her head. Closed the album and caressed her baby's cheek.

"I'm sorry," she said. "This is really hard for me."

"There's no need to apologize," Alison said. She signalled to Krevolin to put down his camera. She walked up to Frankel and knelt down to be at her eye level. "We can stop at any time."

"I want to do this," Frankel said.

"You're brave."

"Am I?" She flipped back to the photo of her mother and her grandmother. "Or is it that now that I have a baby, I don't want to end up like my mom?"

Alison grasped her hand. When she'd realized that it would be impossible to get a homeless woman to go on camera, she came up with this idea of doing a story about the families who got left behind when one of their members ended up on the street. She wanted to show this unseen side of homelessness and the enduring pain it caused. Persaud loved the idea and gave her the go-ahead right away.

Alison had called Frankel and explained what she wanted to do, and she agreed to go on camera on the condition that they not use her name or her mother's. Alison and Krevolin had rushed over to her home and started filming.

Frankel let go of Alison's hand. "I'm ready. This is important for me. For my daughter."

Alison went back behind the camera. She'd placed herself there because she didn't want to be on screen for the interview. Persaud had suggested that she be an unseen voice asking questions so that all the attention would be on Frankel.

"We're filming again," she said. "Gina, are there many supports out there for your mother?"

Frankel snapped the photo album closed. She looked right at the camera. Her whole demeanour changed. To Alison's surprise, she was angry.

"Supports? There's a whole business built around so-called home-less people." She spit out the word *homeless* as if it were a swear word. She was not trying to hide her bitterness. "People like my mother get everything for free. Social workers, drug counsellors, doctors, thera-pists. All the food she can eat. She's classified disabled now, so she gets a cheque at the beginning of every month."

Alison looked at Krevolin. She saw him zoom in on Frankel's face. The dam had burst. Frankel was putting her pain and grief and frustra-tion on full display.

"Don't forget the free narcotics," she said, rubbing her hands across the top of the photo album. "How about the do-gooders who give out sleeping bags and hot coffee? Great, so my mom can live on the street without any responsibility. And who helps me out? Or my dad? Or my husband and our baby?"

"What supports are there for you and your family?" Alison asked.

Frankel shook her head. Clenched her jaw tight.

"You must be kidding. They came to interview us. Once. I could see it in their eyes. We must be to blame for my mother abandoning us. I must have been a bad daughter, Daddy a bad husband."

"How does that make you feel?" Alison asked. It was an obvious question but she needed to stay in the interview.

"Like no one really cares. There's no money for real help for my mother or for us. No real family counselling. Why should we get any assistance? We just get up every morning, go to work, obey the law, pay our taxes."

Alison had learned that once you got the key parts of an interview, it was best to wrap things up. She asked a few more questions and finished.

"One last request," Alison said. "Could we take some close-ups of the pictures in the photo album?"

Alison knew that Persaud would want them. They would make ideal cutaway shots.

Frankel hesitated.

"We'll blur out the faces," Alison said.

Frankel picked up the photo album, and Alison thought she was going to agree. Instead she clutched it across her chest with both hands.

"I can't," she said. Then, in a whisper so soft that Alison had to strain to hear her, "What if one day Mom does get better and comes home? I don't want her to think that I betrayed her."

48

Although Toronto lies on the shores of Lake Ontario, during the city's postwar building boom, civic politicians did everything they could to ignore the waterfront and to keep it from view of the local populace. The most egregious example of this was the Gardiner Expressway, named after Fredrick C. Gardiner, a highway-obsessed 1950s alderman. "The Gardiner," as it came to be known, is a mammoth raised highway that for decades has acted as a barrier to the lake.

The nadir of this ignore-the-waterfront trend came in the late 1990s when fly-by-night builders threw up a pair of Stalin-era-like concrete condominiums on the narrow strip of land between the Gardiner and the lake. This happened in the era when there was a gradual awakening to the notion that cities did not have to be only about cars. At the same time, the 1950s highway started to crumble. Since then, seemingly endless debates have raged about the raised road: an eyesore to most downtowners, a transit lifeline for most suburbanites. Ideas were tossed around ranging from burying the damn thing to ripping it out to simply leaving it alone.

In the end, a small part was torn down, most of it stayed, and massive development sprang up on both sides: glass towers and a regenerating waterfront with widened sidewalks, outdoor cafés, and extensive bike and jogging paths.

The lakeshore was Angela Breaker's favourite running route. Kennicott ran with her whenever he could. She preferred to head east, where the shoreline was underdeveloped and wilder, but today he'd persuaded her to run west, over to the Humber River. He wanted to take another look at the crime scenes.

They hit the crowded path at the foot of Spadina Avenue, near the spot where starving Irish immigrants had once landed, and today small jets arrived at the Island Airport. They ran along, sailboats to one side, the city's iconic fairgrounds, the CNE, on the other. As they headed farther, the path hugged the lake, and the air was fresh. Kennicott began to hit his stride.

"It's beautiful down here," he said.

Angela tapped him on the shoulder and pointed ahead to a modern-looking white pedestrian bridge. "There's the Humber. The running path's on the west side."

He nodded and kept going. Angela was fast, and he didn't want to waste his breath. She'd taught him a new running technique, to lift his foot high over his knee and create a circle so that when his foot landed it was propelling him forward.

"Most people run in a teardrop shape," she'd explained to him. "It's called heel strike. It slows you down and causes injury."

He'd tried it. It felt awkward at first but he was getting used to it.

"Remember Jose Reyes, the baseball player who used to play for the Jays," she told him. "He learned this growing up in the Dominican Republic by running downhill."

They'd gone on YouTube together and watched highlights from his career. Reyes was what the commentators called "sneaky fast." Angela said it was because of his stride.

The bridge was packed with families and kids in strollers, bike riders, and joggers. They dodged their way through the crowd, cut down to the path below and headed north.

The trees and underbrush on the side of the river were thick. They kept running, the sounds and the feel of the city falling away. Except for the occasional kayaker paddling on the water, they were in near-complete wilderness. It was remarkable, how quickly they'd gone from the noise of the city to near-total silence, the only sound the slap of their feet on the path, the huffing of their breath. Well, his breath. Angela didn't even seem to be breaking a sweat.

They came to a short, steep part of the path. Angela scampered up it. Kennicott didn't even try to keep pace with her. She waited for him at the top. There was a clearing where someone had made a bench out of cut logs.

"This is a good lookout spot," she said, not showing the least sign of fatigue. Kennicott was inhaling hard to try to lower his heart rate.

He was grateful to sit. Angela kept standing and stretched. She carried a few small water bottles in a special belt around her waist. She took one out, shot some water into her mouth, then squirted some on Kennicott. It was one of their fun rituals, which dated back to the first time they'd run together before they became involved.

"Hey," he said. "Don't waste it."

"Then open up."

He opened his mouth, and she squirted some water into it. It was warm but he was thirsty and it tasted good.

"There's the golf club," she said, pointing across the river. "Down below is the homeless encampment. Every time I run by, it seems that there are different homemade tents. But no one has ever hassled me."

"I don't think anyone's left there," he said.

The path turned steep heading down. Kennicott focussed on his Jose Reyes technique. It seemed to work: he was keeping up with Angela.

They hit the bottom and started alongside the river. There was scattered debris in the woods, some plastic sheeting that had once been makeshift tents, a few burnt-out fire pits.

"No one's home," a man's voice said, as they rounded the bend.

Angela pulled up to a stop, and so did Kennicott.

A man stood beside the path leaning on a long stick. He was dressed in old clothes but didn't look malnourished. He seemed calm. Kennicott thought he looked vaguely familiar.

"Good morning, Detective Kennicott," he said.

"Do I know you?" Kennicott asked him.

"Fraser Dent. A friend of Detective Greene. You might recall I helped him out when you charged him with murder."

Now Kennicott remembered. Greene had told Kennicott the man's tragic life story and how from time to time Dent was Greene's eyes and ears on the street. He'd been in court on the last day of the trial, but had been much better dressed.

"Hello, Mr. Dent. This is my girlfriend, Angela Breaker. She's the real runner in the family."

"Nice to meet you, ma'am," Dent said politely. "Detective, you here for another look around?"

"It never hurts. Angela knows this running path. I got her to forgo her usual morning run, get into work early, and run with me over her lunchtime."

"There's not much left to see," Dent said. "But if you're looking for a place to build a home, with the price of housing so high in the city, you might want to buy a lot here. It's a prime location. Any day now the real estate agents are going to name this place 'Humber West Village by the Water.'"

He laughed a deep hearty chuckle and started walking down the path with them.

"Why don't you give us a guided tour?" Kennicott said, playing along.

As they strolled together, Dent pointed his stick up the valley at an orange plastic sheet that was strung between two trees. A few dirty-looking sleeping bags lay discarded underneath. There was an open fire pit with cans of food littered all around.

"This two-bedroom beauty features an all-purpose kitchen, a sunken family room, and central air conditioning," Dent said.

"Don't forget the riverside view," Angela said, joining in.

"A great feature. And how about that one?" Dent aimed his stick at a lean-to made from pieces of plywood nailed haphazardly together. The ground below it was littered with newspapers and garbage. "An architectural gem. Great views of the golf course across the river. This modern-design beauty is perfect for a young couple like you two."

They all laughed.

As they kept walking, the hovels on the hillside looked more and more decrepit. One was made out of cardboard. Someone had dug out some earth and had been living in a small cave. But everything had been abandoned. There wasn't a soul around.

Dent pointed his stick at a rock face that was filled with graffiti. "Humber West even has a local art gallery," he said.

"True," Kennicott said. "But no people."

"You can blame your friend Detective Greene for that. He got me to shoo everyone out of here," Dent said, lifting his big stick and swinging it as if it were a baseball bat. "I'm leaving too. Everyone's headed to the Don River Valley, and no one's coming back here until you guys catch this killer."

49

Toronto Police Headquarters was a classic 1980s-style, heavy-on-concrete building, featuring a spacious plant-filled atrium soaring up ten stories, three banks of glassed-in elevators, and lots and lots of pink granite covering the walls and the floors. Street cops referred to it as either the Pink Palace or the Pink Whorehouse, depending on their point of view. Already, it looked dated compared to the sleek, glass-fronted condos and office buildings sprouting up all over the city.

Parish had only been here once before, a few years ago when she'd surrendered a client who was on the run and wanted for the murder of a young boy hit by a stray bullet. It was early in the morning. After she brought him in, she'd gone to the basement cafeteria and ordered a chocolate croissant and a large coffee. She'd just taken a bite out of the croissant and the chocolate had oozed out of the end and smeared across her cheek, when she met Detective Greene for the first time.

She couldn't talk. Nor could she shake his hand because some of the chocolate had also dripped onto her fingers. With someone else it might have been embarrassing, but Greene was quiet and considerate and had a twinkle in his eye. She swallowed hard, drank some of the very hot coffee, and used two napkins to wipe off her fingers and her cheek before she shook his hand.

It was comic, and they laughed about it once they got to know each other, but there was nothing to smile about this morning. One of the elevators opened and Greene walked out and headed toward Parish.

"Saying 'I'm sorry for your loss' is trite," he said. "This is terrible for you."

She closed her eyes and nodded.

"I'm not going to ask you, 'How are you doing?'"

"Thanks." She shook her head. "I was shocked when Detective Kennicott told me Melissa was your source."

"She talked about you all the time," Greene said. "'If it wasn't for Nance,' she used to say, 'I'd be a goner.'"

Parish shook her head. "My friend Zelda said Melissa was my black hole. That she would suck me dry. That I had to stop trying to save her."

Greene looked straight at her. Unwavering. His eyes were warm. Bluish-green eyes with flecks of yellow in them.

"You had to try," he said. "There are some people we'll never be able to reach. Letting go is the hardest part."

"It's going to take a long time," she said. "We need to talk in private. I have something important to show you."

"Follow me." They took one of the elevators up to the fifth floor, past the smiling woman at the homicide squad reception desk, to Greene's office overlooking College Street. He led her to a round table away from his desk.

As Parish reached into her briefcase and pulled out Melissa's book, she told him how she'd found it in the bag of clothes Melissa had left in her office.

Greene was close with his emotions, but he looked upset when he saw the cover of the diary. He read it slowly, page by page. Parish watched him, not saying a word.

It took him about twenty minutes. When he got to the last page, titled "J'Accuse," he looked up at Parish. Then he finished the diary and closed it.

"Has anyone else seen this?" he asked.

"No one. What do you think?"

"About her treatise on homelessness, or her accusation that Lydia is the killer?"

"Both."

"Your friend was an excellent lawyer," Greene said. "She made a convincing argument about the homelessness situation in the city."

"And Lydia the murderer? What did you think about her theory about that, Detective?"

"You know the history between them better than I do."

Parish felt sad. "I can't believe Lydia would kill anyone," she said. "Or that she'd ever hurt Melissa. I pray I'm right."

Greene didn't react. Parish knew that this was the way homicide detectives worked. They never played their cards until they were ready. "Every homicide investigation is a process of elimination," he said. "We start from the inside and work out."

"Meaning?"

"Meaning, always begin with the family. Sometimes that's painful."

He hadn't answered her question. It was too horrible to even contemplate, Lydia killing Melissa and the other two people.

"I need to keep this for a while," he said, putting his hand over Melissa's book. "What else can you tell me?"

"Lydia came to my office this morning. She wanted to talk. She's totally broken up about this. I'd just read Melissa's diary, so before she arrived, I clicked on the record function on my cell phone. I put it in my pocket so she wouldn't see it."

This got Greene's attention.

"You recorded your conversation?"

She shook her head. "When I saw her, we both started to cry, and I felt so guilty I turned it off."

Greene kept his eyes on her. He seemed to understand. "What did you two talk about?"

"We reminisced about the great times the three of us had together. How hard we worked all those crazy years at the law firm. How close we were. I didn't have the heart to tell her about Melissa's accusations."

"How long was she there?"

"About half an hour. There's this goofy handclapping game called

'I'm a Little Dutch Girl' that she used to play with Melissa when they were kids. They taught it to me when I met them. Before she left, we played the game. It was kind of our own way of remembering her."

Greene sat back. He opened Melissa's book again to the "J'Accuse" page and started rereading it.

Parish inhaled deeply. Relax, she told herself. Greene is thorough.

"I have something to ask you," he said.

"Anything." She had no idea what was coming.

"When is the next time you're going to see Lydia?"

"This afternoon. We're going to have a late lunch at three o'clock at an old diner where we used to go for comfort food."

Greene looked up at her. "Would you wear a wire?"

Parish hadn't expected this. She didn't know what to say.

"Melissa's still your client," Greene said. "If Lydia really is the killer . . ."

"I know," Parish said.

"If you decide to do this, Detective Kennicott can wire you up," Greene said. "Take your time. I'm fine with any decision you make."

"Thanks for that," she said, standing to leave. He stood and opened his office door for her before walking her to the elevator. There was something rather old-world about Greene that in someone else might be annoying. But she'd seen he was equally polite with men and women. In a strange way it was reassuring. And persuasive.

He insisted on riding down in the elevator with her and walking her to the front door. He gave her his business card and wrote out his personal cell number on back and told her to call him any time, night or day. By the time she shook his hand to say goodbye, it was unspoken, but they both knew what she was going to do.

50

"Good afternoon, Ms. Dennison," Alison said, as she sat across from her at the drop-in centre. The homeless woman was sitting in the same chair at the same table, writing away in her diary in her tiny script. She peered up toward Alison, looking past her, avoiding eye contact.

Alison had learned much about this mysterious woman. Her full name was Rachel Dennison. Until two years earlier, she'd been the executive assistant to the CEO of a large company. Her husband worked as an installer for Bell, and they had a daughter named Gina who worked at a bank. Life seemed perfectly normal until one weekend when Dennison went missing. Then it was for ten days, then two months, and now she was homeless.

"Did you talk to my husband?" Dennison asked.

"I tried. He didn't return my call."

Dennison's lips curled up in anger. "He's too busy fucking that whore of a girlfriend of his."

She started writing again. The movement of her hand was swift, precise.

Alison waited until she stopped before she spoke again: "I talked to your daughter."

Dennison gave out a loud harrumph. She turned a page. She still had not made eye contact. "What did Gina say about her crazy mother?"

"She said that she wished you'd get better and come and see your granddaughter."

Dennison put her pen down, whipped her head up, and stared straight at Alison. "She's furious at me, isn't she?"

Alison met her eyes. After the interview with Gina she'd talked to her Grandpa Y. Ever since she'd become a full-time journalist, Alison would chat with him about the stories she was working on. It amazed her how much he understood about people and how they think. She'd told him about the now-homeless woman and her daughter, Gina.

"What did she tell you about her mother?" he'd asked.

"That her mum had worked for years as an assistant to a top executive. She was super organized and efficient. They don't even know why she started to disappear."

"What did her father do?"

"She said at first he would cover up for her. Tell friends she was away at a conference. When she'd come back home, Gina would hear them at night having horrible fights in their bedroom. Her dad would plead with her mom to see a therapist. She'd threaten to leave and never come back if he made her go."

"What happened next?"

"Gina's dad spent more money than he could afford on treatment."

"Did it work?"

"For a while, Gina said, things were almost normal, then a week before her wedding, her mother disappeared again, and since then she's dropped in and out of her daughter's life, never showing up for more than a few days. Her dad has a new girlfriend and wants nothing to do with her. Gina just had a baby, and her mum hasn't seen her. Gina's so angry at her."

"Understand, my dear," Grandpa Y had said, "in life we save our greatest anger for the people we love the most."

Dennison stopped writing. Her dark eyes bore in on Alison. If she was going to gain this woman's confidence, Alison knew she had to be honest.

"Yes. Gina is very angry with you. She had the baby without her mother to help her. And you've never even seen Hunter, her daughter. Your only grandchild."

Dennison kept staring. Then ever so slowly, she began to nod.

"She truly cares about you and wants to see you," Alison said. She felt as if she were pleading. "Your daughter misses you so very much."

"It's terrible," Dennison whispered.

"What's terrible?" Alison asked.

"That she has me as her mother."

"No, no. Don't you understand? Gina's only angry because she cares so much about you."

Dennison picked up her pen. She covered her notebook so Alison couldn't see. She wrote for a few minutes without pausing, and then stopped.

"You're young, and you sound British," she said to Alison without looking up. "Where does your mother live?"

"My mother is dead. I live here with my father."

Dennison started writing again before she looked up.

"Is that why you want to do a story about us?" Dennison swept her hand out across the room. Her face red. Her voice nasty. "We lost and abandoned women? Do you think you can save any of us? So you can have a feel-good story on TV of you reuniting us with our families?"

This must have been what it was like for Gina and her father, Alison thought. These sudden mood swings. This flash of fury from out of the blue. Her attack on their character.

But maybe Dennison was right. Why was Alison so determined to do a story about women and poverty in this city? About women who abandoned their families to live on the street, and the families they left behind? What was she really doing? Rebelling against her father? Filling the void left by her mother's death? Working out her anger at her mother for leaving her? Trying to find answers to questions that couldn't be answered?

She pushed back her chair and stood. "Thank you for your time," she said. "I won't bother you anymore."

If she was expecting Dennison to object or to try to stop her from leaving or to magically say, "Yes, yes, I want to see Gina and my grand-daughter," Alison was sorely mistaken. Instead, Dennison curled back into her notebook, her head even farther down than before, writing furiously.

Alison walked carefully through the tables of silent, homeless women, making herself not rush. None of these women wanted anything to do with her. What was she thinking?

She pushed her way through the heavy front door. There was the stench of urine on the sidewalk. The wind whipped down Adelaide Street, sending a chill right through her as she buttoned up the top two buttons of her overcoat. The low November sky was dark and foreboding.

51

This was the last thing Parish wanted to do. The very, very last thing. But she was doing this for Melissa. Wasn't she? Following Melissa's paranoid fantasy that Lydia was a killer. Parish was sure she would prove Melissa wrong. But what if? What if?

She was talking to herself as she walked over to the George Street Diner, a classic diner that the Three Amigas used to go to once a month when they needed some good home cooking. They hadn't been here for a long time. Whenever she and Lydia had met in the last few years—and it happened less and less often—Lydia always wanted to go to the newest, trendiest, most expensive restaurants.

Parish's coat wasn't warm enough. This happened every November, when the temperatures dropped and she was still in denial that winter was coming. The tape that held the recorder to her chest felt itchy as she walked. Be sure not to scratch yourself, Kennicott had warned her. He was in a van around the corner with a technician and would be listening in. She checked her watch. It was a few minutes after three. Lydia was always late, so she wasn't worried.

At the door of the diner she saw there was still a lineup inside. Cold weather, people wanted comfort food. Damn, she should have got here earlier to get one of the booths by the window.

"Well, would you take a good long look at whom the cat dragged in," she heard a familiar voice say before she saw Ash, the spirited Irishwoman who owned and ran the diner. She grabbed Parish's sleeve. "Your *amiga* is already here. She got here half an hour ago to get a booth," Ash said.

Lydia never got anywhere early.

Ash tugged Parish through the crowd. The diner was long and narrow, with the kitchen counter on the left and red-cushioned booths on the right along the sunny south-side wall. Lydia was in the last booth, not on her cell phone, not looking at her laptop, not checking her watch. Waiting quietly. That was another first.

"I'm so sorry about your Melissa," Ash said in her warm Irish accent. "She'd come by here when times were rough, and we'd feed her."

"You did?" Parish said. All these things she was learning about Melissa's life. Now that it was too late.

"Family. You never give up on family."

Lydia stood and Ash looped her arms around both of them for a group hug. "Now the Three Amigas will be the Dynamic Duo, right?" Ash said.

"Nance, thanks so much," Lydia said, when they sat back down alone.

"We've been friends for . . ."

"Sixteen years," Lydia said. "And you know what all this has made me realize?"

Lydia teared up and brought her hands across the table. Parish held them.

"All those rich people who wanted to chummy up to us once Karl won the trial and got elected. They all think he's going to be the next mayor. Guess how many of them have called?"

She formed her forefinger and thumb into a circle. "Great big zero. But you, even though I've been such a lousy friend for the last few years—"

"You haven't been, Lydia. Our lives have changed—"

"Not true. I have been terrible. And who is the only person I can talk to? You."

Yes, me, Parish thought. Trying to trap you and get you arrested for murder. Some friend she was being. She could feel herself start to sweat. The stupid tape was itchier and itchier.

"It shouldn't have taken Melissa being killed to wake me up," Lydia said, still holding Parish's hand. "I'm not asking you to forgive me or believe me. Please give me a chance to show you how important you are as my friend."

She let go of Parish's hand.

What was she doing here? Parish asked herself. She picked up a menu from the metal holder by the window. "Why don't we start," she said, "by having some food?"

52

Just as the Humber River ran through the west side of the city down to the lake, the Don River did the same thing on the east side. Although over the years politicians had tried to make hay with campaigns to "Clean Up the Don," it remained a vast, wild, and overgrown river valley right in the middle of the city. And an ideal place for the homeless to camp out or hide. Greene had gone down into the valley many times.

From the west end of the Danforth Bridge, he took the narrow path that led to the river far below. The footing was slippery. There were still remnants of the snow and ice from the recent storm. He picked his way down until he was about halfway and arrived at a long, flat plateau. Someone had built a bench out of wooden branches in the middle of it, and for years Greene and Dent had met at this spot. Dent must have come up from wherever he was staying in the valley, because he was sitting there waiting. He stood when he saw Greene.

Not a man for greetings or introductions—a holdover, Greene thought, from his years as an overseas bond trader handling calls and people and money for fourteen-hour days—Dent never bothered to say hello. Or goodbye.

They shook hands. Greene had a fifty-dollar bill in his palm, and Dent pocketed it. The preliminaries over, it was time to get down to business. Greene reached into his pocket and gave him a handful of Tim Horton cards.

"Give her these too," he said. "Tell Daphne that they're from her dad."

Dent slid them in his pant pocket. "She's a survivor, I'll tell you that," he said.

"You got her to talk to you?"

"No problem."

Dent might have lived on the street for about ten years now, but it hadn't destroyed his self-confidence or his bravado.

"She in danger?" Greene asked, as they sat down together.

"Come on, Detective. Everyone who lives on the street is in danger. Especially the women."

Dent picked up a long, thick branch from the ground. In one swift motion, he broke it in half over his thigh and passed the thinner piece to Greene. He smacked his stick into Greene's, making a loud bang.

"There, now we're armed with a weapon that's not outlawed in the criminal code," Dent said.

Greene pointed to the far end of the plateau. "She living down there?"

"Made herself a plush mansion of plastic sheeting and old newspapers. You'd never find her. The valley goes on for miles. There are so many paths and hiding places that if you know your way around down there, you could get yourself lost for months, no problem."

"Can I tell her dad that she's left the Humber Valley completely?"

"Everyone's left the Humber. Even the stubborn old goats. It's one thing being homeless, it's another getting killed."

"She knows you're working for me?"

"Took her about ten minutes to figure it out."

"She didn't run away?"

"She said, 'Tell Ari I need a tent.' A tent can be the difference between life and death down here. It's only November, and it's snowed already."

As if on cue, a gust of chilling wind whistled through the valley. People who lived in southern climates imagined that January and February were the worst months in Canada. But for Greene it was November. The days getting shorter, the light disappearing behind deep clouds, and that first taste of the cold when your blood has not thickened and your mind is still filled with summer memories.

"I'll get a tent, and you can give it to her tomorrow."

"She's got the gift of the gab, likes to crack jokes. She's got a theory of what's behind the killings. I'm sure you've already heard a bunch."

"We put up a tip line, and we're getting flooded with calls."

Dent was right. Everyone had a theory: the killer was a deranged mental health patient who had been out on a day pass from the facility where he was housed and had never come back; the killers were a Chinese gang who wanted to harvest organs from the homeless; the killer was the abandoned child of a homeless woman who had died mysteriously and now was exacting revenge; no one had really been killed and this was all a conspiracy by the newspapers to boost their circulation.

That was the problem with tip lines. The public and the politicians yelled and screamed for the police to set them up, without realizing the enormous amount of manpower needed to chase down each and every lead. If buried in this morass there happened to be one useful tip that was not fully investigated, the police would be accused of negligence. The net effect of it all was valuable time and energy was wasted.

"At least sixty calls a day. Not one of them from a homeless person."

"She says you should look at the type of people who are being knocked off."

"What does she mean, 'type of people'?"

"I told you. The Hospital Ward. A doctor. A nurse. Maybe they had information that someone wanted to keep secret."

Dent stood. Pointed his wooden club at the downtown towers where he used to work. "I was born in this town, Detective. Toronto used to be an easy, soft place to live, but not anymore. It's become a tough, hard city. You make it, or it breaks you."

He slung his club over his shoulder, Robin Hood style. "Meet you here tomorrow. Don't forget the tent, and make it a two-person tent," he said with a smirk.

Before Greene could even say thanks, Dent had disappeared over the edge.

53

"Nance, this is great. It's still so delicious."

They had both ordered the diner's classic all-day Irish breakfast. Two eggs, Irish sourdough bread, sausage, fried tomatoes, and baked beans.

"Every once in a while you need some comfort food," Parish said, feeling more and more uncomfortable by the minute.

Lydia soaked up the remaining sauce from her beans with a corner of her piece of bread, then looked around. Parish could see she was checking to confirm that no one could hear them.

"Can I tell you a secret?" she said, leaning over the table, half whispering.

"Sure," Parish said, thinking, Oh no, what's she going to say?

Lydia chuckled. "I'll buy you lunch, then this will be solicitor-client privilege."

"Don't be silly, we'll go Dutch."

"Little Dutch Girls, but no, I'm buying. I already gave Ash my credit card. You get it next time."

This was turning into a disaster, Parish thought. Lydia was going to ask her to be her lawyer. She could practically hear Ted DiPaulo screaming in her ear, "Nance, conflict of interest!" She couldn't represent Lydia and Melissa. But there was no way now to stop Lydia from talking.

"You won't believe it," Lydia said. "Mel thought I killed those two poor homeless people in the valley."

"She did?" Parish said, trying to act surprised. "Ridiculous." Parish felt utterly disingenuous. "How do you know this?"

"How?" Lydia dug into her purse and pulled out her cell phone. "She was texting me like crazy for days."

"She was?"

"If I'd wanted to breach her bail for contacting me, I could have done it a thousand times."

Lydia kept talking while she showed Parish her phone.

"When the first homeless person, a man, was killed, she scanned a little article in the *Sun* and sent it to me. Look what she wrote."

Parish read it out loud. " 'Good work, you murderer.' Oh my. What did you do?" She was terrified to think what Lydia would say next.

But Lydia laughed. "What do you mean, what did I do? I wrote her back right away. Nance, you don't know. She's been accusing me of everything under the sun for years. Here, look."

Parish kept reading. " 'Mel. I'm in Miami at a conference. This is tragic. Take care.' Were you?" she asked.

"Was I what?"

"In Miami."

Lydia looked at Parish, taken aback. "Yes, I was in Miami. What do you think? I'm a murderer?"

She took back the phone and scrolled down to another text.

"Mel became so crazy," Lydia said. "Listen to what she wrote me when the nurse was killed. 'I know you were home and murdered Nurse Deb. All to save your failing company. Who's next?' Unreal, isn't it? Here, look."

She turned her phone for Parish to read again. Parish did her best to act shocked.

"The funny thing is that I was supposed to come home Sunday," Lydia said. "But there was that freak snowstorm that closed the airport. We got rerouted to Buffalo. I had to get up early Monday morning and rent a car to get back home to get things ready for the party. I didn't get back until after lunch, and you wouldn't believe how much I still had to do with the party planner. I think that Mel somehow got into my calendar. She can do anything with a computer."

Let's hope this tape recorder is working, Parish said to herself as she handed back the phone to Lydia. "I'm sorry you had to go through all this."

"I haven't told Karl about any of this. He's got enough on his plate. There's one more thing he doesn't know. Promise me, you can't tell anyone, okay?"

"Solicitor-client," Parish said. What had she gotten herself into?

"The night of the party, when they played Karl's over-the-top video about Britt?"

"I had too much to drink to remember most of the night," Parish said, trying to make a joke, "but that was memorable."

"Well,"—Lydia looked around the restaurant again to make sure they were not being overheard—"I got the party planner to get me a food package from the kitchen, and I snuck outside. There's a door in back of the stage."

"Lyd, what are you saying? Mel was killed out there."

"I know, Nance, I know. That's why I'm only telling you. If anyone found out, it would look bad."

"Yes, it would."

"I had to bring food out to Rachel. She was in a total panic."

"Rachel?"

"Don't you remember Rachel? She was my dad's executive assistant, who used to bring us those care packages of pills when we did those killer overnight closings at the law firm."

"Oh, I remember her."

"Didn't you see it last night on TV? It was all over the news. Her daughter was talking about her homeless mother, and how she'd left the family to live on the street. That was her."

"Rachel? She was such a kind person. What happened?"

"No one really knows. One day she was at work, the next day she disappeared. My poor dad, she did everything for him. She's been living on the street off and on for two years now. Heartbreaking for her daughter, Gina, who just had a baby."

Parish felt sick to her stomach.

"You wouldn't recognize her," Lydia said. "She's skinny as a rail. She's too embarrassed to talk to my dad, so she keeps in touch with me, like a shadow, slipping in and out of my life. I don't give her money anymore, but I give her food. She saw the interview on TV and was hysterical."

"I had no idea."

"She's begged me not to tell people. She's too proud. It's like when she worked for dad: she keeps a notebook and records everything I give her. She keeps promising me that she'll get help so she can pay me back one day."

"It's so sad," Parish said, barely getting the words out. "I have to hit the loo."

She scrambled out of her seat and practically fell on her face navigating the long, narrow staircase leading downstairs. The diner only had one washroom and thankfully it was empty and no one was around. She rushed in, locked the flimsy door behind her. Her hands were shaking as she tried to unbutton her shirt. She got enough undone so she could reach inside and rip the tape off her chest. It hurt like hell, but she didn't care.

She thought she was going to vomit. She ran the cold water and splashed her face, then took out her cell phone and called Kennicott.

"Ms. Parish," he said, picking up on the first ring. "I couldn't quite hear everything that—"

"Call off your damn dogs," she said, hearing her voice rising. She clutched the recorder in her hand. She wanted to smash it to pieces on the porcelain sink. Or flush the thing down the toilet. "Lydia is innocent!"

Parish was screaming.

"Completely and utterly innocent. Melissa was insane. Lydia has a total alibi. I have it all on tape."

WEDNESDAY MORNING

54

"**D**etective Greene, I'm glad to see that you are up early."

"I guess that makes two of us," he said to Dr. Ramos, who'd just called him at the office. "What can I do for you?"

"Your forensic officer, Detective Ho," she said. "The gentleman is quite a character, but he is also very thorough."

Her accent sounded even more charming on the phone, Greene thought.

"I've been told you are thorough as well," he replied.

"There is something important for you to look at. Can you come over?"

"Urgent?"

"I believe you will want to see this as soon as possible. I will give you my cell number," she said. "Please give me yours and text me when you are around the corner so I can come down in the lobby to meet you. This will save you having to go through our friendly security desk."

Perhaps it was her accent, but her sarcasm made him laugh.

"Are your referring to that friendly young man at reception?"

"Friendly with his phone, you mean," she said, laughing back.

They exchanged numbers. "I'll leave in five," he said.

"It will be good to see you again," she said.

Did she mean this professionally? Or personally? Was asking for him to call just a way to get his phone number? Or was she being efficient? Most likely he was imagining things. Wasn't he?

Instead of leaving right away, he slipped into the bathroom and looked at himself in the mirror. He loosened his tie and slipped it over his head. He took off his jacket. Did that look better, or too informal? He put the tie back on and pulled it halfway down. Too casual? He looked ridiculous. He felt foolish. Enough of this. He settled on wearing the jacket, his shirt with the top button unbuttoned, and no tie.

Ramos met him in the lobby. She was wearing high leather boots, a black-and-red patterned fitted skirt, and a stylish silk blouse. Her black hair was tied back in a simple red hair band. It was a good thing that he'd ditched the tie and undone his shirt, Greene thought.

She gave him a warm handshake and brushed his shoulder with her other hand. "Let's go to the lab," she said. "I've already signed you in."

The surly kid behind the glass got off his phone long enough to press whatever buzzer he needed to push to let them in the main door.

In the lab she directed him to a long desk. There was a large microscope in the middle of it, and beside it were three piles of shattered glass, on separate white sheets. Above each there was a typewritten label: VICTIM 1, VICTIM 2, and VICTIM 3. On the other side of the microscope there was the handheld vacuum cleaner that Greene recognized as one of Detective Ho's favourite pieces of equipment.

She put her hand on it. "I'd never seen one of these before. Detective Ho swept up every bit of the glass at each crime scene. I examined them all under the microscope." She pointed to the VICTIM 1 pile. "All of the glass was consistent with the vodka bottle. Same for victim two."

"Yes," Greene said, looking at the VICTIM 3 pile. Copeland's pile. What had Ramos found?

She directed him to the microscope. "Take a look. Use this knob to focus."

He kept adjusting it until the image of the glass became clear. It was a small piece with a nearly invisible line running through it.

"What am I looking at?" he asked.

"Glass found on the ground near victim three's body. Do you see the line?"

"Barely. What is it?"

"It is not glass from a vodka bottle. Quite subtle, but the glass is from corrective lenses."

Greene pulled his head back.

"Eyeglasses?"

"Yes." She pointed to a small pile of broken pieces of glass beside the larger one. He hadn't noticed it before. "There are seven other fragments that I separated from the vodka bottle pieces. Not enough to make up a whole lens."

"The killer could have been wearing glasses and they broke in the fight with victim three," he said. "The killer picked up some of the pieces but Ho was able to sweep up what was still there."

"You have to do the detecting, Detective," she said, smiling at her own little joke. "I am only the scientist."

They looked at each other.

"Another thing," she said, breaking the silence.

"Victim one had a dangerously low platelets level."

"I read your report. He was close to death."

"Victim two, she was filled with cancer."

"Close to death as well?"

"Extremely."

"Coincidence?"

"That's for you to decide. But here's the point. Victim three was very healthy."

This was something new.

"One more thing," she said, walking across the room. "I've been trying to come up with some ideas of what the weapon could have been to cause this blunt force trauma. Come to my desk."

She'd laid out three photographs side by side. Each one had been labelled with the victim's name.

"These are close-ups of the back of the heads of all three victims."

Greene took his time studying them. They were hard to read.

Before he could say a word, she leaned over the desk and with a thin red marker drew a line on the outside edge of the wound of the first victim.

"See this shape," she said.

Greene nodded. He looked up at her but she was concentrating on drawing on the second photo.

"And this one," she said.

"Yes."

"And the third," she said, as she drew on the last photo.

Greene picked up the photos one at a time to get a closer look, an idea forming in his mind. "They're all the exact same shape."

55

" **I** have something to tell you," Alison said, as she lay back on the pillow in her bed.

Burns propped himself up on one arm and looked at her.

"I'm all ears," he said. Grinning.

"I should have told you this before, but, well, you need to know who my father is."

"Your father?" he said, showing no emotion.

"He's Detective Ari Greene. The head of the homicide squad."

Burns didn't flinch.

"You've been leading protests outside his office, claiming the police aren't trying to solve these cases."

"I know," he said, so calm she found it annoying. Didn't he get it?

"You know what?"

"I know he's your father."

"How the hell?" Now she was angry.

"It wasn't hard to figure out. For one, you both spell your last name with an *e* on the end. I've seen him on TV. You have his eyes." He reached out to tap her on the nose. She swatted his hand away, grabbed the top sheet, and pulled it up to cover herself.

"You knew all along, didn't you?"

"I had no idea who you were when you showed up at the first protest on College Street."

"But then you put two and two together. Why didn't you say something?"

"Because I didn't care."

She thought back to how from the moment they'd met, he'd been feeding her statistics. The stories about the homeless that he'd encouraged her to do. She rolled away from him, swung her legs out of the bed.

He put his hand on her shoulder. "Where are you going?"

"I'm getting dressed. Maybe you should get on your bike and leave."

"Why?"

"You found out about my father and thought, Great. You could use me to get inside information. Didn't you?"

"No."

She swivelled to stare at him.

"If you weren't using me, prove it. Tell me the secret location of this big pop-up protest you're planning."

"Aha," he said. "Who is using whom?"

She shook her head. "Are you going to tell me or not?"

"I don't know the location yet. I swear. It's a committee decision." He gently pulled her back toward him. "The minute I know, I'll text you. Before anyone else. I promise."

She let him ease her back onto the bed. He lay on the pillow beside her.

"What about your family?" she asked him. "I'm an open book, but I don't know anything about you."

"My family. Long story. I'm the rebel of the clan."

He caressed her cheek.

"I'm sure you are," she said, smiling, loosening her grip on the bed sheet. "You're going to tell me all about them, aren't you?"

"One day," he said.

She heard the sound of her dad's car coming into the driveway and parking outside her door.

"Who's that?" Burns asked her.

"That will be him. My dad. When he's on a case like this, he works crazy hours."

"I guess he'll see my bike parked outside."

"Don't worry, he won't care."

She heard her father walk up the outside staircase and come in the front door and call out "Dad" to Grandpa Y.

"Who's he talking to?" Burns asked.

"My grandpa. He lives here too."

"Nice."

"I'm lucky."

A few minutes later she heard her father come back down the steps outside, get in his car, and drive away.

"That your father again?" Burns asked.

"You're wrong to say my dad doesn't care. He's hardly slept for days. I know him. He's determined to catch the killer."

"I can see that," Burns said, getting out of bed and starting to get dressed. "I probably should get going."

She got up too and began putting on her clothes, and then heard the door to the upstairs open.

"Alison," Grandpa Y called down. "I'm making breakfast."

"Be there in a minute," she called back.

"Join us," she said to Burns. "My grandpa is a great cook. I already told him about you."

"You did?"

"He thinks you're very committed."

"Thanks," Burns said. "But I've got so much to do."

"Okay." She walked him outside and gave him a hug before he unlocked his bike and rode away. "Make sure you let me know where the pop-up demo is going to be this afternoon," she called after him.

He gave her a thumbs-up as he rolled down the hill.

She rushed back inside and ran upstairs. Grandpa Y was there, a big smile on his face.

"You have a good night?" he asked.

"Wonderful," she said. "I'm starving."

56

This was something that Greene had taught Kennicott and the other homicide detectives whom he'd mentored over the years: always return to the scene of the crime to take another look. It was surprising what you could see from the perspective of time. Much like when you watched a good movie for the second or third time, and picked up on things you hadn't even noticed the first time.

He hadn't called ahead to the Humber River Golf Club. It was better to simply show up unannounced and see the place and the people who lived or worked there going about their normal day.

Instead of parking in the big lot, he left his car on the street a block away from the entrance at an empty lot with a boarded-up candy store on it. He walked down the long tree-lined driveway to the front entrance. He suspected that none of the members had ever walked into their club.

The wind was sharp. Greene pulled his coat tight around his neck. He wished he'd worn a scarf. He strolled past the main entrance to the parking lot. The lot was ringed with tall light stands, and he easily spotted the few cameras mounted on them. It wasn't a professional system. This didn't surprise him. Over the years he'd found that most places underestimated their security needs and that rich people were often the most parsimonious about spending their money.

The upshot was that if someone who knew what they were doing wanted to sneak in here and break into a car or slip around the clubhouse and get to the back of the building, where Copeland was murdered, it would be easy to do.

He wanted to see if the security system was activated and how well it worked. He paced around the lot, making sure he was visible. The wind seemed to whistle up from the valley and whip right through him. He turned to go back to the clubhouse and saw Waterbridge coming out the front door dressed in his usual grey flannel pants and blue blazer uniform, cleaning his glasses with a handkerchief. He'd obviously rushed out and not bothered to put on an overcoat.

This confirmed Greene's suspicion. Whoever was monitoring the security cameras in the parking lot wasn't doing it full-time or wasn't paying much attention. Exactly what he'd expected at this time of day at this time of the year.

"Good morning, Detective," Waterbridge called out, as he rushed across the lot, his tie dancing in the wind. "To what do we owe the pleasure?"

"Nothing in particular," Greene said, meeting him halfway with a firm handshake. "Just want to take another look at the crime scene."

"Crime scene," Waterbridge said, with a nervous trill in his voice. "Not quite the moniker we'd want for our club."

"I'm sure not," Greene said, walking ahead of him up the clubhouse steps and opening the front door, without waiting for Waterbridge to invite him in.

It was an old police ploy he'd learned during his days of doing foot patrols. They called it "lead with your feet." Project that you have the right to walk inside someone's home or business and assume that you won't be stopped.

Legally, anyone could deny you entry, unless you had a warrant or reason to believe a crime was being committed at that moment or that someone was in danger. But few people knew the law. Even those who did usually wanted to play ball with the police. Most people didn't want to be seen to be hiding anything.

Waterbridge caught up with him inside the door. "Can we hang up your coat?" he asked Greene.

"No, I'll be going in and out for a while."

Greene called this technique "land and expand." Once you were in the door, exercise your authority, take your time, and get a good look around.

Waterbridge looked shaky. If he'd been a younger cop, Greene might have thought his demeanour was significant. But he'd learned over the years not to put much stock in the way people acted in the presence of the police. Some were naturally calm. Others were worriers. Whatever their personality, no one liked having a homicide detective poke around in their lives, even if they had nothing to hide. And everyone, Greene knew, had secrets.

"I'd like to see the ballroom." He'd viewed the video of the party and all the photographs, but still Greene wanted to get a feel for the room.

"Certainly," Waterbridge said. "I'll get security to unlock the door."

The security guard arrived. He was a clean-cut, short-haired, muscular man in uniform, mid-twenties. He had a notebook and pen in his hand.

"Detective, this is Oleg. He's worked security for the past two years."

"Hello, Oleg," Greene said.

"Hello, sir," Oleg said, sounding polite but officious. He had a hint of an accent, perhaps Russian or Ukrainian.

Greene had seen many young men and women like Oleg. Wannabe police officers, who worked security details to get experience to try to get into police college. They tended to be humourless.

"The detective wants to see the ballroom," Waterbridge said.

"Certainly, sir." Oleg brought out a large ring of keys, and Greene noticed that each one had an identifying tag on it. He quickly opened the door.

The room was enormous, bigger than it appeared on the video. Greene spent some time walking around, looking out the window to the pathway across the grass where Roshan had found Copeland's body.

Besides the main door, the only other door into the room was across from the windows. Greene went through it, and Oleg and Waterbridge followed. Greene found himself in the kitchen. He looked around. There was a service door on the far wall.

If someone other than Hodgson wanted to sneak out of the party unseen, it was unlikely they'd come through what would have been a busy kitchen.

Greene went up to the door. It had a large circular button warning that if it were opened, the alarm would go off.

"Is the alarm always set?" he asked Oleg.

"Yes, sir."

Greene put his hand on the door. "If I pushed through it now?"

"It would ring. It's loud, sir."

"How about on the night of the party? Would it have been set?"

"Yes, sir."

"Where does it lead?"

"To a service road off the parking lot. It is used for food and linen deliveries, sir."

Greene took his hand off the door and smiled at Oleg.

"Oleg."

"Yes, sir."

"You can call me Ari or Detective. You don't need to call me sir."

"Yes, S . . ." He smiled. "Yes, Detective."

"You have a record of the times it's opened accidentally?"

"Absolutely. Any time that happens, it's logged, Detective."

"And Monday night?"

"Nothing. That hasn't happened for more than a year, Detective."

Greene thought about telling Oleg he didn't have to keep calling him Detective.

They left the ballroom and Oleg dutifully locked it up. Greene led them down the hallway that went out to the back lawn, where Kennicott had seen Hodgson walk back inside, and into the men's bathroom, where Greene checked out the mirror and the stalls.

Waterbridge and Oleg looked on, curious, but didn't say a word.

Greene went back to the lobby. An idea occurred to him.

"Can we go back in the ballroom?"

"Certainly, Detective," Oleg said. He unlocked the door.

Greene went straight up to the stage and walked behind a set of curtains. There in the back was another door. There was no emergency lock on this one.

He turned to Oleg.

"I don't see an alarm on this door."

"No, there isn't one, sir," Oleg said, slipping back into his old habit. "It's hardly ever used and we don't have the budget for it."

Greene opened it and found himself on the side of the building, steps away from the back lawn. He scanned the side wall. There were no security cameras in sight. If the killer had come from inside the ballroom, this was how they would have got outside.

Or if the killer wasn't at the party but had snuck onto the grounds, they could have gone to the back lawn unseen. He walked out the door and found himself at the end of the parking lot, where it would have been dark at night.

He had an idea. He crossed the lot to where a line of cedar trees formed a natural border between the club and the road beyond. The trees must have been planted many years ago, because they'd grown close together, making a formidable natural barrier. Step by step he walked along the edge, keeping his eyes peeled at the base of the trees.

Waterbridge, clearly uncertain what to do, had come outside and stood by the door, not following Greene any farther.

"Detective," he called out. "Can I help you?"

"Not necessary," Greene said, moving slowly. Then he saw it. The lower branches of two of the trees were bent back the way a constant flow of traffic would have reformed their shape.

He ducked in between the trees and found what he was looking for: a frozen-over path.

57

Every funeral was sad, but this had to be just about the saddest one that Parish had ever attended. To think, in her prime, when Melissa was one of the most successful young lawyers in the city, she had so many friends, so many colleagues, and so many hangers-on: salespeople in high-end shops who would call her weekly about the latest fashion that was "perfect" for her—some would even come to the office when she was working nights and weekends; jewellers who would do the same; hair stylists, masseuses, makeup specialists. There was even a woman who gave Melissa a facial every month.

That wasn't all. There were personal health consultants; personal trainers and nutritionists; a concierge who took care of her travel arrangements and front-row tickets to shows, and even had her dry cleaning and laundry picked up and delivered to her, and had her shoes repaired. When Karl stopped coming to the office with Britt, her personal chef would bring in meals for her almost every night.

Then there were her law partners, who marvelled at her energy, her commitment, and her firm-leading billable hours. Year after year she brought in a river of money they were all happy to dip into.

Where were they all now? Parish thought as she looked around the near-empty little West End church where Karl had chosen to hold the funeral. He'd told her that they wanted to do it quickly for Britt's sake.

The only person here from their old law firm was Isolina Marciano, the older Italian receptionist who had been there forever. The year the Three Amigas began as articling students and were working insane hours, Marciano would bring them all large lattes at five o'clock when her shift ended. "Go, you girls, go," she'd say, often in a half whisper. "My papa would never let me go to law school, so you show them."

As for all the lawyers at the firm whom Melissa had worked with, mentored, made money for, not one of them had the nerve to show up. Or perhaps they didn't want to sacrifice their precious billable hours. Cowards.

Isolina saw Parish and rushed up to greet her.

"Oh, Nancy, Nancy," she said, embracing her in a firm hug. "You three girls were my most favourite, all so smart, so beautiful. And our Melissa."

She shook her head. "Every year on my birthday. Even this year. She would come. Draw me a card. I would buy her a latte."

"I never knew that."

"I would save up for months. Give her a package with socks and underwear and bras and well, you know, ladies' things. She still wore those stylish clothes but now they all looked like rags."

"I know."

"Melissa, she said to me so many times that you were her only true friend."

Parish spotted one more person she recognized. Violet, the kind Vietnamese woman who used to give Melissa her facials.

"Thanks for coming," Parish said to Violet.

"Of course, love. Melissa was one of my oldest clients."

"When was the last time you saw her?"

"Two days before she died, love."

"Really?"

"She was going to court with you the next day. We did it all. Facial. Nails. Eyebrows. Mani. Pedi. She sure needed it. She was rougher than usual."

"How often did you see her?"

"First Wednesday of every month."

"Still. Even when—"

"Never missed."

"And, if you don't mind, how did she pay—"

"She didn't. Karl paid. He'd give me an envelope with cash for her."

"He did?"

"He still cared for her, you know that, love."

Parish shouldn't have been so surprised. Melissa always seemed to have enough money when she needed it, and over the years, any time she saw Karl, he'd ask Parish if she'd seen Melissa and how was she doing. And her skin. Well, that explained why despite her living rough it always looked so good.

The rest of the pews were filled with a smattering of people Parish didn't know. Many of them looked like homeless people who were doing their best to look proper. She suspected at least one or two of them were undercover cops. There was a police security detail outside the church, and thankfully they'd kept the horde of reporters and TV cameras at bay. She saw Detective Greene join Detective Kennicott, who was already seated in a back row.

As the service was about to begin, a handsome young man with longish blond hair approached her. He looked familiar but she wasn't sure why.

"Excuse me, you're Nancy Parish, aren't you? Melissa's friend, her lawyer."

"I am," she said.

"I'm Dr. Burns, from the People on the Street Health Care Clinic."

That's where she recognized him from. He was the doctor on TV who was leading all the protests.

"I've seen you on TV," she said.

"Melissa would come to the clinic and give the women legal advice. Landlord-tenant, fights with welfare about their benefits, disability claims, child welfare when the CAS would try to grab a woman's kids."

Parish remembered how from time to time Melissa would call her from the clinic and ask her to help some homeless woman facing minor criminal charges, such as shoplifting, mischief, and fraud. She hadn't made the connection between the clinic and the doctor.

"She spoke highly of you," he said. "Thank you for the pro bono work you've done for many of our people."

"You're welcome," Parish said. She took a seat alone in the second-row pew and shook her head. So many things she was learning about Melissa only after she was gone.

The preacher came in from a side door, followed by Karl, Lydia, and Britt. Britt saw Parish and rushed over. They held on to each other tight, like two overboard passengers stranded on a lifeboat in frigid, turbulent waters.

58

"Dad," Alison said, as she sat down to eat with her father and Grandpa Y at the little table in the kitchen. "You must be exhausted. I heard you leave early this morning."

"I'm fine. The first days of an investigation are non-stop, and I had to go to a funeral," he said. "Grandpa Y made your breakfast, didn't he?"

"Yeah. It's called *shakshuka*. His new Israeli girlfriend taught him."

"Baked tomatoes and poached eggs," Grandpa Y said, bringing out the serving dish. "We saved you some."

"Thanks, Dad," Ari said, and dug into the food.

This was the first time the three of them had been together in days. Her father looked tired. She'd been holding off talking to him about her new relationship with Dr. Burns. She felt guilty bringing it up and bothering him when he was so preoccupied with his cases. But she also felt guilty keeping it from him.

She knew it was time to do it. Before she could say a word, he turned to her.

"I'm sure you'll be covering the demonstration when it 'pops up,'" he said. "Wherever that turns out to be."

"Full network coverage. There'll be a lot of police there, won't there?"

"It looks as if the mayor and maybe even the premier are going to show up. We'll have tons of security."

He finished his food. "Thanks, Dad," he said. "Better than what your Russian girlfriend had you cooking."

They all laughed. Grandpa Y had found a website for older Jewish men and women, and he seemed to have a new girlfriend every few months.

"I've got to get rolling," Ari said, about to get up.

"Dad." Alison grabbed his arm.

"Yes," he said, surprised. "What's wrong?"

"I need to tell you something."

He looked at her, smiling.

She let go of his arm. "Well, you know, I mean you've always been respectful of my privacy. And I really appreciate it."

"Why wouldn't I be?" He looked confused. He traded glances with Grandpa Y.

Alison looked at Grandpa Y too. He tilted his head so her dad couldn't see and winked at her.

She looked right at her dad. "I've started seeing someone."

"Great."

"It's kind of complicated."

"In my experience relationships are always complicated. Congratulations." He started to get up again.

"Dad," she said, grabbing his arm a second time. "It's Dr. Burns."

"A doctor?"

"Burns."

"Am I supposed to know him?"

"He's the man leading all these demonstrations. The one who had the crowd screaming the cops don't care outside your office."

She tensed. He was sure to be angry when he found out that she was attracted to someone who had made him a target.

"Oh," he said. "The guy on TV with the bicycle."

Since Alison's initial report, Burns had been doing the rounds of interviews. Reporters loved the image of a bicycle-riding physician who was so committed to the homeless.

"Yes, Dad. The guy on TV."

He shrugged. One of his dad shrugs, as she liked to call them. She was sure he'd inherited them from Grandpa Y.

"So it was his bike that I saw locked up outside your door when I left early this morning?"

Grandpa Y laughed. "Alison, your father is a detective! He doesn't miss a thing."

She smiled. "Yes, it was Arnold's bike. He rides it all year long."

"Good," he said. "He seems really committed to his cause."

"He is."

"I thought so too," Grandpa Y chimed in.

Her father wasn't upset. She was gobsmacked.

"Aren't you angry at me for seeing him?"

"Why would I be upset?"

"He's saying all these terrible things about the police."

"Seems to me he's doing a good job. Look at the hornet's nest he's stirred up. This protest is getting publicity for homelessness right across the country and beyond."

She shook her head. This was exactly the argument she had planned to make in Arnold's favour to fight with her dad.

"You finished?" he asked her, picking up his plate and kissing her on the top of her head. "I've got to hit the road."

"Thanks, Dad." She'd never called him Daddy, but for the first time that word almost popped out of her mouth.

He rinsed his dishes and was gone. She looked over to Grandpa Y.

He was laughing.

"What's so funny?" she said.

"Life," he said. "And the pursuit of happiness."

WEDNESDAY AFTERNOON

59

Over the years Kennicott had learned that Greene had different places scattered throughout the city where he liked to meet when he wanted to get out of Police Headquarters and have a conversation off the grid. One of his favourites was Caldense, a Portuguese bakery near Greene's home. They'd met there many times, usually early in the morning when construction workers gathered to get their first daily shots of espresso, eat a croissant, and catch up on the latest scores of their favourite soccer teams on the TV on the back wall that was constantly blasting out game highlights.

Today the midday crowd was mainly older men, sitting in small groups, talking away. When Kennicott arrived, Greene was already sitting at his regular table by the window. The corner TV was filled with news from the Portuguese parliament. Mostly what appeared to be politicians gesticulating with their hands and shouting at each other.

Kennicott sat across from Greene. As usual with Greene, when he wanted to talk like this off the grid, Kennicott had no idea what the meeting was about.

"I ordered you a double espresso," Greene said. "And only one croissant for each of us."

They had a running joke about how the small croissants served here were too hard. Greene hated them but could never let on to Miguel Caldas, the owner, who treated Greene like a king.

"Nice of you," Kennicott said, taking a large sip of the cup of coffee.

"Nora is coming to join us in a few minutes."

The fact that they were meeting here, with the chief, and not at

Police Headquarters told Kennicott that something was afoot that Greene wanted to keep very close to the vest.

"Why are we meeting her?" Kennicott asked.

"To give her an update. She wants to know if we have a suspect. And we are going to tell her that we do not."

"But we don't have a suspect, do we?"

Greene fixed him with his eyes. "We are going to tell her that we don't have anyone."

Kennicott understood. Greene was working on something.

"Who?" he whispered.

Greene pointed to the door. "Here she is. I'll tell you later."

Kennicott looked out the window and saw Bering striding purposefully down the sidewalk toward the restaurant. In the distance he could see the limousine that must have driven her over to this side of town.

Kennicott and Greene stood as she entered the café. Bering's eyes lit up when she saw Kennicott.

"Daniel," she said.

Although their paths had crossed less and less often over the years as they'd both climbed through the ranks, they were always glad to see each other.

Kennicott smiled back and gave her a hug.

She looked around the little café. "Man, oh man, it's great to be out of the Pink Palace and back on the street," she said.

Caldas, a short man wearing his usual white shirt, black tie, and black vest, scampered over to greet them.

"Chief Nora, such a pleasure!" he said with genuine excitement. "You and Detective Greene, now in charge of the whole city. Such an honour."

Bering put her arm around Caldas's shoulder. Bering was tall, and she towered above him. "You took care of us when we were two young pups."

"I knew you were both special ones." He looked up at Bering. "Single shot latte, one sugar coming up."

"You remember," she said, delighted.

"How could I forget?"

"Make it a double shot today," she said.

"With pleasure," he said, and hustled off.

They all sat. Bering's face turned grim. "I know this is the last thing you two need right now," she said. "The mayor's chomping at the bit. She wants a report. She's holding a press conference in an hour."

Greene shrugged, the way Kennicott knew he did when he was thinking of what to say. Or when he had nothing to say.

"This is getting real political, real fast," Bering said. "Homeless advocates are coming in from across the country for this pop-up rally of theirs. We have no idea where it's going to be yet. All we know is they plan to disrupt the afternoon rush hour. I'm cancelling holiday leaves and bringing in an extra two hundred officers."

Greene pointed across the table at Kennicott. "Daniel, give Nora an update?"

"We interviewed Hodgson this morning," he said.

"Already?" Bering asked, looking hopeful.

"He came in on his own, with his lawyer, Cutter."

Bering grimaced. There wasn't a cop in the city who liked Cutter. "Make my day. Please tell me Hodgson confessed."

"Only to his love for his ex-wife," Greene said, joining back in on the conversation. "And to a traffic violation."

"He was the driver of the SUV who knocked Jember Roshan off his bicycle," Kennicott said.

"That puts him in the vicinity of the second murder early Monday morning," she said.

"There's something else, but you can't breathe a word of this to the mayor," Greene said. "The autopsy on Copeland was done top priority. Hodgson's fingerprints were on her neck, and we're pretty sure she had his DNA under her fingernails."

"Phew," she whistled.

"Don't get too excited," Greene said. "Hodgson will say he was driving in to the course on his way to play his usual early-morning round, and he gave us an exculpatory explanation for the DNA that we're pretty certain will hold up."

Kennicott saw that Greene didn't mention the golf balls with Hodgson's initials on them. This was his way, always keeping something back, even from the chief.

Bering looked back and forth between Kennicott and Greene. She was dying of curiosity to find out more. But she was too much of a pro to ask. Now that she was the chief, Bering had to tread the fine line of keeping the politicians—and the public—happy, while not stepping on the toes of her detectives and hampering their investigations. Kennicott knew that when push came to shove, she'd come down on the side of her own people.

"If this gets out, it could be a disaster for our investigation," Kennicott said.

"I see that," Bering said. "And it would look as if the mayor leaked this and was using this crisis for political gain against Hodgson."

"That's why," Greene said, "it's better that she not know."

Caldas appeared with Bering's coffee and a croissant and disappeared again. If the chief of police was here, there had to be some very private conversations going on, and he knew when to get out of the way.

Bering bit into one of the croissants. "They're harder than ever," she said in a stage whisper.

They all smiled.

"Ari, in all my years on the force, I've never seen anything like this. We're getting media requests from CNN, BBC, and a bunch of European stations. Australia, New Zealand, South Africa. Homelessness is an international crisis, and thanks to this, right now we're the poster child for the problem."

"Toronto wants to be a world-class city," Greene said, with a sly grin. "Now we've got a world-class murder story."

"'Serial Killer Targets Homeless Women,' that's the headline. The mayor is desperate for something to say. Are there any other suspects?"

Greene picked up the menu on the table, cleared his throat, and—mocking himself reading from prepared notes at a press conference—said, "The Toronto Police Force is presently working full out on this investigation. Every available resource is being used to maintain the safety of our citizens and bring whoever is responsible for these heinous crimes to justice."

Bering grinned. "What about, 'We will leave no stone unturned'?"

"That stone has been turned over so many times that it's got an even tan," Greene said.

Bering started to chuckle.

They trusted each other to the core. They could laugh about almost anything.

"We're giving this one hundred ten per cent," Kennicott chimed in.

Bering shook her head. Amused. "In other words, you have nothing."

"*Nada y pues nada*," Greene said.

"Or to be precise, nothing you're going to tell me about at this time."

"You'll be the first to know," Greene said.

Bering took a long sip of her double-shot latte. "Mmm," she said. "This place hasn't changed a bit, has it? I sure miss it."

"It's lonely at the top," Greene said, grinning.

"I've seen your daughter on TV," Bering said with a Cheshire cat grin. Kennicott recognized this as her way of trying to charm information out of someone. "Congratulations. She's a good young reporter."

"Thanks. She works hard at it."

"Strange, isn't it," Bering said, "that with all the media coverage, she seems to be the one getting all the scoops?"

Kennicott had been thinking the same thing about Greene and his daughter. What was Greene up to? Helping his daughter with her career? Or using her to control the story in the press? Or, as Kennicott suspected, both?

Years ago when he was new to the force, Greene and Bering had shown Kennicott that sometimes it was necessary to deliberately mislead the media to send a false message to a suspect. In one of their most celebrated cases, a young girl who lived downtown disappeared while walking to school. People were terrified, and the pressure on the police to find the child and solve the case was extreme. An all-out search came up with nothing. The girl's distraught mother was headline news for days.

Then, horribly, parts of the young girl's body were found in a ravine. She had been brutally raped and mutilated. People were in an uproar. The press demanded the police be open with the public and provide some answers. Parents were keeping their children home from school, and the city was gripped with fear.

What no one knew was that the pathologist had discovered a green rug fibre in the girl's clothes. Greene and Bering were determined to jealously guard this clue. Secretly, they sent out an army of trusted street cops to knock on doors in the little girl's neighbourhood and look for a place with a green carpet. Kennicott was one of the cops.

On the third night he rang the bell on the door of a bachelor apartment. A man opened it partway. He looked nervous. Kennicott managed to worm his way in far enough to peer inside and spot a green carpet on the floor.

The next day, Greene and Bering held a major press conference. The media was there in force expecting breakthrough news. Instead, Bering and Greene wore deep frowns. Kennicott still remembered exactly what Greene said.

"Despite the hundreds of hours the dedicated men and women of our force have worked on this case, we've hit a wall. Right now, we have no leads. Once again we are appealing to the public to come forward if you have any information that can assist in this investigation. And keep your children close."

The hardest part was the girl's distressed mother. Greene warned her in advance of the negative message he was about to tell the press. But he couldn't reveal that, in fact, they now had twenty-four-hour surveillance on the man in the bachelor apartment. It was better for his ploy that she tell the media how hurt and disappointed she was.

For two days the man didn't leave his apartment. Newspaper commentators and radio talk show hosts were vitriolic in their criticism of the incompetent Toronto cops.

On the third day he emerged with a pack on his back. He took the ferry over to the Toronto Islands, and when he tried to dump the rest of the girl's remains into Lake Ontario, Greene and Bering were there to arrest him.

Bering downed the rest of her latte. "The coffee here is so good. Ari, you don't know what you're missing only drinking your tea."

"Maybe I'll try it one day."

"So no suspects. No leads. That's the message you want me to give the mayor and for her to tell the press."

"No. Tell the mayor to hold off and that we'll talk to the media instead."

Kennicott watched transfixed as their eyes met. So much meaning conveyed. All unspoken.

"The mayor won't be happy," Bering said at last.

Greene didn't move.

"Ari, you got a green fibre?"

Greene just kept staring at her.

Bering nodded. Took another sip of her latte.

"Okay," she said.

"Good," Greene said, taking a bite out of his croissant. "Now listen, this is how we're going to do the press conference."

60

Greene sat with Kennicott and Bering to wait until the media gallery on the second floor of Police Headquarters was filled with reporters before they walked in. All three of them were dressed in full uniform.

"How do I look?" Kennicott asked Bering.

She smiled at Greene. "Ari, remember how green Daniel was when he started? Now he looks like a real cop, doesn't he?"

They all laughed.

"Thanks to you two," Kennicott said.

"No, Daniel," Bering said, "you put in the work. You ready?"

"As I'll ever be."

"You, Ari?" she asked.

"Let's go," he said.

They walked out and the room filled with noisy reporters fell silent. Kennicott and Greene sat on either side of Bering, glum looks on their faces.

Bering introduced them, then picked up a piece of paper and started reading from a prepared statement. "Toronto remains one of the safest cities in Canada, with by far the lowest homicide rate per capita of any large city in North America."

The reporters looked impatient as she read through the rest of the bland prepared statement.

She finished and looked up.

"Questions?" she asked them.

In unison they raised their hands like a pack of eager grade-one students asked, "Who wants a cookie?"

"Sam," she said, pointing to the journalist from the *Toronto Sun*. Sadly, in the last few years a number of top court reporters in the city had passed away or retired, leaving Sam as the most experienced of the bunch. By picking him first, Bering was signalling to the press that she respected their work and their unspoken pecking order.

"Chief, do the police have a suspect at this time?" he asked.

Bering shook her head. "Not at this very moment. But I can assure the citizens of Toronto that the men and women on the force are working night and day on this investigation."

"Do you have any leads?"

"Sam, I'll let Homicide Detective Kennicott answer that question. He's been on this case from the beginning."

There was only one microphone. Bering passed it to him.

"We need to be frank and transparent with the public," Kennicott said. "Our team is diligently following up every lead. The tip line is getting more than seventy-five calls a day. And we are appealing to the public for help."

He was handling it perfectly, Greene thought. Being obtuse and not answering the question. This was going to provoke the reaction they wanted.

"But do the police have any solid leads?" the reporter asked again.

Before Kennicott could answer, Greene reached over and took the microphone, exactly the way they'd rehearsed it.

"We don't want to mislead the public about this dangerous situation, so let me be clear," Greene said. "The Metropolitan Toronto Police Service is suggesting in the strongest terms that anyone who is homeless seek a spot in one of the city's shelters. Immediately."

"Are you saying the streets are not safe?" another reporter asked.

"We are saying people must be alert and cautious. And if they see anything or anyone acting suspiciously, contact the police."

"In other words," the first reporter said, exasperated, "you have no leads."

Bering took the microphone back. This was what Greene wanted. Make it seem as if the press was dragging it out of them. Never give an absolute denial because that might be too transparent a ruse. Let the press fill in the blanks.

"Do we have any leads?" She turned to Kennicott first, then Greene. They returned cold stares. "Unfortunately, we are not at liberty to discuss the specifics of this particular investigation at this time. That is why we are appealing to the public for help. But I want to personally assure the people of Toronto that we will leave no stone unturned to solve these terrible crimes."

Bering picked up her paper and stood. Greene and Kennicott did the same. Even though reporters were still shouting out questions at them, they turned and left the stage.

"Quite a performance, gentlemen," Bering said, when they were alone in the room behind the stage. Her shoulders sagged, and she wiped her brow. Greene could see the pressure weighing down on her.

"I don't suppose now you'd let me know who the suspect is?" she asked Kennicott.

"You'll have to ask Ari," he said.

Greene's phone buzzed. He read the text message from Alison and then looked up at them.

"The 'pop-up' demonstration just started on the Danforth Bridge. Let's go."

"Follow me," Kennicott said. "I've got the best driver on the force on standby." As he spoke, he punched in a speed-dial number on his phone.

"Officer Sheppard," he said, "we're heading out the door."

61

"I am standing on an historic bridge here in Toronto, Canada," Raymond Handbolt, the BBC Radio correspondent, was saying, speaking into his mic and broadcasting live. "Known locally as the Danforth Bridge, the true name is the Prince Edward Viaduct, and it was named after the former Prince of Wales, who arrived in 1919 to officially open the bridge. A tremendous demonstration has popped up, closing down one of the city's main bridges at rush hour. It is a chaotic scene. With me now is Ms. Alison Greene, the crusading young reporter who first broke the story of the so-called Homeless Serial Killer, which has galvanized the issue of homelessness not only in Canada but across industrial nations around the globe."

Alison stood beside Handbolt in the middle of the bridge, right across the street from the place where she'd first kissed Burns. They were crowded in amongst the growing mass of demonstrators, who had seized control of the bridge and created a major traffic jam in the afternoon rush hour. The protesters were holding banners and chanting slogans: "Homes Not Golf Courses," and "Homes for Everyone, not Holes in One."

Burns was leading the crowd. He'd sent Alison a tip with a coded text—"location of first kiss"—which had given her enough time to text the location to her dad, get to the bridge with Krevolin ahead of other reporters, and seize a prime spot for their coverage. She'd done a great live stand-up when the cop cars arrived just as Burns and his band of demonstrators took over the bridge and shut it down.

"Ms. Greene," Handbolt said, "Three homeless people have been murdered in Toronto in less than a week. All in approximately the same location."

He put the mic uncomfortably close to her mouth. She'd never done a radio interview before. "Yes," she said, "in a valley in the city called the Humber, where there was a large homeless encampment."

"There have been no arrests," he said, pulling the mic back before shoving it back in her face.

"No, there have not been."

"And the police, how have they responded? Do they have any leads?"

"No, at the moment they seem to have nothing."

"Only adding to the anxiety and the protests," he said.

As if on cue, a group of protesters, seeing Alison being interviewed, moved closer and started singing the John Lennon song "Give Peace a Chance," with their own lyrics:

"All we are saying, is give us a home . . ."

Handbolt's eyes lit up and he tilted his mic toward them.

Alison recognized their leader, Cassandra Amberlight, a veteran activist she had met the previous year while covering a protest by a local residents group against a large condominium project going up in their neighbourhood. Amberlight was a tall, gawky woman, famous for carrying an old brown leather megaphone and leading crowds with her booming voice.

"As you can hear," Handbolt said, "the people are demanding action. Reporting live from Toronto, Canada, this is Raymond Handbolt for BBC Radio news."

He clicked off his mic. "Thank you," he said to Alison.

The singing stopped, and Amberlight stepped forward. "Hello, Ms. Greene, I told you I'd see you at the next demonstration."

"You certainly did." It was said of Amberlight that she never saw a microphone she didn't want to speak into. Alison knew she'd seen the BBC label on Handbolt's mic, and she was honing in on him like a hawk.

Alison introduced the two, and Amberlight began to chat him up.

Alison stepped away. She waved to Krevolin, who'd been taking cut-away shots of the protesters' signs as the bridge was filling with people. She'd lost sight of Burns.

"Have you seen Dr. Burns?"

"He's over there," Krevolin said, pointing his camera at the spot where Alison and Burns had kissed. Burns was climbing up on the ledge, grasping the suicide barrier wires to hoist himself up above the crowd.

62

Parish was of two minds about having a TV in her bedroom. She'd once heard that the only thing former prime minister Pierre Trudeau had in his bedroom was a light and the book he was reading. Nothing else.

It would have been nice to be that aesthetically pure, but the reality was that some nights she wanted to crawl in under the covers and binge on Netflix or watch Colbert.

She was also a closet news junkie, and this afternoon all the news was about the massive demonstration that had popped up on the Danforth Bridge. She wasn't usually in bed in the middle of the day, but she was sleeping with a community college student who, she'd just discovered, had no sympathy for the plight of the homeless. Chalk it up to his country-club upbringing.

She'd been watching the protest on TV while he slept, and snored, beside her. He was awoken by the sound of the protesters chanting, "The Homeless Need Homes," "We Are Citizens Too," "Homes Not Golf Courses."

Jack groaned and groped over to the bedside table to find his glasses. "Do you really want to watch this stuff?" he asked her.

"I think it's important."

"Always the same old crap with these people. They don't want to work. They just steal stuff, get high, and kill each other."

Parish hadn't told him that the third victim, Melissa, was her close friend. He was here for diversion, not sympathy.

"Not everyone has had your pampered upbringing," she said, not really wanting to get into a political argument with him but not able to stop herself.

"Well, not everyone from my family turned out the same. Look, there's my older brother, Arnie."

He pointed to the screen at the man leading a group of protesters.

Parish looked closer at the TV. There was a close-up shot of Dr. Burns, the man Parish had met at the funeral. He had climbed up on the bridge railing and was leading a large crowd of protesters in their chants.

"He's your brother?" she asked Jack. "His name is Burns, not Water-bridge."

"My mother's last name was Burnside. He shortened it to Burns."

"Was?"

"She died when we were kids. Funny thing is Arnie was a better golfer than me. Dad named him for Arnold Palmer. I'm named after Jack Nicklaus."

"Oh," Parish said, half listening. Riveted to the TV.

"Now he wouldn't set foot on the course if his life depended on it."

"He wouldn't?" she asked, distracted, not really paying attention to him.

"My therapist, she says Arnold's homeless crusade is his way of act-ing out his anger at my dad."

"Does she?" Now she was listening.

"That subconsciously he blames my dad for Mom's death. I hardly recognized him. He's not wearing his glasses. We all have crummy eye-sight in our family. We all need bifocals."

"And he's not wearing his?"

"Dad calls Arnie a champagne socialist. Working for the poor but he rides a specially made bicycle, drinks the most expensive coffee you can buy, and wears custom-made, one-of-a-kind glasses."

"One-of-a-kind, specially made?"

Her robe was on the floor. She slid out of bed, slipped it on, and reached for her phone.

"Hey, where you going?" Jack said, tugging at her robe.

"Give me a minute," she said. "I have to make an important phone call."

She rushed downstairs, sat at her kitchen table, and called Greene on the emergency number he'd given her.

63

Kennicott was right about Officer Sheppard, Greene thought as she flew through the city, siren blaring, horn honking.

He'd just gotten off the phone with Parish and briefed Kennicott. Alison had been texting and had warned him what to expect, but as their car approached the bridge, the scene was even more chaotic than he'd imagined. TV vans, police cars, demonstrators, and cars stranded in the middle of it all were packed on the bridge.

"Good work, Officer," Greene said to Sheppard, as she threw the patrol car into park. "Stick with us."

"Sure thing," she said, hopping out of the car with them. They rushed up to the front of the bridge.

"You two get in position," Greene said to Kennicott, "but wait for my call."

"Where are you going?" Kennicott asked him.

Greene pointed to a path by the bridge. "I need to confirm something. It won't take long. Grab some officers to help you and be ready."

He headed down the path. Dent was sitting in his usual spot on the bench waiting for him.

"You forget the tent, Detective?" Dent said as his way of greeting.

"It's been a little busy," Greene said.

Above them they could hear the noise from the demonstration on the bridge.

Dent still had his club-like stick with him. He pointed it skyward. "Doc Photo Op has sure kicked up a shit storm, hasn't he?"

"You mean Dr. Burns?"

"Doc Photo Op. That's what everyone on the street calls him. The

guy is everywhere. Shouldn't you be up there? You're missing the pa-
rade."

"I've got people covering it."

They shook hands. Greene had two fifty-dollar bills in his palm, and
Dent pocketed them.

"Give one to Daphne," he said.

"She'll like that better than Tim Horton cards."

"Did you know Melissa Copeland?"

"Law Lady? You see that headline in the *Sun*? 'Hodgson's Homeless
Ex Murdered'?" Dent spit on the ground in disgust.

"I saw it." Greene had seen all the tasteless headlines about Copeland. The press only cared about the politics and the money and ignored what had happened: someone had died a terrible death. To say
nothing of the fact that she was leaving behind a young daughter.

"I hadn't seen her for a while," Dent said. "She helped everyone
with their legal problems. I asked Daphne about her for you. She told
me the word on the street was that Law Lady got crazier and crazier."

"We heard that."

Dent took his stick and pointed toward the office towers downtown. "Once upon a time she worked there. Big firm. Top biller." His
voice trailed off.

They sat silently for a while. Greene knew that Melissa's story
echoed Dent's own.

"Daphne said she had a kid she never got to see," Dent said.

"Daughter. Daphne tell you anything else?"

"She said no one really knew when Law Lady would appear, and
no one knew where she stayed most nights. I wish I had more for you,
Detective."

"When was the last time Daphne saw her?"

"The day before she got herself killed. Everyone was leaving the valley after the second murder. Law Lady was telling people they didn't
have to go. She said she knew who the killer was, and that she knew

a cop who was real high up. This cop was going to take care of things. Any idea who that might have been, Detective?"

Dent rarely made eye contact but he turned and looked straight at Greene.

Greene stared straight back at him.

Dent chuckled. He had a loud, hearty laugh.

"Detective," he said, "you're one of a kind."

Greene laughed. He pointed back up the path. "Is this the only way down here from the bridge?"

"To this spot." Dent swung his stick back behind him. "Get over this ridge and there's a million ways to go."

"Thanks," Greene said, taking out his cell phone to call Kennicott. "Do me a favour, keep an eye out for the good doctor for me."

"Will do," Dent said. "And Detective, it's getting cold. Don't forget the tent next time."

64

Alison had covered demonstrations before. They were tricky because you could get caught in the middle of things and not be able to tell what was really going on. Or find a quiet-enough place from which to report. As the bridge filled up with demonstrators, she'd found a spot near the west end of the bridge where Krevolin could film her with the colour and noise of the demonstrators in the background.

People were protesting everything under the sun: the homeless demanding more housing; a group of cyclists demanding better bike lanes; daycare workers demanding more daycare spots; university students demanding lower tuition. Burns was the ringleader, perched on the railing high above the crowd.

Amberlight had passed him her megaphone, and he was leading the protest sign–toting demonstrators in a new chant: "Stop pampering the rich. House the poor!" "Stop pampering the rich. House the poor!"

"We're live in two minutes," Krevolin told Alison.

She adjusted her hair and took one last look across the bridge. She spotted a group of police officers in a V-shape formation moving through the hordes of people. Usually Toronto cops stayed on the edge of demonstrations as long as they were peaceful, as this one was.

She scanned the crowd and noticed Burns. He saw them coming. Even from a distance Alison could see the surprised look on his face as they moved towards him. He threw the megaphone back to Amberlight, jumped down, and started pushing his way through the demonstrators, away from the police toward her side of the bridge.

What in the world was going on?

Her phone was on vibrate, buzzing in her pocket. She grabbed it. It was her dad.

"Ninety seconds," Krevolin said.

The cops were chasing Burns through the crowd. He was well ahead of them and getting closer to her.

She grabbed her phone. "Dad?"

"Where are you?" he said.

"The west end of the bridge."

"Turn around. I see you."

She whirled around. Her dad was running toward her. Her father never ran. What was going on? He'd just come up from the path down into the valley. She looked back. Burns was pushing through the crowd. Her father's partner, Detective Kennicott, was chasing after him.

"Allie," her dad said, coming up to her, breathing hard.

"Dad?"

"I know it's your personal life. But I have to know. Monday night, the night of the third murder, were you with Dr. Burns?"

Why was he asking her this?

"Thirty seconds," Krevolin said in her ear.

"Yes," she said to her father. "We worked at a church feeding the homeless and then walked across this bridge. Why?"

"And after that?"

"After that?" Then she remembered what had happened when Burns walked her to the streetcar.

"We parted. He said he had something planned for later."

As the words escaped her mouth, Burns burst through the crowd running at full speed. Their eyes met.

Her father jumped in front of her. "Don't move," he yelled at her.

"Daddy," Alison said. Shocked. "What?"

Burns ran past her and disappeared down a path at the edge of the bridge where her father had just been.

A moment later Kennicott tore by them, steps behind Burns. A young female officer emerged from the crowd and followed him.

Alison turned back to her dad. The look in his eyes told her everything.

"Is he?" she asked him.

"I'm sorry," he said. He grasped her hands and squeezed them briefly, then ran after Kennicott.

"We're on in five," Krevolin said. Cool and professional as ever.

Alison lifted her mic.

"Follow me," she said to him, walking over to the top of the path as fast as she could.

"This is Alison Greene," she said when the green light went on. "Reporting live with breaking news."

65

It's a good thing he learned that downhill running technique from Angela, Kennicott thought, as he hit the end of the bridge and headed down the steep path into the Don River Valley. He could tell Burns knew the way because he was taking it so quickly.

That was a problem. If Burns got away now, he could hide out here for a long time. The woods were thick and there were trails leading off in all directions. The guy was smart and probably had a hideout stashed away.

Focus on your running, Kennicott told himself. Keep your knees high. Form circles not teardrops. Don't land on your heels. Breathe. Think Jose Reyes running downhill, training for the major leagues.

He was keeping Burns in sight and starting to gain on him. Angela would be proud.

About halfway down into the valley, the path came to a long, flat plateau, with a man-made bench off to the side. Burns looked back over his shoulder, stumbled, and fell hard to the ground.

"Stop! Police!" Kennicott yelled.

Burns pulled himself back up and turned toward Kennicott.

"Okay," Burns yelled, putting one hand out in front of him. "Stay right there and let me talk."

Kennicott stopped and caught his breath. Their eyes met. They were at opposite ends of the plateau. It felt as if they were frozen in time.

Burns made a fist and pounded his chest with it.

"I didn't kill those people," he yelled across the open space between them.

Kennicott took a deep breath.

Burns hadn't moved.

"I'm not a judge, I'm not a jury," Kennicott yelled back. "If you have a defence, you'll have a fair trial."

"Fair? Nothing in the system is fair."

Kennicott heard footsteps coming down the path. That would be Officer Sheppard. He put one hand behind him and motioned for her to stop. That silenced her. Good. He didn't want Burns to see her, but now she could listen and be a witness if Kennicott could get the doctor to confess.

He had to take this slowly. Keep Burns talking.

"We know your real last name is Waterbridge," Kennicott said, no longer yelling.

"So what? It's legal to change your name."

"And we know that your dad runs the golf club."

"I despise that place. Playground for the privileged few." Burns spit on the ground.

He was still being a showman. But he was still talking. Time to ramp up the heat.

"You know your way around the club, don't you? The secret ways to get in and out. All about Hodgson and his initialled golf balls. You stole them from his car and thought you could make him the suspect by stuffing them down the mouths of the people you killed."

Even across the distance, Kennicott could see a flash of anger cross Burns's face.

"You have no proof."

"You hand-picked your first two victims because you had their medical records, and you knew they were both at death's door."

"The system killed them, not me."

Kennicott didn't react. Think of how Greene would handle this. Use the silence.

Burns looked behind him. Kennicott thought he was going to take off and dug his feet into the ground, ready to spring into action.

But Burns didn't move. He looked back toward Kennicott, and now he clenched both his hands into tight fists.

Kennicott had to make a quick decision. Should he try to wait Burns out? He could feel Burns still had something else he wanted to say. Time to play dumb, play to the man's ego.

"There's one thing I still don't understand," Kennicott said at last. "Melissa Copeland."

Burns glared at him, but Kennicott could see he'd hit his mark.

"Why did you kill her? Melissa was perfectly healthy."

Burns shook his head. But he was still standing there.

Time to tie the knot.

"She fought back, didn't she, and broke your glasses? We discovered some of your trifocal lenses on the ground. You rode your bike across the city Monday night to the golf club and went down that path through the trees. Bad luck for you. Your special winter bike tires left a set of very distinct tracks in the mud. Detective Greene photographed your tires and forensics confirmed they were a perfect match. And your square bike lock. It's the exact same shape as the blunt force trauma on the back of the heads of your three victims. Your little gambits of pretending these killings were just a few drunks fighting over a vodka bottle, or that Hodgson was the killer—neither of them worked."

Burns shook his head. He looked up at the bridge, where the demonstration that he'd orchestrated was in full swing.

Kennicott could sense his anger turning to frustration. Today should have been Burns's moment of triumph, but instead he was here, down in the valley, a fugitive.

"The doctor. The nurse. They were believers. I chose them to make a sacrifice for the cause. Melissa was going to expose me and ruin it all." He pointed up to the bridge. "The press, the politicians, no one gave a damn before I did this. Now look, the whole country, the whole world, is talking about homelessness."

Burns was breathing hard.

Kennicott let Burns's words hang in the air. He'd just confessed to three murders.

Burns looked behind him. "I've gone down in this valley more times than I can count to help people," he said.

"Stay right there," Kennicott said, beginning to walk toward him.

"Never," Burns said. "Good luck finding me." He pivoted and ran, disappearing over the edge.

Kennicott took off after him. He ran as fast as he could to the end of the ledge. Burns was going at full speed and approaching a fork in the path when suddenly he flew headfirst to the ground.

"Ahh!" he screamed, clutching his leg.

A man emerged from the bushes, with a club-like stick in his hands. He smiled up at Kennicott. It was Fraser Dent.

"He's not going anywhere, Detective Kennicott," Dent said.

"My knee," Burns moaned. "You crushed my kneecap."

"Good work, Mr. Dent," Kennicott said.

Kennicott heard footsteps behind him. Greene and Sheppard came up beside him, and they all looked down at Burns, who was still on the ground writhing in pain. Sheppard already had a set of handcuffs out.

Kennicott winked at Greene.

"Officer Sheppard," he said. "Why don't you walk down there and make the arrest?"

SIX MONTHS LATER

66

Standing in the hot sun, Alison had the top two buttons of her shirt undone. She flicked her hair back over her shoulder and held the mic up. She nodded an okay to Krevolin, who was standing below her on the courtroom steps. The green light went on.

"Good morning. We are reporting live from Ontario Court of Justice. Minutes ago Dr. Arnold Burns pled guilty to one count of first-degree murder, bringing a dramatic conclusion to the Homeless Serial Killer case that held the country in its thrall six months ago. *T.O. TV News* has learned that Burns's lawyer, Phil Cutter, worked out a deal with Crown Attorney Albert Fernandez. Burns agreed to plead guilty to one of the three counts of murder that he faced. He will serve a minimum of twenty-five years in jail, not the potential seventy-five years of incarceration he faced had he been convicted of all three."

Krevolin panned his camera away from Alison, across the courtyard in front of the main courthouse doors. It was packed with other cameramen, reporters, and spectators. Everyone was waiting for the lawyers and the victims' families to emerge. Alison took the few seconds she was off camera to grab a sip from her water bottle. Stay calm, she told herself. No one knew about her brief affair with Burns, except her father and grandfather. And they would never tell anyone.

For months after his arrest, they'd never mentioned it. Alison could sense they knew she was beating herself up enough about the whole thing. How could she have been so naive? How could she have been so taken in by him? And how had she let him use her for his cause?

One long night in February, when they were practically snowed in, she made her dad and Grandpa Y dinner. "I feel like an idiot," she said, after her dad had cleared the dishes and they were having tea. "I let a killer into my life."

"You weren't the only one he fooled," her dad said.

"That's no excuse," she said. "I'm done with relationships."

"Why would you let him define you?" Grandpa Y said. "You can't let evil win."

After all he'd been through in his life, Grandpa Y of all people should know that. He was right.

"Dad, I have to ask you one question," she said. "I understand in his demented way Arnie, I mean Burns, could justify killing the first victim. The doctor was a patient at his clinic, and he knew that with his low platelet level, he was on the verge of death. And you have to admit Burns was right, no one noticed, no one cared. One homeless murder didn't even cause a ripple."

"Kennicott cared," Greene said. "He worked it the way he'd work any case."

"True. But the press, the politicians ignored it."

Wasn't she still parroting Burns's argument? But it was true.

Grandpa Y shrugged. "Even a broken clock is right twice a day," he said.

They all laughed. He knew how to break the tension.

"When he killed the nurse, the story exploded," she said.

"He knew that the murder of a homeless woman was a bigger story," her father said. "And two former professionals who'd ended up on the street made it even better."

"That insured the press would lap it up, which we did. He played us all, didn't he?"

"He was a master manipulator."

"You're pretty good at it too," she said. "That press conference you gave when you said you didn't have a suspect sure convinced me that you were nowhere on this case."

"Convinced Burns too. We were afraid that if he knew we were on his trail, he would disappear."

"When did you figure out about his bike and his bike lock?"

His father blushed. She'd never seen him do that before. "The morning before his arrest. He'd parked his bike in your bike rack."

"I heard you come in and leave pretty quick."

"I photographed the tires and the bike lock. I had to go to the golf course to take some pictures of his bike tracks, and then forensics confirmed we had a match for both."

"Your daddy's a detective," Grandpa Y said. "He doesn't miss a thing."

She shook her head and laughed.

"Now I get it. That's why Grandpa Y made me breakfast just after I heard you drive away."

"Your father wasn't going to leave you alone with a man he suspected of three murders," Grandpa Y said.

"Thank goodness." She put her face in her hands and covered her eyes. "But I still don't understand one thing. Why did he kill the lawyer, Melissa Copeland? She was healthy."

Her father gently pulled her hands from her eyes and held them.

"The reason is tragic. Melissa was telling people in the valley that she knew who the killer was. She was wrong. She thought it was someone else, but Burns wouldn't have known that."

"Oh no."

"He killed her thinking she was going to expose him. His next victim would have been another sick homeless person from his clinic. There are plenty of them. Melissa just got in his way."

"And left her daughter without her mother. Daddy, it's so awful . . ." Alison closed her eyes, her voice trailing off. She heard her father's chair moving back and then felt his arms curl around her shoulders and hold her tight.

67

"The grief counsellor said this is a good idea," Britt told Parish as they walked through the cemetery gate and started up the path. "She said I need to learn to remember Mom in my own way."

They were holding hands, as they had done each time on their monthly get-togethers since Melissa's murder.

"You know," Parish said, "your mom was brilliant."

"That's what everyone tells me," Britt said. "Maybe that was her downfall. Maybe it would have been better if she hadn't been quite so smart."

Pearls of wisdom from an eleven-year-old girl. "You might be right, but we are what we are."

Britt stopped in her tracks. Turned to Parish.

"Did she really have to be that way?"

Parish reached out to hug Britt.

"Your mom was one of my best friends. I know she didn't want to be ill. I know she fought against it. Try to understand, Britt, she couldn't stop herself."

Britt buried her head in Parish's shoulder.

"I want to see it," she said at last, pointing up the hill toward the graves.

"I was here last week to make sure the stone was up before you came," Parish said.

They walked in silence. Britt was a quiet young woman. That was her survival strategy to deal with her verbose father and unpredictable mother. Parish liked that about her. They felt comfortable being together without words.

"Down this row," Parish said, once they'd crested the hill.

Britt didn't speak.

The gravestone was simple. Hodgson, to his credit, had insisted on that. Under Melissa's name and the dates of her birth and death, was the inscription *She Cared*.

Britt knelt down and touched the stone. She reached back, took Parish's hand, and placed it beside hers. It was a hot day, but the stone felt cool.

"Don't ever doubt how much she loved you," Parish said.

"Can I tell you something?" Britt stood quickly, a determined look on her face.

"Anything."

"You won't tell my dad?"

"Never." Britt was pretty. Had she already discovered boys?

"Because I'm going to tell him myself."

Oh no. Was this about drugs at her young age?

"I'm going to quit golf."

"Oh."

"You're the first person I've told. I have to work up the nerve to tell him."

"Can I ask you why?" Parish said. But she already knew the answer.

"I don't care about being a champion. I want to be normal."

Britt spoke in an angry way Parish had never heard her speak in before.

"I know Dad is going to be mad. So will Lydia, but I don't care what she thinks. It's my life, and I don't have to keep playing golf all the time. The kids at school talk about a show they've binged on Netflix or a great YouTube video everyone else is watching. I say I don't have time to see it because I've got to go practice. Or I don't say anything. Now Dad wants me to go to a special golf camp this summer. All my friends are going to regular camps. I want to go to where I can sail and swim and ride horses. He's going to be so angry when I tell him."

Her words spilled out in rapid fire. As if they'd been dammed up inside her for years and now they were gushing out.

"I have to ask you a big favour," Britt said.

"Anything."

"I mean, you're my godmother, right? If my dad kicks me out because I won't play golf anymore, can I come live with you?"

Parish couldn't help smiling a little. "Your dad would never kick you out. He loves you more than anything in the world."

Britt frowned. "There's something else. I'm not supposed to tell anyone this yet."

"What's wrong?"

"Lydia's pregnant."

"Oh, I didn't know that."

"But what if you are wrong, and he does kick me out after the baby is born?"

"He won't. But you always have a home."

Britt hugged her. Then pulled away.

"I've got one more thing to ask you."

"Anything," Parish said again.

"You know that game you and Lydia used to play with Mom?"

Parish had no idea what she was talking about.

Britt put her hands up to her chest and opened her palms.

"Oh," Parish said, getting it. She put her hands up too. "First you clap your hands together, then your right hand to my right hand, then your left to my left, then both."

She clapped her hands.

Britt did the same. And smiled.

Parish began to sing and soon Britt joined in with her:

> I am a pretty little Dutch girl
> As pretty as pretty can be . . .

68

"I have to warn you," Greene said to Dr. Ramos as he took his usual seat at the Caldense Bakery. He leaned over the little table and whispered, "The little croissants here are as hard as rocks."

"But the coffee's good, correct?"

"So I've been told. You'll have to try it yourself."

She shook her head, her black hair shining in the light coming in from the window. "I've never dated a man who does not drink coffee."

"Detective, good morning." Caldas, the owner, rushed up to greet them. "And to whom do I owe the honour?" he added, a giant smile on his face as he turned to Ramos.

"This is Dr. Ramos, a brilliant pathologist."

"*Bom dia, senhor,*" she said.

Caldas's eyes lit up.

"Brazilian?" he said. "Such a lovely accent."

"Not quite. Northern Uruguay."

Instantly the two jumped into an animated conversation in Portuguese. Ramos began pantomiming someone drinking from a cup, and Caldas nodded enthusiastically. Then she imitated someone eating. Caldas smiled. They were laughing together as if they'd been friends for decades. At last they shook hands, and Caldas bowed and rushed off toward the bar.

When he was gone, Ramos turned to Greene with a blank look on her face, as if nothing had happened.

"Well?" Greene said.

"Well?" Ramos said back.

"You spoke to him for about two minutes."

"Yes. He's a lovely gentleman." She looked over Greene's shoulder. "Here he comes."

Greene turned and saw Caldas approach taking quick steps, holding his serving tray.

"Detective Greene," he said. "I am most happy. After these many years, the beautiful doctor explained to me that at last you have started to drink coffee. And you wish to try mine."

Greene looked across at Ramos, who stared back at him straight-faced.

Caldas put two cups of espresso and the inevitable pair of hard croissants on the table.

"Oh, did she?" Greene said.

"I was going to bring you sugar, but the good doctor told me you take it straight."

"Do I? Well, thank you, Miguel," Greene said, hoping that Caldas would now disappear and he could pass the coffee covertly over to Ramos and they could laugh about her little gambit.

Instead, Caldas crossed his arms in front of him, holding the round tray to his chest. "Dr. Ramos assured me that you would wish me to witness this historic event."

Greene shot Ramos another look.

She smiled back at him with her perfect teeth. Under the table he felt her kick his leg.

"*Excelente!*" Greene said, grasping the little cup and throwing the coffee back in one gulp. He reached for the croissant and took a bite to cut the bitter taste in his mouth.

"Bravo," Caldas said, swinging his tray down by his side and gliding away.

"You are very brave, Detective," Ramos said, once they were alone. Instead of kicking his leg, now she was rubbing it up and down with the side of her shoe.

Holding her eyes, he reached across the table, took her cup of espresso, brought it to his lips, and slowly sipped it dry.

THE NEXT DAY

69

It was Babita's idea, of course. It all started a month after the accident, when Detective Kennicott called Roshan and said the police no longer needed his damaged bicycle as evidence. Did he want it back, or should they destroy it?

Mr. Hodgson, the former club president and the driver of the black SUV who had accidentally knocked Roshan off his bicycle on that most unfortunate morning, had insisted on giving Roshan two thousand dollars to buy a replacement, and for what he called Roshan's pain and suffering. They'd used the money to buy the twins snowsuits and Babita the new rice cooker she had always wanted. They'd put the rest into savings.

"If it is not too much trouble," Roshan told Kennicott, "please, I would like to have it returned in order to do the repair."

The bike was in rough shape. Later Roshan joked that the bike was in even worse condition than his bruised knee. There was little room in their one-bedroom apartment, and with the twins now crawling everywhere, he couldn't leave the bicycle on the floor. He hooked up a pulley system to the ceiling that allowed him to lower it when he was doing work on it and pull it out of the way when he was not.

Soon word spread in the housing complex about Roshan's bicycle repairs, and Babita's specially made reflecting shirts. Within a month Roshan had five bicycles hanging from pulleys throughout the apartment. Babita became so busy with orders that she bought a second sewing machine, and a neighbour came by every day to work with her.

For months they had tried to get Detective Kennicott to come over for dinner so they could thank him for all his help through the ordeal.

But each time they'd asked him, the detective had been too busy. Finally, he was free, and he'd brought his girlfriend, Ms. Breaker, with him. Babita made a delicious eggplant and dhal dish, with okra and spiced rice. As they were teaching their guests how to use their fingers to eat the meal, Ms. Breaker asked about the bicycles and Babita's reflective shirts.

"Have you ever thought of opening a bike repair and clothing shop?" she asked.

"But where and how?" Roshan asked.

"We are running out of room," Babita said. "We have only money to pay the rent and clothe the children."

Ms. Breaker listened, nodded, and said, "Let me work on this. I know ways to find you start-up grants."

A week later she'd come over, and together they'd filled out a pile of government forms to aply for grant money to rent an old building that had once been a candy store down the street from the golf club. To get the funds, Roshan and Babita had to agree to hire four homeless people, who would commit to come to work sober and show up at least fifteen hours a week.

Mr. Waterbridge, the golf club manager, collected funds from members to pay for a sign. His younger son helped him with the fundraising.

Detective Greene had a friend named Mr. Dent, who was their first homeless employee. He seemed to know everyone who lived in the valley and helped pick people he thought were reliable to work as other employees. The best seemed to be a young woman named Daphne.

The shop opened in March, and business was good right from the beginning, thanks mostly to the club members who brought their children's bikes in for repairs. Babita's shirts were popular too.

Daphne started off so well. She watched the others like a hawk, and if someone tried to steal something, or money from the tip jar, she was on them in an instant. Then one day she disappeared, and it turned out she'd been siphoning off the tips for weeks and had stolen yards of Babita's cloth.

A few weeks later, Detective Greene's daughter came by. She was a TV reporter and wanted to do a story about a shop that hired homeless people.

"That would be most helpful," Roshan said.

"But I do not think they will want to have their faces on television," Babita explained.

"We'll film it in such a way as not to reveal their identity," Ms. Greene said. "The audience will only see their hands at work."

The story was on TV the next week, and after that, business doubled. People drove from all over the city to drop off their bicycles and buy Babita's shirts. Now she had four sewing machines.

Sometimes on Saturday mornings Ms. Breaker stopped by on her early morning runs through the valley, and once in a while when he was not on a case, Detective Kennicott would run with her.

The previous week Ms. Breaker had asked Babita, "Could you make me a shirt for running?"

"It would be my pleasure," Babita said. "I will have it for you next week."

Early this morning, Ms. Breaker came into the shop with Detective Kennicott. Babita had hoped he would be with her, because she had also made a shirt for him.

"These are great," Ms. Breaker said, pulling Babita's shirt on. "All my running friends are going to want one."

"Fits like a glove," Detective Kennicott said, when he tried his on.

They thanked Babita and insisted on paying for the shirts. When they were done, Roshan walked with them outside. The sun was rising, and the air was warming.

Detective Kennicott's cell phone rang. It had an unusual ring tone.

Roshan saw him exchange a knowing look with Ms. Breaker before he turned away and answered the phone.

"Ari, what have we got?" Roshan heard him say, before he walked down the road out of range.

A few seconds later he was back. "I have to run over to the nearest division," he said to Ms. Breaker, pointing down the road.

"I'm going to head back down to the valley," she said, gesturing the other way.

"Have a good run," he said.

"But first, Daniel." She put her hands on his face and kissed him.

Roshan smiled as he watched them run off in different directions.

"Roshan, we have a new customer," Babita called out to him from inside the shop.

"I'll be right there," he called back.

Instead, he turned and looked up to the clear blue sky and let the sun caress his face. It had been a cold spring, but at last it was growing warm and there was a faint smell of lilac in the air. Something above him caught his eye. He spotted a bird winging past him, clutching a large twig in its beak. It was heading home.

Acknowledgments

It is a few minutes after five a.m. at the Caldense Bakery on Dundas Street West. Outside snowflakes are falling, dancing through the streetlights. It is not cold enough for them to stick to the ground. Instead they paint the street with a glimmering wet sheen. I've come here to put the final touches on the first draft of this manuscript, which is due today.

In the far corner of the café, TV commentators are having an intense debate about Portuguese soccer. Three men have just come in, wearing work boots, heavy coats, and safety vests, for their morning hits of espresso. A lit-up, bauble-filled Christmas tree is at my side.

People often ask what I do for research. Mostly it involves this: walking through the city, going to places, looking, listening.

There are many people to thank for their countless hours of assistance to help me with this novel. After having the privilege of seeing this, my sixth book, published, I prefer to thank them privately.

On my early-morning drive over to this café, I counted fifteen building cranes towering over new building sites. Soon I'll head back home, where, within two blocks of where I live, five new condominium high-rises are under construction. I walk to work and I know I will pass at least that number of people begging on the street.

Another working day in this hard-working city.

Robert Rotenberg
Toronto
December 6, 2019